FALL OF THE ANCIENT GODS

RISE OF THE ANCIENT GODS SERIES: BOOK 6

CRAIG ROBERTSON

FALL OF THE ANCIENT GODS

RISE OF THE ANCIENT GODS SERIES: BOOK 6

by Craig Robertson

If you think it cannot get worse, you haven't met Jon Ryan.

Imagine-It Publishing

El Dorado Hills, CA

ALSO BY CRAIG ROBERTSON:

For specifics as to the correct order for reading the Ryanverse, click here.

BOOKS IN THE RYANVERSE:

THE FOREVER SERIES (2016)

THE FOREVER LIFE, Book 1

THE FOREVER ENEMY, Book 2

THE FOREVER FIGHT, Book 3

THE FOREVER QUEST, Book 4

THE FOREVER ALLIANCE, Book 5

THE FOREVER PEACE, Book 6

THE FOREVER BOXSET, Part 1, Books 1 & 2

THE FOREVER BOXSET, Part 2, Book 3 & 4

THE FOREVER BOXSET, Part 3, Book 5 & 6

GALAXY ON FIRE SERIES (2017)

EMBERS, Book 1

FLAMES, Book 2

FIRESTORM, Book 3

FIRES OF HELL, Book 4

DRAGON FIRE, Book 5

THE WHALES OF TIME (2023)

Ryan In UnWonderland, Book 1

How Ryan Saves Time, Book 2

Saving Alice Ryan, Book 3

NON-RYANVERSE BOOKS:

A Teenager's Guide to Saving The Earth (2025)

An Apocalypse and Then Some, Book 1

How to Survive Surviving the Apocalypse, Book 2

Is This Apocalypse Over Yet?, Book 3

TIME DIVING (2024)

Letters From Hell, Book 1

Purgatory's Best Shot, Book 2

Heaven Says Wait, Book 3

Into the Nexus, Book 4

ROAD TRIPS IN SPACE SERIES (2019):

THE GALAXY ACCORDING TO GIDEON, Book 1

THE EARTH ACCORDING TO GIDEON, Book 2

OLDER, STANDALONE WORKS:

THE CORPORATE VIRUS (2016)

THE INNERgLOW EFFECT (2010)

WRITE NOW! THE PRISONER OF NaNoWRiMo (2009)

ANON TIME (2009)

For more information about Craig, his books, various series, or to see images and videos for some of his wild alien

characters, please visit his website. You'll be glad you did: https://craigarobertson.com/

To sign up for Craig's newsletter to get announcements, updates, and his recommendations for other great Sci-Fi reads go to: https://preview.mailerlite.io/forms/2369493/188634426375144501/share

ISBN: 978-1-7331137-1-7 (E-Book)
978-1-7331137-2-4 (Paperback)
979-8-7754144-7-4 (Hardcover)

Cover design by Jessica Bell
https://www.jessicabelldesign.com/

Editors: Michael. R. Blanche
Forest Olivier
Charles Pitts

Formatting services by Drew Avera
drewavera@gmail.com

First Edition 2019
Second Edition 2020

I dedicate this book to the dream that is Jon Ryan. For all the hope and love and charity and commitment we wish there were more of in our lives. Too often, those positives are blinded by the negativity that can surround us. I wish everyone would be a little more Ryanesque. The world would be a much nicer place. Jon'd tell you that—straight up.

PRELUDE

Bethniak's heart was colder than the midwinter South Pole. Her arrangement with the outside world suited her just fine. It was symmetric. She loved no one, and no one loved her. She assumed she'd had parents, but Bethniak had never met them, heard tell of them, or desired to know factoid number one about any of that dubious trio. As to her sexuality, it was straightforward. There was none. Many a Cleinoid lusted after the many billion year old because she always *appeared* to be a sweet little ten year old child. Bad Cleinoids. But Bethniak had zero interest in males, females, alien monstrosities, or any combination amongst those extremes.

Bethniak had but one pleasure in her very long life. Being mean. She loved making, wanted to make, and had always striven to make others suffer. It was her sole vice, her only joy. That helped explain her love of flatco hunting. She spent most days, if there was no one or nothing else to molest, engaged in the hunt. Flatcos were roughly the size of a double-decker bus, and twice the width. They were similar in form to a triceratops. Thick skinned, tiny brained, and easy to piss off. Unlike the dinosaur, flatcos were vicious predators, and, in place of horns, they had multiple whip-like antennae that were razor sharp and injected a deadly poison.

Specifically, Bethniak loved to hunt *baby* flatcos. A mother flatco would lay a clutch of eggs only once every ten or eleven years, from fifteen to twenty in number. She brooded her clutch deep inside a cave or cavern, sometimes many kilometers from the opening. She wanted her babies to be safe when she was out hunting for them. Mother flatcos had to bring a fairly good sized catch back every week or two to please her offspring. Generally that meant the eggs or young were alone for days at a time.

What Bethniak called "flatco hunting" was actually bashing the incubating eggs or dismembering the young chicks. Yeah, she was not a very good sport. The real challenge of it for her was to commit her mayhem while the enraged mother was able to witness the carnage. If Bethniak located a nest while the mother was away, she'd wait until mom was back to finish off her "hunt." The very best, most satisfying times, were when Bethniak chanced upon a mother tending her new hatchlings. The little ones were so cute in a chirp-chirpy way and mom was especially maternal, early in the bonding period.

Bethniak would dance side to side, taunting the mother. When mom inevitably charged Bethniak, the god would rush around her and throttle a chick. That would force the mother to remain close to the nest. But, having only a pea brain, mother flatco would always end up lunging for the attacker, and that cost her another offspring. Polishing off twenty young could entertain Bethniak for hours. Being not just a Cleinoid, but a particularly powerful one, Bethniak was immune to the poison in the antennae, and the whip ends never even broke her skin. Once all the young were dead, Bethniak made every effort to then escape without having to slay the rampaging mother. Bethniak passionately hoped the parent had enough brain power to remember the gruesome details and to feel remorse for a very long time. She intended for flatco hunting to be the ultimate horror for the mother. Yes, Bethniak was just that sick.

On a hunt, one particular morning, Bethniak found her treasure. Far back in a dank cave, barely wide enough for her to pass through, she found a mother flatco ripping lengths of flesh off some prey animal and feeding them to her riotous chicks. Bethniak observed the blissful, domestic scene for several minutes, wanting to take in all the wonder and hope she was about to terminate. Then, because fun was not a matter to delay much, Bethniak stepped forward so the mother could see her. At that exact moment, Bethniak felt a wave pass through her body. It was like a vacuum sucked all the electricity out of her. She nearly passed out, but quickly found her wits. Luckily for her, it was not a moment too soon. Mother flatco had dashed toward Bethniak and was only a few meters away. Her antennae popped like firecrackers and a piercing screech came from her throat. Mom was pissed off.

Bethniak jumped to one side. She was instantly stunned. Normally she'd have bounded ten meters. That time she leaped maybe a foot. Whatever short distance it was did not place her outside mom's snapping jaws. The mother sank her teeth into Bethniak's thigh and tossed her into the air.

For her part, Bethniak screamed in pain. She reached down to find her leg was bleeding briskly. Once she'd landed, she tried to stand, but her injured leg collapsed. With the intruder lying face down, the mother pounced on her back. Her antennae slapped and snapped, basically peeling Bethniak's skin off, starting at her neck and proceeding down to her waist.

The Cleinoid raged in anguish and fury. She tried to flip over, but the flatco was too strong. It began gouging deep holes in Bethniak's torso. After a minute, all was still. Realizing the assailant was dead, the mother issued a victory squawk so loud the walls of the cave shook. Debris filtered to the ground. When mother flatco had that out of her system, she dragged the lifeless Bethniak back to the nest. Methodically, she began peeling strips off of the former child god and feeding them to the eager chicks. With the eternal-life-providing Clein gone, Bethniak was nothing more than a light snack.

Payback was a bitch.

CHAPTER ONE

A brave new world, or a dying old one? My to-do list really was never going to end. With outstanding teamwork, even better luck, and maybe, just maybe, a favorable nod from Fate, we'd taken out Clein. It cost us Casper. That I'll regret, forever. I mean, dude was dead. He died two billion years ago. It wasn't like he'd been short-changed, or anything. But ... I wish I'd known before I acted. He was a good man, er, ghost. Then again, you might be thinking, ah, *hello*, Jon, he was *you*. Of course, you thought he was a good egg. I can prove *that* assumption to be false. I can't stand EJ. He's a punk and his feet smell bad, and he's also me. See, I am *discerning*. Yeah, a big word meaning I'm picky.

"Come on, honey," Sapale said with a gentle tug. "We need to go. Someone's going to be coming, soon. We don't want to be here when the Clein Fan Club arrives and finds out we just ruined their upcoming annual picnic and barbecue."

Even when in dire peril, my brood's-mate was the best.

If you get a chance to marry a Kaljaxian, I'd highly suggest you do.

"Staring at that *spot* isn't going to bring him back?" I responded.

"No. It's not. He's finally at peace."

"I sure hope not."

She stepped back in a huff. "I beg your pardon. Why on earth would you wish poor, long dead *you* a nasty afterlife? Pig."

"No, I mean I hope he parties and there's no possible end. Boogie down, all around." I displayed, briefly, my winning dance moves.

"Yuck," my loving wife exclaimed. "You move like a worm on fire."

"Hey, I'll have you know—"

Then I looked at her. She was giving me the stop-speaking-immediately glare. "Let's go."

I offered her my elbow. She hesitated, begrudgingly grinned, and accepted my offer. We returned to *Stingray*.

"Head count. Al, is everyone aboard?"

"Yes, well," he lowered his voice, "except for Casper."

"Where's Cas—" Daleria started to ask. Then she fell silent, having answered her own question.

"Clein was what sustained him," Mirraya spoke up with reverence. "I sensed him depart. He is in a good place. He is *happy.*"

"Wife," began Slapgren, "remember we've talked about you not creeping people out with the witch-speak?"

"No. I don't recall us ever having that conversation." Then she stuck her tongue out at him. Good girl.

"Speaking of departing, *Stingray*, take us up to Beal's Point," I called out as I touched my fibers to the deck.

"What?" just about everybody blurted out, incredulously.

"Hey, I want to go somewhere we'll not be surprised by a crowd. Especially with Clein gone, no one, but no one'll be at that awful place."

"*We* will be in that awful place," scorned my wife.

"And won't it be wonderful. Als, make the magic happen."

Mild nausea came and went.

"Status," I asked.

"Aside from the *lovely* artwork, Pilot, we're perfectly alone."

"Excellent. Slapgren, Toño, you're with me. Grab some rifles and let's sweep the plateau."

"For what?" asked Sapale. "Al just said we were all by our lonesome."

"Which I'd like to verify. I also wish to see what's happening in the new, post-Clein reality."

"And I'm not coming because?"

"Because you're in command when I'm gone."

"Of course, I am. *Duh*. And I'm not coming because?" she repeated. "Wait, you want me to babysit EJ?"

I tried not to move a muscle or change expressions.

"I so hate you," she snarled. "I hate you *this* much." My spirited mate opened her arms as wide as she could.

"I'll report back every five minutes, *Captain*," I responded in conclusion.

As I made for the exit, I heard a mumbled, "More than this much, now." What a gal, that wife of mine.

My initial impression was that nothing had changed. It was midday, but the air was dim, like there were clouds, but there were none. And a dry, abrasive wind swirled. What a dreadful place.

"Let's head to the center," I announced, and took point.

The path wound around a bit, due to the slope. We made good time, however. About halfway up, Toño asked,

"Did you notice that's the third random pile of sand, back there?"

"Fourth," I corrected. "Two were heaped together."

"I don't recall them from before."

"Neither do I. Maybe vandals?"

He harrumphed. "*We're* the only vandals to visit here, my friend. No one else would go to the trouble."

"Not your ideal family picnic venue, I'll grant you that."

"It's gotta be this wind," Slapgren said as he batted a hand at flying dust. "It must make small dunes."

"Hmm," responded Toño. "We'll see."

We stopped in front of the statue to—you guessed it—Jéfnoss tra-Fundly. Yeah, I missed the little prick already. "Well, I'll be damned," I remarked with a sigh.

"Aside from having stated the very obvious," Al piped in, "is there more meaning to your remark, Pilot?"

"No, just commenting."

"Well, I'll be damned, too," marveled Toño. "I don't feel ill."

"Me, neither," I confirmed. "The neutral matter in the statue isn't working."

"Or it's not been replaced," Toño cautioned. "Remember, this is one of those we stole from, a while back."

I trudged over to another monument. Then another. Nothing. They were all duds.

Toño, who'd followed me closely, said, "I guess they're all on the fritz. I think that's a positive sign."

"*Hell*, yes," I snapped. "No more Clein seems to mean no more Cleinoid magic." Then an odd thought struck me. I'd forgotten about something. Something big.

"Al, what's the status of our cargo lobster?"

In my rush to get to Beal's Point, I'd neglected to check on Gáwar. He was so pleasant to forget, after all.

"Ah, I'm A) not certain you want to know, and B) not going to clean up, this time. It's your turn, big guy."

"Al, grow up and report."

"Gáwar appears to have joined his fallen brothers in the Great Beyond."

"He's dead?" asked Slapgren.

"Oh, he's dead," scoffed Al. "Dead, actually stinkier, and, oh my, he's leaking."

"Please do *not* tell me what he's leaking," I ordered.

"It's so gross, I won't even analyze it, pilot." He sounded like he was about to toss his cookies. Nice.

"Sapale," I said, "can you take a look and confirm Gáwar's status, please."

"Yes, I can."

Odd response. I waited a sec. "So, what—"

"I *can*, but there's no freaking way I will, swizzle dick. Leaving the little woman at home was bad enough. *You* want a visual, *you* do the visual."

"Jeez," exclaimed EJ, "I'll do it. Everyone else is in the middle of a struggle to survive, but you two have time for a lover's spat." He opened the door to the storage area. "Holy moly," he shouted.

"*What?*" I snapped.

"I cannot tell which's worse. What I'm *looking* at or what I'm *smelling*. Seriously, I should get hazardous duty pay for this."

"Sure, whatever," I responded. "Report."

"First off, Gáwar's *as* dead as he can be. No doubt there. Second, he's decaying much faster than I'd expect. Most of his upper torso has caved in, and his eyes are gone. Third, there's ungodly fluids of any color you choose dribbling away from the corpse. Oh, and did I mention the smell?"

"I recall something to the effect it'd make a bad cologne," I replied. "Can you tell what he actually died of?"

5

"Not without doing a post on him."

"I'll settle for a best guess," I returned.

"The way he's flattened suggests he collapsed in onto himself. You know, like he was too massive for his body to support itself."

"I imagine he was too large for his respiratory system to support his bulk, also," added Toño. "Once Gáwar lost the blessings of Clein, he discovered he was not suitable for mortal life."

"So, Clein leaves. Daleria's fine, but Gáwar dies and the monuments lost their bad mojo," I summarized.

"Daleria's a fairly typical humanoid. She is fit to survive without godly magic. However, once the powers that kept Gáwar alive and the neutral matter stable were removed, they were left on their own. No creature like Gáwar could survive in nature."

"Or flying rock piles, dragons, and boulder gods like Gorpedder. Likely they all had a bad day of it," I speculated.

"Almost certainly," agreed Toño.

"These piles of sand we passed," said Slapgren, "I'll bet those were the golem guards."

"Makes perfect sense," responded Toño.

"We're heading back to the ship," I announced. "We need to figure out what this means for the viability of and potential threats posed by the Cleinoid ex-gods."

A few minutes later we were gathered in the mess. "We took out Clein," I began. "The impossible beasts we've seen are dead, while the fairly normal ones are still alive. I need to know if this universe still poses a threat to ours."

"How can it?" asked Slapgren, more than a little incredulously. "No Clein means no magic. No magic means any stragglers, no offense intended, Daleria, are left to fend for themselves."

"None taken," Daleria replied with a mirthless smile.

"That's likely," I agreed, "but too much is at stake to assume it and act accordingly. I have to know with reasonable certainty if there's still a danger."

"What do you propose?" asked Toño.

"All I can think of is we perform an extensive search of the surroundings. See who's alive, who isn't, and, most of all, confirm that the big nasties are all dead."

"We have our bugs everywhere, Captain," piped in Al. "I can state with confidence the present data very much supports the hypothesis that only naturally viable Cleinoids have survived this crisis."

I pointed toward where his voice had come from. "That's great intel, Al. Keep it up. But, with all that's hanging on this, I'll need to eyeball the results myself. Boots on the ground."

"Reasonable," mused EJ. "We can split into two or three groups. That'll speed up our search."

I breathed deeply through my nose as I thought. "Probably a good plan. Sapale, Daleria, and I can work together. That leaves Mirraya, Slapgren, EJ, and Toño as team two."

I could tell EJ wanted to object to the split. But he didn't go as far as voicing that opinion. He probably chafed over having Toño watching over him, which, of course, was my intention. He *respected* Toño.

"We've already surveyed the capital. Daleria, let's head back to your town. It's a long way removed from here. We'll find out, in detail, what the precise consequences of the loss of Clein are," I announced.

"And when we prove the Cleinoid threat is extinguished?" posed Toño.

"*If* we come to that conclusion, we're free to return home."

"And probably find out there's nothing left," EJ scoffed.

7

"We'll see, Susie Sunshine. There's nothing we can do about the state of affairs back home at this moment." I stood. "*Stingray*, put us in front of Daleria's old restaurant."

"Plotted and executed, Form One."

Super-service. Nice.

"Everyone snag some thunder and let's do this," I called out. "oh, and, Al, while we're —"

"I know. See what we can do about the mess in Storage A."

"You got it, my friend."

"I understand. But friend? Please. You wouldn't ask a *friend* to clean up an epic mess like that."

"You know what? You're one hundred percent correct on that. Smart boy."

Stepping off the ship, I pointed to the right. "You guys go that way," I pointed left, "we'll take this direction. Stay in contact and be back in an hour, tops."

Sapale, Daleria, and I marched ahead. It didn't take long for Daleria to ask, "Can we check out my old place?"

I shrugged. "Good a place as any to start." It was right there in front of us. "Let me go first."

She nodded in understanding.

My sidearm was holstered. I did not want to make a poor first impression. A man with a weapon at the ready suggests either *he's* trouble, or, to him, *you're* trouble. Either way, cordiality is out the window. I entered like a patron. Turns out, the show was for nothing. The place was empty. I ran an infrared scan. One humanoid was in the back room, maybe the kitchen. Otherwise, no one else on either story.

"Someone's in the kitchen." I signaled for the women to follow.

"I cannot believe it," announced Sapale with surprise in her tone.

I froze. "What?"

"You didn't finish that sentence. You didn't say *with Dinah*."

I grinned. "Babe, this is serious business. I need to focus. I'm a serious, focused warrior."

"And you got me to say it, didn't you?" She added such a look.

"Well, you did." I bopped the end of her nose, then headed back toward the kitchen.

The person in the back was Tonflare, Daleria's old sous-chef. She'd taken over after Daleria left to join our merry band. I didn't really know her, but Daleria spoke of her as a good friend.

"Ton Ton," Daleria exclaimed as she slid past me. "How are you?"

Tonflare spun like a trapped animal. She brandished an impressively large kitchen knife. "Stay back, whoever you are. I'll use this. I *swear* I will."

"Tonflare, it's me. Put that down."

"You say it's you. You could be one of the Devils of the East, for all I know."

"Devils of the East? Ton Ton, what's gotten into you?"

I saw the problem. Tonflare was humanoid, like the infrared scan suggested. But she had horns, big horns (and no, I'm not going to make any horny jokes. I'm a serious, focused warrior). Think Texas Longhorn cattle and you'll get the picture. The base of both horns was bleeding. They were another of the unsupportable Cleinoid novelties in the post-Clein world. She must have been in a world of hurt.

"Daleria," I said evenly, "your friend's scared and in pain." I nodded toward her rack.

"Ton Ton, I'm so sorry. Can I help you?" She took one step forward.

9

"Stay where you are." The sudden movement of her knife hand made her head jerk. Poor girl winced in pain.

"Sapale," I said firmly, "knife."

She grabbed it with her fibers and I shot behind Tonflare before she knew what hit her. I put her in a gentle but firm bear hug. "Easy, my friend. We're here to help. That's all. Relax."

Tonflare struggled to free herself, but the added motion was agony.

Wisely, Sapale dropped the knife, placed her fibers on Tonflare's head, and said *sleep*. The cook melted into my arms.

Toño, I said head-to-head, *we have a situation in the kitchen of Daleria's restaurant. Be here.*

On my way, he replied quickly. *Is it Daleria?*

No, her friend. Just get here.

In a few seconds, Toño flew through the door. EJ and my Deft kids were right behind him.

"What do we have here?" he asked as he dropped to his knees alongside me. I was still cradling Tonflare.

"Daleria's friend. She went nuts when she saw us. I think it the horns. They—"

"Got it," he cut me off. "Lay her flat." Doc gave her a general once over, because, well, he's a doctor. Then he coned down on her horns. "Yes. Hmm."

"What?" Daleria pressed.

"The horn origins appear to be infected. They're both hanging on only by degrading sinew."

I didn't need to know what he was saying. Only he needed to, right?

"Slapgren, go back to the ship and get my med kit."

"You got it," he snapped, as he sped away.

"Was she ... no you said she irrationally confronted you."

"I put her to sleep," clarified Sapale.

"Smart work. She has to be out of her mind with the suffering." He placed a palm on her forehead. "I cannot know for certain, but I think she's running a fever, too."

"So maybe she was delirious when we got here?" I asked.

"Quite possibly. However, Cleinoid physiology is undiscovered country for me."

"Yeah. I don't recall seeing a drop-in medical clinic anywhere," I grumbled.

"I'm thinking you will, soon," remarked EJ. "These SOBs are in for some real ch ... ch ... changes."

If they survive at all, I mumbled in my head. I didn't want to alarm Daleria any more than she already was. Life as we knew it was going to be a shock for the surviving Cleinoids. Great. Just great. I'd singlehandedly created a humanitarian, or whatever, crisis. Now I had to ponder and reflect on the moral implications of providing or *not* providing aid. What a screwy universe. I'm a pilot, not a philosopher. *Crapazoid.*

Slapgren trotted in and handed Toño his kit. "I'll need to remove these horns, clean the site, and begin some antibiotics."

"Do you think human medicines will work on ... on whatever species she is?" puzzled Mirraya.

"I, *she*, doesn't have any proper alternatives. Now that I've had a chance to inspect the wounds, I can tell the underlying tissues are necrotic as well as infected. She's likely septic. I'm going to have to revise the area widely and employ broad spectrum antibiosis at high serum levels."

Like I said, only *he* had to know what he was babbling about. The rest of us clammed up and watched.

"I'll remove the horns here. Then let's get her back to

the ship where I can perform the rest in a more controlled environment."

I presume he didn't want to have the dangling horns in the way, and causing more damage, in transport. I also knew better than to say a peep. Toño used a laser scalpel to separate off the horns and—thank you oh so much— handed the drippy things off to me. My first instinct was to toss them out the nearby window. I thought better of that. Daleria might resent the disrespect. Instead, I walked the horns outside and *then* unceremoniously dumped them on the ground.

When I returned, Slapgren was ferrying the still unconscious chef out the opposite door. Toño packed up his stuff and sped to catch up.

"You okay, kid?" I asked Daleria. I think she put up with me calling her kid because, well, she liked me. Honest to goodness, the word just popped out my mouth when I spoke to her. It wasn't like I could control it, or anything. The fact that I was *only* two billion years old didn't annoy my four-plus billion year old friend.

She nodded bravely, but I could tell she was shaken. "Why don't you stay with her. I'm sure she'd appreciate the support."

"N ... no. We have a mission," she protested.

"Sapale will keep me out of trouble. Trust me, we've done this before," I kissed her forehead. "You go be a good friend. Heck, it's even possible the incomparable Dr. Toño DeJesus'll need some help."

"Let's not be silly," she returned with a playful grin. "I'll be at his side. If you need me, let him know and I'm there."

"If we do, we will," Sapale responded, and she gently directed Daleria toward the door. "Well, this is starting off weird, even by our slack standards," my wife remarked.

"Weird, indeed," I agreed. "Let's go see if we can make it even more so." I put my arm around her neck and we went in search of the paranormal.

CHAPTER TWO

Gabaraph The Unholy was one of the more despicable and sordid Cleinoid gods, as witnessed by his name. He was—and you would never, ever have guessed it—the god of teen spirit. For the record, he could care less about teens, spirit, or any combination of the two concepts. He was the god of teen spirit due to some form of bureaucratic oversight, or a practical joke without a punchline. Perhaps that is why teen spirt is so labile and generally unwelcome? Anyway, Gabaraph The Unholy lived alone, raged alone, and was friend to, and of, no other god.

His technical species designation was that of Franbuol. He, unlike that ancient and long extinct race, had changed. Known for epochs as kind, thoughtful, and nurturing, the Franbuol encouraged and supported many galactic species as they climbed from their respective primordial goos. In spite of the Franbuol's outwardly frightening appearance, in their chests—for each had three—beat hearts of gold. A loose characterization of the beasts would be spherical raptors with tiny red lightning bolts of static electricity leaping from their bodies. Oh, and they were trans-physical. They could *be* or *not be where* they where, *when* they were. They were called, long, long ago, the kindest variable species ever to have existed.

Gabaraph The Unholy retained all the external trappings of his kind, while rejecting all the internal good. He replaced it with pulp-fiction-level meanness, disregard, and hatred. Along with being an altogether bad guy, Gabaraph The Unholy was a slow, methodical god. In the years since the transheaval, he'd only occupied and devastated one solitary planet. Partly this was due to his fickleness. He examined and rejected hundreds of worlds before selecting Messimor-α. Gabaraph demanded that the planet he vanquished be cool, have a high oxygen level in its atmosphere, and be densely populated with well-fed masses. He also would only strike a world that had not been fouled by any of his Cleinoid family. He detested them as much as he detested those he would consume.

Unlucky Messimor-α was ideal in all regards. Plus, being far from the egress point, most lazy Cleinoids wouldn't be ravaging the place for generations. By then, there would be but the barest bones to pick. That insight was one of the few thoughts that put a smile on Gabaraph's hideous face. He landed at one pole on Messimor-α and proceeded, in an orderly manner, to destroy the surface of the planet in ever-growing spirals of death, north to south. Yes, his path of conquest began modestly with ice, snow, and the occasional sea creature, but it was *orderly*. Order was, in the mind of Gabaraph, critically important. No actual reason why. He was just OCD that way.

But soon, Gabaraph's thoroughness was rewarded. He began ruining rich patches of happy, living beings who, even he would admit, deserved better. It was marvelous. A large, vivacious city here, a green and luxurious rain forest there, and he was good as gold. No creature, however large or small, important or disgusting, was left alive. He was like one of those tree-limb shredders, only mounted on legs to constitute a horrific lawnmower. Grind, grind, grind. Buzz, buzz, buzz. Gabaraph was unstoppable. Nuclear weapons, vicious native predators, and combined military units were completely ineffective against him. That gave him a warm, reassuring feeling deep in his unholy soul.

One day, into Gabaraph's complete domination lumbered a clanking figure who stumbled occasionally, and fell to the ground once in a great while. Verazz, king of the Stone Witches, had arrived. He lacked only a white steed and a lance to be the very picture of a proper knight of justice. What he did look like was a proper fool in dented armor.

"What, in the flames of damnation are *you*, little one?" challenged Gabaraph the Unholy.

"I am y—" Verazz's visor experienced a technical failure at that point, and fell. To maintain an air of potency, he stopped talking and fumbled with the guard, clicking it up, again and again.

Finally he was ready to continue. "I am your worst nightmare, Gab—"

Damn visor. Verazz ripped it off and threw it at Gabaraph. It sailed off at a wide angle and fell harmlessly to one side.

Verazz slapped his thigh. "Now see what you've made me do?" he seethed.

"What? Make a complete spectacle of yourself, or ruin your pathetic Halloween costume, or miss me badly, because you throw like a girl?" Gabaraph concluded his insult with a low, hardy laugh.

"You will *thrice* regret that mocking, you three-chested abomination. I referred, of course, to making me ruin my magnificent armor. Look at it. It's *ruined*."

Gabaraph grinned wickedly. "I don't think it was all *that* magnificent before you made a spectacle of yourself."

"Thrice plus one. That is how much you will suffer, mouth-breather," thundered Verazz.

"Do you mean *four*? If so, why bluster thrice plus one. You sound like an idiot when you say it that way. *Thrice plus one*," Gabaraph mocked again, more shrilly, this time.

"My name is Verazz. You ruined my entry. Prepare to die."

"This had been a light moment, sperm-spawn, but I'm over it now. Time to meet my stomach lining." Gabaraph launched himself at Verazz.

"Oh, bother," mumbled Verazz, "this is not at all how I envisioned this going down. He reflexively slipped a hand down over his face, hoping to lower his now absent visor. He stomped his foot in anger for the blunder. How was he going to bring greater glory to Carol and little Mari if he was a dodo bird?

As Verazz reflected and self-castigated, Gabaraph plowed into him, with enormous force and his spherical jaws gaping wide. Such a blow would have obliterated any other creature. In the present case, Gabaraph sailed through Verazz as if he weren't there. That was because he wasn't. Being an Apractolith was good, ten times out of ten.

Once Gabaraph passed through the image of Verazz, and skidded awkwardly to a halt, Verazz was there, back where he was supposed to be in the first place. He was still muttering unflattering words *to* himself, *concerning* himself.

"Do not do that again, urine-tower," Gabaraph

screamed insanely. He took one powerful stride toward Verazz.

Verazz turned to him, a sour look on his godly face. "Wait right there."

And Gabaraph did just that. He was frozen in space, but not time.

"I must inform you that, if you hadn't gone too far before, you certainly have *now*." He walked casually toward his opponent, dusting a gauntlet as he went. "You ruin my splendid armor, you mock me, and now you pretend to be able to assault me? As *if*. I actually hate you more because I don't know which offense to kill you for. Hmm. Do you see the untenable position you've placed me in? If I slay you for the *armor* thing," Verazz gestured to one side, "how am I supposed to punish you for the *mocking*?" he gestured to the other side. "I can't reliably revivify you, now can I?"

Gabaraph did not respond. His jaws were as frozen in space as was the rest of him.

"I say, are you adding rude to your ... Oh, my bad." Verazz flipped a hand in the air.

"What have you done?" wheezed Gabaraph.

"What have *I* done? The pot's calling the kettle black now, isn't it?"

"What? I do not speak your language. What are you saying?" Gabaraph was panicking badly.

"Small words for small minds," he said to himself. "You've really pissed me off. I will take minutes to recover. *Minutes*."

"You will—"

The talking portion of Gabaraph's existence was over. Verazz folded him into the fifteenth, the forty third, and the one hundred and twelfth dimensions. One third of Gabaraph per dimension. If you were standing at the wrong spot in any of those dimensions, at the wrong time, you'd be covered in a really nasty muck, and you'd have no intact person to send the dry cleaning bill to.

Back in our universe, Verazz smiled a child's smile. "See, you helped *immensely*," he complimented his armor.

And then he was gone.

CHAPTER THREE

While Toño tended to the sick Tonflare, Sapale and I ghosted down the center of the street. We were both lost in our miseries. We'd labored mightily to destroy Clein and to kill off the Cleinoid scum. Then, what's the first thing we discover as soon as we accomplished the impossible? We caused suffering to a nice person. We knew, by extension, we'd caused anguish to innumerable innocent Cleinoids. Well, innocent and Cleinoid don't belong in the same sentence. Perhaps relatively *not awful* Cleinoids. The few children we'd ever seen, for example, Bethniak excluded twice-over, of course. The workers and at least some of the demigods. Yeah, I've heard it a million times. Omelettes and eggs. War's hell, so shut the hell up. But, crap. That is my final thought on the subject. *Crap*.

"So, do you think they'll all die?" Sapale asked, breaking the silence.

I shrugged. "I suppose so. Some sooner than others."

"I freaking hate this."

"Anyone with a functioning brain does, hon."

"I mean, why'd they—"

"Stop." I stopped and took her by the shoulders. "*They* attacked *us*. They *are* attacking us back home. No one in existence asked for this more than these pig stickers. You know better than to beat yourself up about it. We don't have the luxury of generals and pilots. We're boots on the ground. We see the horror of our actions. But that doesn't mean it didn't need to be done, and done thoroughly." I looked away, into the parched distance. "You remember that family I sort of adopted, back when we were fighting the Adamant?"

"*Cellardoor?*" She looked at me like many of my screws were loose as hell.

"Yeah, her. I latched onto her and her kids, made pretend I was her husband."

"Wow, you went way down the rabbit hole to pull that one out."

"No. My point is this. I needed cover. She was a good choice. But, you know what? I did so without asking. I placed her and those sweet, innocent, kids in harm's way, because *I* needed a cover story." I swept my hand contemptibly in the air. "Yeah. Just like that. I threaten to cause a nice family to die horribly because I, *not they,* felt the *cause* justified my *actions.* Truth be told, I figured at the time there was a fifty/fifty chance they'd be dead that same day. But did I hesitate? Did I search my soul and change my scheme? Did I *look* in that cute little boy's eyes and say, "*Jon Ryan, what kind of monster have you become?*" I had to hold up a second. "No. Under the bus I threw them. And we won and the Adamant are scratching their fleas in the mud now because I played a hunch that could have killed those three innocent souls." I looked away. "This *is* war. A war we didn't ask for, we didn't deserve, but a war we, sure as hell's a bad place for polar bears, are going to win."

"Jon, it's not your fault." She patted my chest.

21

"Wh ... what?" I reoriented to her words.

"It's not your fault. This," she gestured widely, "this war. Or any *other*. Sooner or later Cellardoor and her kids would have ended up in tin cans supporting the Adamant cause the only way they really could. They were dead before you arrived. They were alive after you left. You did good, brood-mate. You did *good*."

My rage flared. I wanted to explode. I wanted to tell her I hated her. I hated *everything*. I wanted to not *be*, with a conviction forged in hellfire.

The forever love of my existence looked into my eyes and saw my pain. She laid her head on my chest, as we stood in the center of that accursed Cleinoid street. "World's so full of assholes, I'm amazed noses evolved. They want, they lie, they steal, and their greed is limitless. Always been that way. Sorry to be the one to break it to you. But, you know what's nice about assholes?"

I started giggling instantly. Here I am raging against the sky, and my girl sees the upside of assholes. "No. What's so *nice* about assholes?"

"Aside from the obvious," she added deadpan.

"Aside from the dietary necessity."

"They have a cure." She bopped my nose. "Me and you."

"Do tell."

"Yup." She mimed a person walking in place, fingers in their waistband, all cocky. "We see an asshole," she pointed dramatically to nothing at all. "We reconnoiter that asshole, and then we remove that asshole from the grand play that is this life."

I fought to suppress a grin. "We do, do we?" I spun my fingers, as if tracing a waltz. "Just like that."

"Yup." She mock-walked, again. "Asshole." She pointed a finger pistol, fired, and blew off the barrel smoke. "Dead and gone asshole. Thank you, Jon and Sapale Ryan."

"Ah, just to be clear, who thanked us?"

She gave an animated shrug. "Heck, everybody. The *universe*, Jon Ryan. The universe thanks us, each and every time we de-asshole it. Come on. You think the universe enjoys being tormented by being chock-full of assholes?"

I started to respond.

"Jon, the ratio of assholes to mouths, it's like seven *billion* to one. What kind of *universe* wants to have zillions more assholes than it has mouths? It's completely unnatural, I say. You and me, Jon, we're naturalizers."

"*Naturalizers?*" I grinned big.

"Hell, yes. That is why the universe loves and thanks us. We labor constantly to naturalize that despicable ratio." She tapped my chest, then hers. "You and me, Jon."

"Yeah?"

"We're good people."

"But you always fight me on that. I call you a person, you kick me and remind me you're Kaljaxian, not *people*."

"You're crashing my ocean liner here, son," she said, à la PT Barnum. "Don't be as concrete as the sidewalk."

"Got ya. No sidewalk thinking."

"Now you got it."

We hugged there, in the middle of that accursed Cleinoid street. I can't say how long we hugged. It got dark. Toño called us, head-to-head. He called us again. Before I knew it, Daleria and Doc stood gawking at us, right there by outside.

"Do you require oil, like the Tin Man of Oz?" Toño asked sarcastically.

"And new radios in your fool heads?" added an angry Daleria.

"Geez, can't a guy hug his wife without the whole town complaining?"

"We're *vertical*," soothed Sapale. "Give credit where it's due."

"It's very late. You're very conspicuous. Could you take a short commercial break and resume the show when we're home, *safely*?" asked Papa Toño.

I pulled back from Sapale and looked at her. "I don't see why not."

She shrugged and beamed, simultaneously. "Me neither. Let's go."

We left them in our dust.

"How long have they been married?" queried an incredulous Daleria.

"Apparently not long enough," replied an exasperated Toño.

Back aboard *Stingray*, EJ was stepping out of the Doc's lab, the makeshift sickbay.

"How's she doing?" Toño asked him.

"'Bout the same. Fever's still way up there. She's still delirious. Neither the Als nor I can make heads or tails of what she's saying."

"Al, play a loop," called out Toño.

"Eh ... the ants ... no the rubber will ... suicide—" was what he heard.

"In my qualified opinion, that there's gibberish," I announced.

"Qualified?" scorned Toño. "What makes you qualified?"

"No, I'm not. If I *knew* what she was saying, I'd have an *unqualified* opinion. I don't, so it's *qualified*, right?"

"No. Er," Toño struggled. "One refers—"

"Don't encourage him," warned Daleria firmly.

"Oh," he snapped his head to her and smiled. "You're right, my dear. You've learned. How grand."

"No, I'm serious," I protested.

"So is bad breath," returned Toño with glee, "but we try our best to ignore that, too, don't we?"

"I don't have bad breath," I defended, for some extremely unclear reason.

"That's good news," replied Sapale, patting my arm. "How about some coffee?"

"No," I seemed to say, "I ... well yes, but I *was* serious."

"Almost every day," said EJ with juvenile wonder, "I wake up and wish I were you, Jonny boy."

"Er ... you—"

Sapale forced a mug into my hands and my butt into a chair.

"How about those Giants?" she asked out of nowhere.

I looked around quickly. "Giants? Where?"

"Yes. The *San Francisco* Giants. Do you think they have the pitching to go the distance this season?"

"Ah, I don't think there's a season any more," I replied, rather confused.

"Hmm. Then I guess their pitching staff isn't all that important. I'm sure glad we had this conversation, though."

"And me? Am I glad, too?" I wondered in her direction.

"*Sure,*" she said slapping my arm. "Why not?"

What were we talking about?

"I think I'll go round on Tonflare," Toño announced.

My hands traced a circle in the air. "Go round on her?" I puzzled to my mate.

Sapale patted my arm, again. "Focus on the Giants, honey."

I started to remind her about no more baseball leagues, so I could defend myself, but I didn't.

Tonflare died the next morning. I'd like to say it was peaceful, but it wasn't. It was fairly ugly, in fact. She got sicker; her fever nearly broke the thermometer, and she grew more and more delirious without ever passing into a coma. Doc said that was unusual. Then again, for Cleinoid ex-demigods, maybe it was the norm. Who knew?

"The antibiotics didn't help?" I asked as a few of us, including a tearful Daleria, stood by the lifeless body.

"Not enough," he replied with a long breath. "Or maybe they killed her." He was frustrated. Man hated to lose a patient.

"Or," Daleria said softly, "it was just her time." She slid her arm inside Toño's. "You did everything you could, love."

I'm guessing Doc was still enough in the puppy love phase to not give her the tell-that-to-the-dead-patient-and-their-grieving-family speech. Lucky girl. I'd gotten it, oh, couple hundred times, by then.

"So, we need to continue to study this Bonzo society. I need to know if we pushed it past the tipping point."

I figured it might help to get Doc's focus off the dead enemy girl and back on task. Then again, I might have gotten my head handed to me on a platter. Luckily, he was in a reasonable mood, it seemed.

"Yes. I'll go over the eavesdropping videos with the Als," he said. "Daleria, you stay with me."

Because—I swear to all that is holy—I could not help it, I started making kissing sounds. Not my fault. Dude made me do it.

"Because you, my dear, can help identify places and things *I* cannot."

"You should be so lucky," I said to my wife, out of the corner of my dirty mouth.

"I heard that," he snapped.

"What?" I responded. "I was asking Sapale to help me discover places and emotions I've never experienced, either. What's the national emergency?"

He gave me such a look.

"Let's the rest of us hit the streets, people. EJ and the dragon people, go one way. Sapale and I'll go another. Happy hunting."

"Good *riddance*," hissed Toño.

We continued our exploring. I was hoping every Cleinoid we ran across was either completely okay, or completely dead. I didn't want anymore tug-at-the-heart-strings-Hallmark moments. We passed Daleria's old place. I made it a point to give it a wide berth. So sue me. I'm easy to creep out. The occasional figure passed us, heading the other direction. But, gone were the flying carpets—not going to miss them—the bizarre cabs, and the golems, naked and otherwise. Might miss the naked ones, just a bit. Sure. The males reminded me of myself, and the females reminded me I was a male. Nice eye candy.

No one, but no one, was in a chatty mood. We didn't stop or approach anyone, and neither did anyone give us more than a furtive glance. Those Cleinoids left alive knew damn well something bad for them had happened. Maybe they knew Clein was gone. Perhaps they just knew death was multiplying faster than bunnies in Spring. The town had a square of sorts. It was not decorated much, or well, but it might have served as a gathering spot, at some point in time. Whatever it was, it was abandoned completely.

"Should we start knocking on doors?" asked Sapale. She sensed the emptiness of the place.

"Maybe soon," I replied. I pretended to knock on a door. "Hi. The missus and I, we were just wondering if you were dead, yet, or not?" I smiled grimly. "Sure. It'll be a breeze."

"If they *were* dead, they *probably* wouldn't answer the freaking door."

I crossed eight fingers and held them up. "Let's hope not. Otherwise, I might lose it."

She elbowed me and stepped ahead. "You ain't got it, to lose it, bozo."

"So unsupportive," I whispered after her.

After a large loop, we were back at *Stingray* in a couple hours. EJ and my kids were already back.

"So, what are we looking at?" I asked, as I sat and took possession of a mug of hot joe.

"I'll start," said Toño. "We were able to process a large number of location images. Using the average density of historical action-hits we were a—"

"Historical action hits?" I questioned. "Like *Star Wars?*"

"No, Jon," he said tersely. "As in a *hit* being an observed individual passing the camera *actively*." He held up a finger with considerable frustration. "One person *passes*, one hit is *counted*."

"Makes sense," I responded with faint nodding.

I then received look number one hundred fifty three in Toño's repertoire of Jon-that-was-a-dumb-question looks. Not a personal favorite, but not the worst by a wide margin.

"As I was *saying*," he continued, glaring at me as he spoke, "We were able to establish that the activity level of Cleinoids is down, on average, sixty five percent, compared to comparable time intervals over the three months proceeding Clein's removal."

"That's impressive," voiced EJ. "Do you assume that sixty five percent are dead, or are the pig farts just less active?"

"From these data, we cannot say. However, using similar techniques where residential observations were

28

made, the resulting decreases are in the fifty seven percent range."

"So about two-thirds of the ancient gods are dead, based only on no more Clein?" I asked.

"That is my belief. Over the next few days and weeks, a clearer picture will probably emerge," replied Toño.

"To me, that sounds about right," stated Daleria. "I always thought that bizarre, fantastical beasts made up around that percentage of the population. The remaining third were humanoid, or at least some other unspectacular species."

"So, gosh, we're right up there with the bubonic plague and smallpox. We, *also*, wipe out seventy percent of a population," I said, with dubious glee.

"Yes, if you feel such an inappropriate comparison is necessary," chided Doc. "Genocide was our *goal*, was it not?"

"Yeah, sure," I sighed. "But *doing* genocide is so much more, you know, right there in your face and on your permanent record."

Daleria leaned over to Toño. "What's our *permanent record* and who's keeping it?"

He patted her hand. "A reference to an academic record and how marks are permanent. It's meant to remind students that grades are important, so they strive for good ones." He smiled, contented with the clarity of his response.

"Ah," she responded politely. She then leaned over to Sapale. She was sitting on Daleria's other side. "What's an *academic*, *marks*, and this *grades* thing?" No school in Godville, remember?

"Not to worry. It's boy talk."

Daleria nodded robustly. *That* she understood and was anxious to ignore.

"Mirri?" I asked.

"On our short trip, we observed that the streets were basically empty, the public houses were either closed or just no one was in them, and there were a few corpses in varying states of decay strewn about randomly."

"Any signs the civil authorities had made any efforts to clear the dead?" I asked.

"None. No signs of public authority at all, in fact. Certainly no golems tromping around," added Slapgren.

"And all the DBs were consistent with the bizarre, unsurvivable species theory we're preposing."

Daleria looked to Sapale. Before she could ask, my wife said, "*Dead bodies*. Boy talk. They *love* their boy talk."

Daleria, again, nodded briskly and knowingly. I was about to protest that clear, efficient communications were not *boy* talk. I decided that my correcting input was not, completely, mission critical, so I dropped it.

"Sapale and I can report more or less the same observations. I can tell you this, we didn't see anyone but ourselves smiling out there."

"Jon," Toño snapped, as he angled his head toward Daleria, "we can be *precise* without being *insensitive*."

"Oh, don't worry about my feelings," she said blandly.

"But we do. We must," Toño said with conviction. "However harsh your opinion was concerning the Cleinoids, some were your good friends."

Good friends. It hit me. "Al," I spoke with hesitation, "do you have a status on Wul?"

Daleria shot me a glance of concern.

"No, Captain. Sorry. There are definitely no recordings of him in public that we reviewed. No bugs were placed in any of his residences, him being a non-key member of the society."

"Understandable. Could you—"

"I just launched ten bugs. I'll let you know what they show, sir." When Al felt the need to be nice to me, I was probably in for a fall of some sort and extent.

"Thanks. Keep me posted."

Sapale leaned into Daleria. "He wants *updates*, not to be tied to a fence *post*."

"Thank you. I was a bit confused," whispered Daleria.

I rubbed my chin, twisting it roughly. "How soon before the remaining population starves to death?" I asked starkly.

Everyone shifted uncomfortably in their seats. It *was* the twenty four thousand dollar question.

Toño looked down and messaged the bridge of his nose. "I've ... we've run some preliminary models on that. Assuming there is no rapid and widespread switch to food production ... uh, and no *outside* assistance, we estimate starvation will take the, er, *bulk* of the population in six, maybe seven weeks."

"Factoring in cannibalism and similar scavenging?" Hey, I was mission commander. I needed hard facts.

"Including the recycling of *all* calorie resources," he replied grimly.

Daleria began to stand, as in, *I'm going to vomit and don't want to do it right here.*

Sapale soothed her arm. "You'll be okay. You're strong. We all knew this was part of the picture."

Daleria nodded weakly.

"In terms of *outside assistance*, I can guarantee there will be none. Zero. We came here to kill off these ... individuals. We're not organizing a Clein-Aid concert, folks."

"Jon," Toño said in a pleading tone, "we know this. The reality ... the reality of it is *still* unpalatable."

"I understand. If anyone cares or asks, this is one hundred percent *my* decision. I'm not taking a *vote* on whether to provide aid, in any form, to the surviving gods. I've made a command decision. That's it. Done, wrapped up, and placed-under-the-Christmas-tree done." I felt like shit even saying the words. I wanted to be tough for my crew, but I was speaking the devil's own words. Yeah, yeah, War ... *smore*. I know. Got the tee shirt in my closet.

"What will your orders be ... um, if any individuals come ... well, present themselves—"

"When we're done surveying the sit rep here and a few other locales, *Stingray* will go back into hiding." I answered, without Toño having to finish his uncharitable thought. "Speaking of which, are you done with the autopsy on Tonflare?"

Daleria's eyes bugged out. She hadn't known that was on the table.

"Yes," Toño replied softly. "Shall I ... dispose of the remains?"

I looked to Daleria. "Your call, Daleria. How do you want to handle this?" I kept the damn command-edge in my tone.

"Toño and I will bury her, if thats—"

"We'll all bury her, dear," Sapale said tenderly. "You name the place and we'll all be there."

Daleria nodded as she began to weep.

"Next order of business," I pressed on. "We'll conduct a limited series of residential inspections. No specific pattern necessary. Just knock, then kick it open if no one answers. We'll work in teams of two. Daleria, you'll stand watch on *Stingray* while the rest of us gather the intel. Any questions?"

"Yes, your *highness*," snarled EJ, "why all the Marines-storm-the-beach crap? We have two AIs and a million bugs. We don't need to do this boots-on-the-ground BS."

"We don't *need* to, you're correct. We will, however, do

the beach landing BS you refer to. We will, lest you inquire, do so because I say so." I let that hang in the air a few seconds. "*One*, it's the best quality intel. *Two*, we can interview any survivors quickly and efficiently, aided by the fact that a rifle barrel will have been placed on their foreheads. *Three*, it saves us the pain of sitting here aboard *Stingray* doing nothing else but wallowing in self-pity and the contemplation of how insufficient we all are as moral ambassadors of our individual cultures. Does that do it for you, Mister?"

EJ nodded with his head lowered.

"Then let's mount up and be the professionals they're paying us so handsomely to be, shall we?"

Was I being a hard ass? Yup, a fairly despicable one, at that. Did I need to be that much of a hard ass? Who can know? What I wanted to do was help my people out as much as I could in a surreal, impossible situation. If allowing them to resent me helped, then I was going to be the best whipping boy there'd ever been. If focusing their anger on me, not themselves, personally, was possible, that was what was going to happen. Sure, it'd have been nice to have someone else to hate for me, too. But, that role was currently unfilled and no applications were pending review. So, I would suck it up and take whatever, wherever, for my crew. That's what Jon Ryans do.

CHAPTER FOUR

Bolstered by his immediate success, Verazz searched the cosmos for more Cleinoids to vanquish. He estimated he was on a roll, so he mustn't stop. He was taken aback somewhat by the sheer number of vermin he discovered littering his domain. Surely someone else, somewhere, would be working to reduce their burden, too. Otherwise it might take Verazz days to kill every single one of them. *Days.* Unacceptable. But, a quest was a quest was a quest. So, he sallied forth, after a quick repair and modification to his glitchy visor.

The open cluster of Gamox was composed of twelve principle stars, a lot of cold gas, and not much else. As a young system, it harbored few planets on which life had evolved or been deposited. It did have one large rocky world, orbiting the third brightest star, Duvona, that had spawned a sentient species. The Premulex were an aerial species, small birds, as it were. Unlike the terrestrial avian species, however, the Premulex had modified aerodynamic exoskeletons with adjustable hollow plates, as opposed to feathers. And, as clever as a parrot may *sound* asking for a cracker, the Premulex were proficient at multidimensional mathematics and could fabricate all types of mechanical devices in their sky-bound factories. They never needed to land on the dangerous surface of Duvona. That was fortunate. The entire planet was a predator. A communal vine species had evolved that spanned the globe. Many shapes and forms of tentacles had developed to snare anything that moved on the ground, below it, or even close to it from above.

Carleferder and his brothers Def and Cla had landed on Duvona only recently. They were having the time of their immortal lives. Carleferder was the Cleinoid god of cooperation. He was vile, unworthy in every aspect of his being, and he cheated at cards, dice, or any other activity he engaged in. The cooperation segment of his power had mostly to do with his brothers. He was the alpha. His massive, segmented body said *worm*, along the lines of the sandworms of *Dune*. His very much smaller brothers were *commensal*. That was to say, the brothers obtained food and other benefits from their alpha without damaging or benefiting *him*. They were also fully detachable. Carleferder could carry them or set them down in a resting mode if he wanted to. Why did a species evolve in such an odd manner? Ask Darwin, not Carleferder. It was what it was, as far as he was concerned.

If the brothers afforded their alpha any benefit, it was that they laughed and derided victims as he mauled, destroyed, and consumed everything in his path. His mouth and jaw apparatus opened—ten meters across—and if it was along his path, it was history. Picture them. A two hundred meter long worm with an unstable, mean-spirited mind, sucking up everything in sight, while two appendages giggled and shouted discouraging words the whole while. Really, they were too much. If they'd had a mother, one would hope she'd be mortified. They did, for the record, not have one. Their species only reproduced asexually.

"Hey, Charlie," whooped out Cla (both brothers referred to their alpha as *Charlie* for no obvious reason), "get a load of the volunteer meal." Lacking arms or legs, he could not point at what he was seeing, but the trio shared a low-level telepathy, so they were good.

"Yeah, it's a meal in it's own can. How very convenient of it," chided Def.

Verazz ignored the brothers' taunts. He was in what he now called his *combat mode.*

"It's a small snack," hissed Carleferder. "If I didn't hate it, I don't think it would be worth the trouble swallowing it."

"Yeah, all that tin's going to give you such *gas,*" teased Cla.

"And I'm downwind. *Please* skip the shiny idiot," mocked Def. He was neither downwind nor bothered by gas. He was just an asshole.

"If you are done flapping your gums, or whatever, please make any provisions or consideration for death you need to. But, and I'm standing firm on this one, you have only *two* minutes to prepare. I'm pressed for time," announced Verazz, fairly triumphantly. His one-victory-in-a-row had gone a bit to his head.

"You know, Charlie, eatin's too good for this ton'a fish bait," snarked Cla.

"Maybe we should hang him up to dry. Make an example out of him, for the others," affirmed Def.

"What *uthers,* you simp. Charlie eats dem all. No one's left to *see* his examples."

"Oh, yeah. Charlie, *charge,*" shouted Cla.

And Carleferder did just that. He opened his maw and

careened toward Verazz. For his part, Verazz was toying with—you got it—his visor. He was having difficulty lowering it. Without witnessing it himself, Carleferder engulfed Verazz, along with several trees and a large swath of the communal predatory vine. He slammed his mouth shut with authority, and dived straight down. He ate his meals above ground, but he preferred to digest them on home turf, far below the surface.

Verazz blinked his eyes. Still, all was dark. He felt rapid, wriggling movement. He smelled such a foul odor he wished he hadn't. Almost comically, he reenacted the moments before the lights went out. Ugly worm yells at him. He graciously offers said worm to make peace, or whatever, his visor sticks, he readjusts it, unsuccessfully, there's a loud scraping sound, then he was wherever he was, in the dark rolling around in rancorous air. Ah ha! The stupid worm ate him. Oh, that was going to factor negatively as to how unpleasantly this fool died.

Verazz made to stand outside the insolent insect.

Nothing. The world was still dark and smelly. Verazz said he was to be on the surface of his home world, standing next to Carol.

Nothing.

Well this was unacceptable. Verazz willed the slime-monger to be on the surface, torn open and bleeding.

Nothing.

Hmm. He experienced a things-that-make-you-go-*hmm* moment. Was it possible his powerful magic did not work *inside* a Cleinoid, at least *this* Cleinoid? That would be awkward. Well, discretion being the better part of valor, he sent a thought-wave to Carol: *Sorry to bother, but I'm in a bit of a fix. Could you pop over and, well, I'll just say it, rescue me?*

Nothing. A chill ran up his spine. He'd never *not* been

able to communicate with Carol. This was vexing. If he couldn't free himself, and couldn't contact Carol, how was he going to get out, in order to slay this pompous beast?

Maybe he *wasn't* going to escape?

Where did that thought come from? It was certainly unwelcome and extremely unhelpful. Verazz tried to turn, so he was facing what he imagined to be the worm's mouth. He couldn't move. Something restrained him. It was a vine, wrapped around something on his waist. Oh, he realized by feel, it was that silly sword he'd worn for the show of it. The one he'd personally forged from neutron star core matter, imbued with the vengeful spirit of the Valkyrie, and sharpened to a microns width. He'd also plated it with gold, and inscribed ...

He was wearing a lethal weapon. Talk about your lucky foresight, coupled with unbridled vanity. Verazz drew his blade. Though he had little room to move, he was a Stone Witch. He used his inner power to force the sword side-to-side in expanding arches. Soon, he was slicing freely through his immediate surroundings. He willed the throat of the monster to have light. It did. His magic worked *inside* the beast, just not to *exit* the abomination.

Verazz spied the side of the gullet. He swung at it viciously, and it splayed open like tissue paper. A roar passed Verazz, as he stood in the throat. The worm stopped descending, in fact, it stopped moving altogether. Verazz swung, wildly at first, more confidently as the wound in the hell-spawn grew and bled.

Carleferder shot for the surface. His brothers slowed his progress, so he jettisoned them a hundred meters underground. As their digging abilities were nominal, he was basically leaving them to die. The harder he struggled to rise, the more the gaping gash in his throat grew, and it gorged itself with dirt. Larger and larger it swelled.

Carleferder began turning toward the injured side, it grew so massive. If he didn't make the surface soon, he never would. The best he would be able to manage was to move in circles, waiting for death to take him.

Carleferder angled his nose in the direction of the wound, and powered on. Then a slash parted his lower throat. Then his upper throat. Before he had moved ten meters, his head was more *unattached* than it was *attached*. It swiveled in ghastly spirals. Finally, with his last, best muscular effort, Carleferder's head slumped to one side, and tore free. True to his wormy nature, the headless tube continued to power upward. Now Verazz was standing astride the grotesque opening. His magic, unrestrained again, protected him from being crushed by the tons of rock and dirt he saw spread to allow his passage.

Verazz had a big smile on his face as the slowing remains of Carleferder cleared the surface, stopped advancing, and began wiggling spasmodically. Verazz stepped down as if exiting an airplane by way of a ramp. Standing clear of the death throes, he slapped his armor free of dirt. When the corpse moved no more, Verazz tried to lift his visor. It wouldn't budge.

Speaking through his face guard, he dressed Carleferder down, but good. "I warned you, vile scum, not to mess with me. But, *noooo*. You had to mess with the best. See what it garnered you?"

Carleferder didn't answer, especially since his severed head was still twenty meters underground.

"Next time, if there were one possible, I would slay you with less courtesy and more zeal. Alas, that is unlikely. But, be warned. Were it to happen, you would like *that* death less than you did *this* one."

Verazz considered his rebuke. He didn't actually know how much, or, more precisely, how *little* the wormy

Cleinoid had enjoyed his death. Perhaps he was being more spiteful than accurate. That would go against the chivalry he imagined was spelled out in the many books he'd seen, but not actually read, concerning the subject. He felt some small measure of remorse, briefly.

"Well—" he began to say to the headless, dead worm. Then he realized any words he might speak were fairly extraneous, so he didn't speak them. Instead, he beat a quick retreat ... er, *return*, to Carol's side. He just needed to get the rest of the dirt off, before she noticed it, and inquired how he came to be covered in it. That was a need-to-know topic, and she didn't.

CHAPTER FIVE

I knocked on the door, hard. Nothing. I knocked again, hard enough to nearly splinter the damn thing. One-two-three. "Okay, let's see what's up," I said to Sapale as I twisted the latch.

The door squeaked open. Locks, in the land of the gods, were basically unheard of. I stepped in and backed away from the opening area of the door. I swept the room with the barrel of my rifle. Empty.

"Clear," I called to her.

Sapale entered, and assumed my position as I advanced toward the nearest passageway. The kitchen was clear. So was the head and a bedroom. That left a large closet and one bedroom. We cleared the closet quickly. There was nothing inside it, whatsoever. I repeated my backing in coverage of the master bedroom.

"Cl—"

Something moved in the shadows of the far corner.

"Freeze," I shouted. "I see you and I have a gun trained on you. Arms up, slowly advance toward me," I stated loudly and clearly.

The shape took greater form as it advanced, slowly, arms in the air as directed.

"Slowly, pal," I said to what became clear to be a male. "We mean you no harm."

"Sure. Most people who break into my home with guns don't, either."

Funny guy. "Okay, stop there. My partner's going to frisk you. Turn your back to her."

"Do I get to frisk her after she does me?" he asked with no fear in his voice.

"That'd be a resounding *no*," Sapale shot back.

"This just keeps getting worse," he whined.

"You got a big mouth, buddy. If I were you, I'd be the nicest guy in town, not a smart ass. You know who likes smart asses?"

"No, but I bet you're about to tell me."

Dude just killed my, *I don't either line*. I *loved* that come back.

"He's clean," Sapale said as she backed away.

"That's it? Clean. No comments on my godly physique?"

"Why didn't you answer when I knocked?" I challenged, switching subjects.

"Because I didn't want company. Based on what I've seen so far, I can see I was correct to feel antisocial."

"I'm Jon Ryan. This is my wife, Sapale. We're here trying to determine what's going on. Clein is gone. I want to know the effect that has."

"I know you, *Ryanmax*," he quipped sarcastically. "You're one of Wul's friends. We met at a party a ways back."

I studied his face more closely. "Oh, yeah. Counterrup. You were with that beautiful angel."

"Now *dead, was*-beautiful angel," he replied glumly.

"Sorry for your loss," I said flatly.

"Thanks. You sound real torn up."

"You the only one home?" I asked.

"Yes. I live alone. No guests, other than you two."

"Jon," Sapale called out, "I don't think we're going to learn much from Mr. Funny Boner, here."

"I agree. Sorry to bother you, Big C."

Sapale slipped out, and I backed away, keeping my gun on the home owner.

"You know, you can shoot me, if you want."

"You feeling otherwise poorly?"

"I'm feeling realistic. Clein is gone. I'll be dead in a few weeks. Shoot me now or I starve real soon. Makes no difference in the big picture."

"Maybe not. But how do you know help won't arrive?"

"Help? You stupid, or something? Who's going to help me? *Any* of us?"

I realized I might learn something from this guy, after all. "Maybe Clein comes back."

"You are stupid. If Clein was here, and is gone, there's only two ways that happens. One, it left. If it did, it's not returning. Two, it was cast out. If it was, and it wanted to return, it already would have. But, since we treated it like shit, why would it want to return?"

"It likes us in *spite* of our shortcomings?" I asked rhetorically.

"Not hardly."

"Maybe another source of power takes Clein's place."

"Sheesh. Okay, you may officially leave. I don't have much time left and I don't want to spend it talking to a boob."

"What?"

"Another source of powerful magic is, what, on a road trip? It might swing by because it heard from Clein how

43

nice we are? A piece of free advice, *pal*. Don't count on it. You're about to die. Plan accordingly."

"Nice seeing you again, Counterrup."

"I love you, too, Ryanmax. As this is our last goodbye, let's keep it short and sweet. Go screw yourself."

"Back atcha, pal."

I sped out the door, and hooked up with Sapale outside.

"Okay. We have one vote for we're-all-going-to-die," I remarked.

"Couldn't happen to a nicer guy," spat Sapale. "You know, you and I are fundamentally different."

"Do tell," I responded.

"I'd have shot the asswipe. He might not have felt better, but I sure the hell would."

"You know, I got the same vibe from him. Asshole, ass wipe. Way too assy for my taste."

"Do me a favor. When we're safely home, play that back to yourself. Then apologize to me about a hundred times for having said such a stupid thing when I could hear it."

"I'm sorry," I cupped a hand over an ear, "did you say let's press on to another target, gather some more critical intel?"

"Yes, that's exactly what I said. Oh, you're the best man to ever live."

"Why, thank you."

"No prob. Said in the same spirit as the prior remarks."

We proceeded. The next two places we knocked, the owner opened the door and cursed at us before insisting we leave. I took that to mean they were at least healthy enough to be energetically rude. Third one wasn't a charm. We guessed trouble even before we knocked. The smell wafting through every nook and cranny was overwhelming. After a few perfunctory taps on the door, I went in first. Naturally, as a gentleman, I offered for my wife to proceed me. She deferred. I made a show of sweeping the room, but only for a second. My barrel was trained on a puddle of bubbling ooze. With each new popped bubble came a new frontier in gut killing stench. Seriously. Each was worse than the previous one, both in quality and quantity.

The deceased looked to be Avaliry, a land-bound bird that looked distractingly like Big Bird of *Sesame Street* fame. But, I'd met him. He was maybe BB's evil twin. He had no manners or sense of personal space, and he was known to start pecking off body parts of those conversing with him socially. Well, he wouldn't be annoying anyone from here on out, aside from his annoying decay.

"He's not going anywhere," announced Sapale. "I'll clear the rest of the house."

"Which just happens to place you as far from this darkness as possible."

She tilted her hear like she was surprised, "Imagine that. It does, doesn't it?" With that, she sped away.

"So, Avaliry," I asked from the corner farthest from his bubbling remains. "How's it going, lately?"

No response.

"Heard any good jokes lately? No? Say, have you been losing weight? Nice. Who doesn't want to do that? Sure, you look good. Your waist's so skinny I ... I can't even see it. No, absolutely not. This new look does not make your butt appear bigger. Um, I'd hold off going to the tailor, just yet. Sure, you lost, like, half your body weight. But If you buy that custom-fit silk suit too soon, you'll need another before you know it.

"Okay, my turn, I suppose. A man walks into a bar with a juicy hamburger under his arm. He orders a beer for himself and one for the burger. The bar tender yells back, *We don't serve food in here.*" I waited a few seconds. "No, to *serve* alcohol to *food* is being played off the bar *itself* being in the habit of *serving* food items. It a pun. Huh? Look, forget it. If I have to explain my jokes, they become less funny."

I was over this stiff. No sense of humor, period. Fortunately, Sapale returned about then. "You two making friends?" she asked sarcastically.

"Maybe. Just not with each other."

"Give it time, Jon. You tend to force early relationships. Give him some time."

I poked at the goo with a boot tip. "Time does not favor friendship with poor old Avaliry."

"You could be right. I, however, might be, also," she said.

"How so?"

"I say we leave. Once outside we burn these clothes and we get very drunk."

"Sounds like my honeymoon with Gloria."

"You had a decaying DB at your Las Vegas dream wedding?"

"Yup, Her mom." I nodded toward Avaliry. "The resemblance is striking. My soon to be MIL used bottles full of Shalimar, so she smelled worse than Avaliry, here."

"Glad I missed the wedding," Sapale remarked matter-of-factly.

"Yeah. We didn't have space travel then, so it was unavoidable."

"You done yet?" Sapale pressed. "We *do* still have half a town to clear."

"Do you know what Gloria's first words to me were, that next morning, as our bleary eyes eased open while our guts cramped up?"

"Not going to encourage you," she grunted.

"Gloria struggled to focus on me. She actually pawed my face to help identify who she'd just wed."

46

"Do we get to the first words *soon?*" growled Sapale.

"She smacked her dry lips, burped, and said, *Hot damn, Frank. I thought I married* Carl."

"Sounds like Romeo and Juliet, all over again."

"True love. It's a wonder onto itself," I replied mistily.

"I can't believe the marriage only lasted six weeks. You had to be blindsided by her lawyers."

"Lawyers? She had her new husband come kick my ass. He told me to not *ever* return to my apartment, because he was a man who knew how to protect his woman."

"You let her next, drunk-fool boyfriend kick your ass, Ryan?"

"You bet. Hey, I'd lived with Gloria six *weeks* at that point. Marcel, her new hubby, took a swing but missed by two counties. I fell flat on my back and started groaning. They locked arms and staggered away, giggling like the village idiots they were. Never saw either one again."

Sapale powered up her plasm rifle.

"What?" I spun, looking for trouble.

"So you never actually divorced Gloria?"

Uh oh. "*Technically* isn't a word used where love lives," I replied, hopefully.

"So, when you seduced me, you were still a married male?"

"Ah, in *fact*, but not in *spirit*." I smiled big, "And I'm not prepared to say it was *I* who seduced *you*."

She flipped the control toggle from stun to incinerate.

"Sapale, please. The check her mom wrote to The Chapel Of Sexual Love bounced like a rubber banana in a monkey's paw. We were never *actually* married."

Her weapon powered down. "You done yet, again?"

"Lead, and I shall follow."

After I said *lead*, she double-timed it away. By the time I finished *follow*, no way she could hear me. Marriage is such a gift.

We started picking structures randomly. A house here, a commercial building there. A pattern soon became clear. What were offices, places of business, were vacated like a bomb had gone off. Bars, clubs, and restaurants were mostly closed. The few that were open were sparsely populated by quiet humanoids drinking quietly. Even at the rare table with two patrons at it, they didn't exchange words. Interestingly, everyone served themselves. If the owners were normal enough to still be alive, they clearly weren't bothering to run a business with no future.

As the hour-mark neared for our turn around, I selected what the Cleinoids called a love club. Those were, basically, whorehouses that served lots of booze and a few crumbs to eat, for those so inclined, between other engagements. Probably fifty percent of the night spots in Godville were of this ilk. Wul dragged me in once. I left in ten minutes and never returned. And that's not because I feared pissing off the missus. No, it was because the love clubs had nothing to do with love. They were debauchery institutionalized. Not my style, thank you very much.

"This your regular spot?" Sapale teased as we entered.

"Huh. I wish. No, they said I was too lowbrow to enter. Management feared losing their better clients if I was allowed regular access."

"Makes sense," she mused. "Gotta protect your business model."

We were in by the time our banter died off. First thing that was obvious was that no grand celebration was in progress. Quiet as the grave covered the noise level. Scattered piles of sand indicated where a golem had been when the shit hit the fan. For what it's worth, I noted two distinct populations of sand piles. Larger and smaller. Males and females. I'd assumed a golem was a golem, and the illusionary magic used to sustain them accounted for the size differences.

I stumbled, literally, across the first true oddity. Two humanoids were lying dead on the floor. Unlike the other DBs we'd screened, these were locked in mortal combat. Each was choking the other.

"Toño, I'm sending some scans," I alerted him.

"Ah, it appears they killed one another."

"How? Who won?"

"That should be fairly easy. There. Yes. No question, they killed each other. The one in the gray clothes has a broken neck. The other has a crushed windpipe. They probably died within seconds of each other."

"Thanks," I said, and closed the link.

"Maybe they had an old score to settle?" wondered Sapale.

"Around here, that's a safe bet. Or, they went crazy."

"No witnesses, so we'll just have to file the info away."

The kitchen was not empty. A pair of females sat together. They were eating a stew or soup. When they noticed us, they completely disregarded our presence, returning to their meal.

"Hi, there," Sapale called out cheerily.

One looked up and studied her. "We're out of soup. Go away."

"We're not hungry."

"Lies. No stew for you. Leave us."

"If you're out of stew, what's that simmering in that pot?" I grew bolder.

"The last person who asked that question."

"Maybe we'll settle for *him*."

"Won't be ready for hours. You'll be long gone."

"We have nothing but time. When did you say he'll be ready?"

"Ten minutes after you leave."

"Say," Sapale asked openly, "Is that a gun there, to your left?"

The woman shook her head with contempt. "No, Batty Bettie. It's a ladle."

"So, if *I* had a rifle," she held hers up, "while all *you* have is a ladle, what's my motivation to leave unless I actually want to?"

"Not much, I guess."

"Hey," I said to the silent partner, "your friend there's a comedian. Maybe you could use her to reopen this club?"

They both stopped responding. They figured we didn't look too desperate, so we could be safely ignored.

"Let's check the rest of the club out," I said.

The storerooms were half full of boxes and bags, mostly food. The cellar was absolutely stuffed to the rafters with booze. Racked, boxed, or just laying on the ground. Booze, booze, booze. I made a mental note of where to go if I needed a strong dose of liquid courage. There was also something JPW—just plain weird. Way in the back, there was a small chamber, like one a fourteenth century monk might live in. A rudimentary cot, a wooden table, and one wooden stool. There were two piles of sand, one larger than the other, next to each other on the floor. On the cot lay the remains of a most bizarre creature. Seriously, he looked like Thoth, the Egyptian god of the judgment of the dead. An ibis beak curved toward the ceiling, his pencil-neck was almost completely gone from decay, and his chest was caved in because of similar decay. Instead of smelling, well, like a rotting corpse, he smelled of pine resin and rosemary. Weird and a half, right? I could not get out of the room quickly enough.

The building had a second story. Such levels were used for privacy with the golem or god of one's dreams, however briefly one might need the privacy. There were also large rooms, for meetings or banquets. The private hook up rooms were all empty. The first three conference rooms were equally void of inhabitants and looked like they hadn't been used in quite some time. The last had yet another odd surprise. At the head of a long table, in the weak light afforded by a solitary, dirty window, sat a man. Well, a humanoid. He was a couple meters tall and around a hundred kilos. His skin was reptilian. It was even green. His face was Kelly green with small scales, and he had two beady black eyes protruding slightly. If I was doing a guest star role on *Doctor Who*, he'd be a Silurian.

He sat with his head down, supported by one hand, with a flask of a clear liquid to one side. His glass was empty. Either he didn't notice us noisily entering the room, or, more likely, he couldn't care less. We stood there an awkward second or three, staring at each other, then at the silent lizard dude.

"What'cha drinking, pal," I finally called out.

In ultra-slow motion, he head rose, then his eyes rotated up, and finally he coned down to visualize us.

"Water," was all he said. He sounded deeply depressed. Then again, why wouldn't he be deeply depressed?

"Mind if we join you?" I asked with bravado.

He silently gestured to seats on either side of his.

I sat to his right, Sapale sat to mine.

"There are glasses over there," he said with dismal enthusiasm. He specifically did not point, or even look to where he referenced.

"We're good," Sapale replied. "You seem down, or something. Oh, I'm Sapale. This is my brood-mate, Jon."

Dude didn't flinch. He just sat there like a bump on a log.

"Water?" I asked. "The basement's full of *fire* water. You give up booze for Lent?"

Even my mentioning something he could not have known about didn't light a fire of interest under his sorry ass.

"It is the End Times," he finally, and oh so morosely, stated. "Water is appropriate for such a calamity."

"I rather fancy large volumes of powerful intoxicants would be my ticket," I interjected.

That brought his sad eyes up to mine, if only for a heartbeat. "One does not celebrate the end of things. Water," he half-lifted a hand and tossed the back of it at the flask, "is too proper for such an occasion."

"May I ask you a personal question?" I posed.

"You just did."

"May I ask you *multiple* personal questions?" Tough audience tonight.

He shrugged. "Who cares?"

Wow, the guy needed a Prozac enema.

"Why are you so very depressed?"

"You heard me mention the End of Times?"

"Yes. But, look, how old are you?"

He shrugged again.

"Approximately?"

"A few billion years old, maybe."

"So, hang with me here. You've lived a good life, a very *long*, good life. So it ends. Why be so down about it? *Everything* ends."

"We don't."

"We *are*," I played along as a Cleinoid. No need to muddy the conversational waters. "Everything passes."

"You said that already. Hearing it twice does not soften the blow."

"Soften the ... what's your name?"

"Gilbetle," he said with disinterest.

"Gilbetle, how many transheavals have you participated in?"

There was a bit more challenge in his expression. "Four."

"So, four times, you went forth and destroyed, killed, and maimed. Am I right?"

"They *were* transheavals," he replied in a strained tone.

"You ended countless lives, innumerable places. You know death. You know of End Times. What's so different in the present case? We are meeting *our* end."

"You seem to be the only one pleased with the prospect of the fall of the Cleinoid gods."

"Who said I liked it?" That's when it hit me. What sort of nonsense conversation had I gotten myself into, and, more critically, why? My reflex was to shoot this Gilbetle, put us *both* out of our misery.

"You argue in its favor. You scorn me for wanting my existence to not end."

"Whatever." I clearly wasn't going to gain any information or insight into anything I cared about with Mr. Debbie Downer, here. I stood.

"I have a question for *you*, stranger."

"Shoot." I plopped back down.

"There was the prophecy."

"Yeah. I was never a big fan. It wasn't as punchy as a prophecy needs to be, IMHO."

"Was it fulfilled? Did three miracles work as two and perform one task?"

"You say it even less punchily. It's *when three miracles that are one work as two.*"

"Will there be a quiz, later on?"

"Let us hope not."

"Was it?"

"Yes. It was. That said, why do you care?"

He was glum silent for the better part of a minute. "Because *that* makes it official. It is The End Time."

"You needed a slogan to know it was happening, pal? Would you feel better if I wore a tee shirt with the affirmation written on it?" I pointed outside. "Did you not notice the dead bodies, the piles of sand, or the absence of magic?"

"You are a cruel man."

Do not hit the depressed pity-party lizard. No, Jon, show restraint. He's having a bad day. Sensitivity, empathy, love-thy-neighbor, Jon.

Screw it. "Listen up. The Ancient Gods wreaked havoc on *gazillions* of innocent lives. At the end of the party, someone's got to pay the bill. This," I pointed at him roughly, "is what paying a very big bill feels like. If you're sad, it's because you're *supposed* to be. If you'd rather not perish from this earth, well, tough titties. *Y'are.* Buck up and receive your karma. That's life, or, in your case, the end of it."

"I said you were a cruel man. Why are you so cruel? What have *I* ever done to *you*?"

"Are you familiar with the term *vengeance by proxy*?"

He shook his head slowly. "No."

"That's reassuring. I just invented it. Vengeance by proxy is where one agent, *me*, exacts revenge on behalf of another agent, *everyone you wronged or allowed to be wronged*. Traditionally, the *recipient* of VBP is less than enthusiastic about the receipt of the bill, which is, in the present case, sweet revenge. So, you see, my friend, I only *seem* cruel. I am an agent of those who damn well *would* be cruel, if they

54

FALL OF THE ANCIENT GODS

were still alive to be cruel to a piece of shit, such as yourself. If I hurt or offend, please blame the ones you killed for pleasure, *not* the messenger."

"Would it be too much to ask of you, if I insisted you leave me in peace?"

"Thank you for asking. I'm happy to field that excellent question. Yes, it is asking too much. You *deserve* VBP. I, *being* VBP, very much need to remain here and hound you and cause you to be *as* miserable as possible until your cold, black heart stops beating."

"Ah. I thought as much."

"However, I bear good news for you, clone of Gilbert Gottfried. You, as a prime example of a SHPOS, are not worth my time, effort, or bother. So, I will be leaving to try to make *other* Cleinoid dickwads as miserable as you are. I might, with your permission, employ your photo to aid in that effort."

Sapale covered her brow, looked to the table, and mumbled, "Not sure the SHPOS *knows* what a SHPOS is."

"Ah. My wife makes a valid point. I, wanting you to suffer maximally, will inform you that, SHPOS is short for a *subhuman piece of shit*. You are welcome, citizen." I stood and held my elbow out to Sapale. "Shall we?"

"Our work here is done," she returned with a smile.

CHAPTER SIX

Verazz stomped loudly into Carol's chambers. He wanted to make certain she was both awake, and aware, of his glorious entry. His hand was poised on the pommel of Dragon Slayer, the new name he'd given his sword, after having killed a large worm with it. He suspended multiple floodlights above himself as he walked, to provide just the right touch in terms of illumination and show. Shadows might have detracted from his overall splendor. Who was he kidding? Nothing could do that. But, then again, why leave even tiny details to chance?

"Ah, Hulknormous, you're finally here," shouted Carol without rising from the comfort of her elevated bed. "Hurry to my side before my husband returns. I've missed you, so."

Verazz stopped. The lights went out. "I am hoping that is a joke in the worst taste," scorned the jealous husband.

Carol shot straight up and covered herself with her sheets. "Oh, no. I've been discovered in my dalliances. What *ever* shall I do?" She rested the back of her hand on her forehead.

"Very droll. V-e-r-y droll," he sniped. "Here I am, returning in triumph after proving myself to you, and you tease me. I give glory to you. You give headaches to me. How is that fair?"

"Oh, I'm sorry," she declared, "I never got the *be fair* memo."

He huffed. "Are you going to ask me how I *fared* in my exploits?"

"If it would make you happy." She grinned weakly.

"Thank you for asking." He forgot instantly that he was mad and reappeared sitting on the edge of her mattress. "It was grand. No, silly of me. It was gl—"

"Dear, you're covered in mud. At least I hope that's mud. Please sit over there."

A fainting couch appeared atop a pedestal, only slightly separated from hers.

"Thank you," he said, unaware of the slight, "now, as I was saying, I was grandglorious. Wh—"

"Grandglorious? Is that a word, now?"

"It is now, if it wasn't before. Wh—"

"I know of *vain*glory, and *star*glory, and *de*glory. But *grand*glory, not so much."

"Fine, fine," he responded with irritation. "Hyphenate it, if you must. Wh—"

"I'm not certain it's proper to hyphenate just any combination of letters. The adverb *very* and adverbs ending in *ly* are *never* hyphenated. There are rules that apply, in this domain."

Verazz dropped his arms, which had been swinging overhead grand-gloriously. "I wish to relate my triumphs, my victories, which prove my love and my worth to you. I do not wish to dwell on or bog down on grammar."

"Your call, love. Proceed."

"Thank you." He raised his sword arm high. "Wh—"

"Oh, dear. Some of that muck has fouled my favorite fainting couch. Look *there*," she pointed at the large, irregular smudge, aghast.

"*Honey*," he whined. "Can I *please* tell my *tale*?"

"*May* I please, not *can* I please. Of course you *can*. You *are*." She giggled.

"Enough with the grammar," he said with anger. "From now on, whatever I say is, by definition, grammatically correct. I have so willed it."

"Fine. If you feel so strongly as to see the need to change word usage to fit your whims, be my guest."

"I do not need your invitation. The rules are already altered. And mine are not whims, they are innovations, new frontiers of ... of ... I'm sorry. What were we discussing?"

"You had just finished your *grandglorious* tale of your victories and I was saying how very brave you were. Then *you* dribbled that brown ooze onto *my* fainting couch. How do you plan on removing the stain?"

An irritated Verazz backed away from the couch, which left him floating freely in the air. He raised a hand and cast an annihilation spell against the defenseless furniture. It, well, it was annihilated.

"There," he said with angry finality. "That is how I plan to deal with the damn spot."

"Out," she snapped. "That was my—"

"Whatever it *was*, it is *not* any longer. As to the grime you so pointedly remarked upon, over and over, it came from the gullet of a large and most disagreeable worm. I was able to secure a sample after it swallowed me, whole. Were it not for Dragon Slayer," he rattled his sword in its scabbard, "I would have been lost. I hope, as I take my leave of you, to quest again for *your* glory, that my near-death experience pleases and amuses you no end."

Oh, bother, Carol reflected. Perhaps she'd gone too far, pushed a few too many of his buttons.

Naaah. She was good. She should, and might even be, nice, when next he disturbed her rest. But, on this occasion, she was happy to leave the chips where they lay.

CHAPTER SEVEN

After a few days, and only a handful of patrols, a clear, cohesive picture developed as to the state of the Cleinoid existence. It was grim for those who survived a quick but brutal death. Theirs was to be a less dramatic, but more agonizing demise. I was fine with that. Served the sons and daughters of bitches just right. What we needed to establish was how long most survivors had left. Also, and this was a critical twist, was it possible the ancient gods could rally? Might they quickly develop into hunter-gatherers or farmers? Endless epochs of lazy self-indulgence suggested that transition was unlikely. But, if they did turn that caloric-acquisition corner, they might become a self-sustaining culture. That would be bad. If that were the case, we had to factor in the likelihood of their redeveloping magical abilities. That was not an option. If I even got a whiff of that possibility, we'd kill every loving one of them. By hand, if need be.

Obviously, I didn't want to linger in the Cleinoid realm a second longer than necessary. Not only did I loathe the place and its inhabitants, I wanted to help clean up our universe. I knew it had to have suffered mightily while we were gone. The sooner we joined the fray, the sooner the last Cleinoid would face-plant and their threat would end.

"Als," I said, to begin the pivotal meeting we were having in the mess, "please summarize your findings from reviewing the bugging devices we've placed throughout this cursed land."

"We've scanned over fifty thousand hours of recordings. Subdivided as to open-public venues, personal quarters, and public buildings, the results are all basically the same. Seventy one point eight five percent of the Cleinoids present when we first arrived are dead. Only one point three percent of those deaths occurred more than one day after Clein was removed. The bulk of the post-Clein deaths were by suicide, but a small number were homicides. Five were accidental, three by disease."

"And your estimate of their food and fresh water reserves?" I asked formally.

"Potable water is not currently a limiting factor. Running water has basically ended, but the vast cistern system still holds much clean water. Additionally, there are enough streams and lakes to support the present population indefinitely."

"And the food situation?"

"Somewhat challenging to estimate. There are many basements and storage facilities housing untold amounts of consumables, not counting intoxicants. There are even greater stores of those. Though the Cleinoids used magic for most of their food production, they, for whatever reason, believed in larding away stores for future use. If we assume all food chambers are full, and estimate the number of such sites based on extrapolations of a random sample of structures, the longest the current provisions could evenly support the entire population is six months."

"Wait, I thought you said they'd starve much quicker," I protested.

"It is *likely* they will all starve in a shorter time period. It is, however, the worst-case scenario for us that they *might* have six months worth of provisions."

"Maybe we should make it our main focus to destroy consumables?" suggested EJ.

"That would be an efficient use of our time and effort, I agree," I replied.

"Once we start degrading their food supplies, we have to assume they'll start to defend them, quite literally, with their lives," stated Sapale.

"True, but they have few weapons, no advanced technology, and most of their more fearsome members are already dead," responded Toño.

"True," she added, "but hunger is a great motivator. They'll become vicious animals."

"Vicious animals with plasma holes in their foreheads," remarked EJ.

"Let's move on," I said firmly. "How will we monitor the possible return of magic?"

"The bugs will probably be the best tools for that," said Toño. "The Als will know pretty quickly if anyone begins using magic."

"Agreed, Form Three," responded *Stingray*. "We have extensive records of magic performed in the past. Algorithms to scan for similar patterns will be easy to establish and extremely accurate."

"Good," I said. "Make it so."

"Aye, Captain," shot back Al.

"Toño, any electronic scans that might help?" I asked.

FALL OF THE ANCIENT GODS

"Possibly. We established that Casper and Jéfnoss had similar spectral characteristics. I should be able to set up an array to monitor for those types of emissions."

"Good. Then I think we have those issues covered. That leads right to the subject of when it will be safe to return home. We don't actually need to see the last starving wretch drop dead. We only need to remain here until the society passes the point-of-no-return, so to speak."

"I've given that some thought," said Toño. "We cannot, as of this moment, predict that time frame. However, it will be quite easy to monitor the average weight loss per individual, using our bugs. Once statistically valid lines are established as to the pace of calorie deprivation, the crisis point will become obvious."

"Huh," grunted EJ.

"What?" I asked.

"For billions of years we've all fought like hell. We've killed *millions*, between the lot of us. And now, we sit like morticians waiting for a population to dwindle away, quietly. It sucks, that's all."

"Winning the war is all we're about," responded Slapgren. "A win is a win is a win."

"True that," I snapped. "Any victory won without losses on our side is a righteous victory."

"Sure," EJ mused, "just a pathetic one, though."

"How about we keep it to ourselves, never tell another soul. Would that make it better?" I teased.

He shrugged and dropped the subject.

"I won't hold you to it, Doc, but give me your best guess how long we need to wait, assuming we don't place a finger on the scales in our favor?"

"Whatever I say, you will hold me to it. You always have. That said, I think we're committed to at least two months of monitoring. Between three and four months is my actual estimate of how long until matters become unambiguous."

"Okay," I said standing. "We have a few months in a shithole with nothing to do but incur unnecessary risk if we drop our guard. Bored, but in danger."

"For us, that's Tuesday," responded Sapale, with a wicked grin.

"Tuesday it is," I concurred robustly.

We were all soldiers. Even Toño was more warrior than wizard by then. Enduring boredom, often uncomfortably, was our stock in trade. At least we weren't sitting in mud being rained upon, with leeches crawling up our hooches. But, months of hiding away in a metal cube was no vacation. The Als kept it perfectly clean and odor free. The heads, for the few that needed them, were never gross. The meals were always warm and free. Still, once boredom gored you with its nasty horns, you were in trouble. Add to the picture that we needed to stay sharp, because, *hello*, we were the ones who sentenced everyone currently in the process of dying. At the very least, the public at large would like to include us in their impending deaths. So, the merry crew of the happy ship *Stingray* hunkered down for grim times.

For a few days, I assigned people to "review" the videos the Als had screened. Yes, it was make-work, but I hoped that keeping people busy would stave off interpersonal friction. That plan didn't survive contact with reality. A couple rotations in, everyone griped that the Als had committed zero oversights or errors, and that watching hours of dull recordings was worse than mixed-doubles colonoscopies.

I toyed with the idea of sending out milk-run patrols, you know, ones where it was impossible to encounter danger. But my crew was too seasoned to fall for that. Plus, it's the mission where nothing can go wrong that breeds Charlie foxtrots. In the end, I just kept an eye on my people, watching for signs of undue strain. I didn't have to wait long. And you'll never guess whose temper flared first. EJ's. Alert the media, right? He was watching *Mr. Ed* reruns in the mess. You know, *a horse is a horse, of course, of course?* He was on his fifth revisit—and science cannot explain how any sentient could watch four complete volumes of *Mr. Ed* and want to watch it a fifth time—when Slapgren asked *politely* if EJ might select another viewing option.

"Hey, shit for brains, could you turn that soul-killing drivel off and watch a blank screen. It'd be more entertaining and less annoying."

EJ glanced over at Slapgren. "That's right. You dipsticks didn't have TV. You just played charades by changing shapes, then screwing whatever squirms to life."

No way a version of me would escalate a tense situation, right?

Slapgren took a moment to reflect, and calm himself. He understood the importance of crew unity.

"I'll show you some fancy shapeshifting, then you can screw this," flared Slapgren.

He held up his flat hand, and *shifted* it into a fist. Then he threw it at EJ. He had to vault halfway across the room to do so, but he did so with speed and commitment.

EJ was on his feet in a burst. I happened to be in the room. I elected to negotiate a peaceful settlement to the minor misunderstanding. I grabbed either participant in my probe fibers and pinned them, respectfully, against the ceiling.

"Since you two are so bored, I thought maybe you could clean the roof. I've been meaning to, but, man, have I been busy."

"Put me down," wailed EJ. "I'm going to strangle you."

"Well there's my motivation to free you. I love being choked." I set him down, but didn't release him.

Sapale, my trusty straight-man, said, "He means he wants to strangle the neck below your head and above your shoulders, numbnuts, not the one you're thinking of."

I looked surprised. "Oh. In that case." I repinned EJ to the ceiling. I let him hang a moment. "Okay, people, this ends one of two ways. Y'each grow up, calm down, and go your separate ways, or your mail starts being delivered up there."

"I don't get much mail," Slapgren mumbled, his mouth being, for some reason, pressed against the ceiling.

Mirraya came in. "I can only speak for one idiot, Uncle. But," she pointed to Slapgren, "hand me that one and I promise he'll behave himself. Otherwise he'll spend a week living as a toad. A very small, very lonely toad."

I dropped Slapgren into her waiting arms. Dude was smart. He didn't even pretend to try to wriggle free. Nice toad.

After they were in their cabin, with the door sealed, I set EJ down. "What say we watch us some more *Mr. Ed?* I loves me my *Mr. Ed* face time."

He smoothed his jumpsuit out while glaring at me. "I hate that show."

"Then why the devil were you starting *Mister Ed* Season 1, Episode 1, *The First Meeting,* all over, again?"

He tossed his head to one side. "I was bored."

"No shit?" I thought a sec. "You and me. Shore leave. Now." I thumbed over a shoulder.

"Shore leave?" he derided. "Gee, wait, let me go to sick bay and grab some condoms."

"Think of it as a *working* shore leave."

"No condoms?"

"No condoms," replied Sapale with great emphasis.

I had *Stingray* move us close to Blind Faith No More. I wanted to check on an old friendoid. EJ could come alone. Hell, it was a dive bar. Maybe he could get in a couple fights. It'd do him a world of good. Plus, I did want to see the look on Queeheg's face when we both wandered in.

The place looked, and unfortunately smelled, the same. But it was empty, aside from the large, burly owner. He stood behind the bar, scouring the surface with a dirty, wet rag. His intense focus on one poor spot in particular was impressive. That had to be one hard wood.

We stood across from him for several seconds before he noticed us. Have you ever seen *Hogan's Heroes*? Specifically, remember Sergeant Shultz? Picture him looking up at us. Queeheg shot his glance back to the spot and started polishing again. "I see *nothing*, I hear *nothing*. Colonel Hogan, I was not even *here*." Yeah, that Sergeant Schultz.

"Are you open for business?" I teased.

"Ah, Master Ryanmax. Goods to seez ya, as always."

I extended my hand across the bar. "Hi. My name is *Jon Ryan*. I was born on a planet called Earth, in a different universe, over two billion years ago."

Poor guy. He was dumberstuck. Instead of shaking, he gave me a tiny finger wave. "Nice to meet youz, I'm sure."

"This is my alternate timeline self. His name is also, *surprise*, Jon Ryan. But you can call him EJ."

"No he cannot. My name is Jon Ryan."

"He's the one you clobbered," I said with a large

grin. "Nice move. He was possessed by Jéfnoss tra-Fundly at the time. But, you probably didn't know that."

The mention of the evil one got a bug-eye expression out of old Queeheg.

"I ... I attacked Jéfnoss tra-Fundly?" Queeheg said weakly. I was hoping he didn't pass out.

"Not to worry," I said with a grin, "he's dead now. Jéfnoss, not EJ."

"Do *not* call me that in public," snapped EJ.

"Ya mindz if I sits?" asked a queasy bartender.

"I'll grab a stool," EJ quickly offered.

"Better?" I asked in a perky tone.

"No, but not swoonin'," he replied slowly.

"Seriously, Queeheg, I came to see how you were doing," I said warmly. "I consider you a good friend."

He nodded. "Honored to be thought'a as such. Mutualality, to be certain, extends to you, lord."

"*Jon.* Never lord."

"Earth, ya says?"

"It was destroyed, but, yes, *Earth.*"

"Nice place?"

"I thought so," I responded, looking to EJ.

"Top flight," he added. "Big oceans. Lots," he opened his arms wide, "of oceans."

"Oceans er nice, if ya likes um," Queeheg reflected.

"Especially so," responded EJ.

"Your, vacationing 'ere, Jon?"

"Not *exactly*," I said cautiously. "It's probably not a good idea to, you know, dwell on the *whys* of it."

He furrowed his massive brow. "Not best to dwells on da whys of it? Why?"

On boy. I didn't want to have him vaulting for my throat. "Well, you know, what with Clein ... you know—"

FALL OF THE ANCIENT GODS

"I do? What do I knowz about Clein, dat I don't know I knowz?"

"Clein's gone, right?" EJ asked incredulously.

"It *is*?" he gasped. "Where'd it go, 'n why'd it *go* dar?"

"Long story, probably not mission critical to explain," I responded.

"It tiz?"

"Oh, yeah, totally gone," replied EJ. "You didn't, like, notice Clein wasn't present?"

He bobbed his head side to side. "Has been a might slow lately, come a'mentions it."

"Slow?" I asked with a slack jaw. "Queeheg, when was your last patron present?"

He gestured to us. "Now."

My eyes fluttered. "And before us?"

He looked up and counted on his stumpy fingers. "Six .. no, seven days."

"And that didn't strike you as *odd*?" I pressed.

"In a sense, surely. But I didn't think's Clein'z da cause."

"And you feel, normal?" EJ asked.

"Bones ache. But dats not uncommon't my age."

"Okay, then," I sighed. "I bring bad news."

"Oh, no, Jon. I hates bad news. Ya keeps it, if ya pleases."

"No, I already gave it to you. Clein is gone. It's never coming back."

"Ah, *dat* bad news. Er, too late fur ya to keeps it, I'm supposen."

"Probably."

"Dat said, can I gets anyone a drink? I think I needs one, quite likely more."

"Us, too," EJ shot back quickly. "More, *definitely*."

Queeheg produced an oversized bottle of nectar and three tall mugs. We were going to do some drinking! Alright, already.

After a couple mugs consumed in silence, I asked Queeheg the hard question. "So, my friend, now that you know about Clein, what'll you do?"

There was a glint in his eyes. "What does ya mean? I'll stay open extra late, open extra early, and sleep in a'tween."

"And if there're no customers, because, they're like, too scared shitless?"

He grinned wide. "Then'll be more for me." He toasted. "Me and you, Earth friend Jon."

"Sounds like a plan." I clanked his mug soundly.

"Ya 'member when ya asked about me and da transheaval?"

"I do indeed," I replied.

"And I tole ya I wasn't partaking?"

"Yes. You said you didn't have anymore pillaging and destruction left in your heart."

"Probably did'na say precisely dat, but you're close enough to claim victory with da truth." He looked out the swinging doors. "I'm a very old man. I done tings I best shouldn'ta. Dars a weight on me soul, to dis very day. I figure I gots atoning to do. I'm not afeared of da prospect nor the consequences I freely brought on meself." He thumped his chest with a fist. "I owns da evil I done. I'm a man not afeard to pay da tab he's run up. If dis is da end a'old Queeheg, so bez it. I can't tink of a better time, meself." He gulped down his firewater and slammed the mug down so hard it shattered. "And *dats* de end'a da philosophical portion a'tonights entertainment."

"Let me guess," I said toasting him. "Da rest'a iz drinkin'?"

"A man after me *own* fancy," he responded, slapping my shoulder.

"Who ever you were, my friend, you're a good man

now. I'm proud to have known you," I said with stone-cold sincerity.

"Tanks, Jon. Dat does ease me thinkin', if only a bit. Here," he burst out jubilantly, "I sees glasses in need a'fillin' and long faces. Dat will ner'a do."

EJ and I lingered a good long while. He was mostly quiet, which was unexpected. Civility was unexpected when it came to that me. In the end, I made an empty promise to return soon, and often, and I said my final goodbye to my biggest fan in Godville. Him, I was going to miss.

CHAPTER EIGHT

Gafel and Torent were twins. They had spent almost every single second of their immortal lives together. Neither could recall their childhoods, if they'd had one, their parents, or their planet of origin. All they knew for certain was each other. As creatures judged to be undesirable by most other living beings, they spent much of their time alone, apart from a disdaining universe. That was fine with the brothers. The Listorians felt everyone around them was *as* revolting as they were repeatedly told they were by everyone around them.

Throughout all space-time, wherever sentience has arisen, one of the first concepts to be wrestled with was that of good versus evil. In nearly every instance, good was pictured as graceful, alluring, and inviting. Evil, on the other hand, was depicted as vile, frightening, and merciless. Horns, sharp teeth, and an off-putting appearance were near universal standards. The Listorian brothers owned that dark end of the physical spectrum. Most any species, anywhere, would take one look at them, and commence with the running and screaming. Three meters tall, four hundred kilos of tough, red hide, with spiraling horns, pointy tales, and rock-hard feet made them unforgettable, if nothing else. And, though they were clairvoyant and rarely spoke, when they did, their voices were the very images of demon voices we all carry in our DNA. Basso deep, full of echos, and unmistakably malevolent.

Gafel and Torent were the actual last two Cleinoids to exit on the one and only transheaval to Prime, with the Rage, long ago. They waited for all their brethren to pass through Dominion Splitter before sailing in. They *wanted* to be apart from the swarm. After the masses of ancient gods rallied in Prime, and then dispersed, the brothers, again, lingered. It wasn't until they were completely alone, floating in deep intergalactic space, that they began discussing which direction to strike out in. Loners, to the end.

For a few years, Gafel and Torent traveled inseparably and destroyed together. It was so natural. To do otherwise was inconceivable to either twin. And, oh, how they marauded. As if laboring to live up to their devilish outward appearance, the brothers ravaged reality with a vengeance, a cruelty, and a lust that was unparalleled by any other pair of Cleinoids. If destroying lives and property were Olympic events, they'd share the gold medal in the doubles competition.

But, as with all matters concerning lives, family, and cooperation, there came a time when Gafel and Torent began to desire to be apart. A rift had developed between them, not surprisingly, born of competition, rivalry, and, above all, unquenchable greed. They began to feel their other half was getting the better share of the spoils, and not by accident or chance. They both equally knew with a certainty only insanity can spawn, that scheming, trickery, and deception were the tools of their treacherous brother's attempts to take what was rightfully theirs.

So, after leaving a once verdant, thriving world in ruin and despair, they parted ways. Strong words were spoken, the kind that cannot be taken back, by both twins. Curses, warnings, and threats were exchanged, and then they went in separate directions. Gafel went one way, and Torent went in the perfectly opposite direction. For a time, each enjoyed victories over lesser beings. But the dominations were less ... satisfying, less ... rapturous. Soon, each twin was having trouble recalling precisely why he thought the other had acted in bad faith. They began to miss one another.

Gafel called out across the endless void of space to his brother. "Are you there, brother?"

Torent smiled. "Yes, dear brother, I am. I was just thinking how much I missed you."

"We were fools, were we not?"

"Grade A, certifiable fools, good brother."

"We ... we should journey again, Torent, together," spoke Gafel.

"Yes. That would be ... agreeable."

"Where, then, are you, brother of mine?" asked Gafel.

"I am in the Third Quadrant assigned to Rage. I am near the Peramabic Parallels."

"How far have we traveled apart, we fools? I am approaching Red 8 in the Second Quadrant."

"And how have you faired?"

"Well," he laughed maniacally. "I have killed so many, so cruelly. You would be proud of me."

"I am, even without the details."

"Torent, I am turning to join you as we speak."

"That is acceptable. You are far, presently, from a suitable victim?"

"Well, one is all but in my grasp, but I cannot wait to rejoin you. I shall forego the destruction of this vile world, at least until we can consume it together," affirmed Gafel.

"Well, here's the deal, brother. I, too, am within one foul intention of a place called Rivule. It orbits the Peony Star. I have longed to destroy it, truth be told. There is something wondrous about the planet. I know it to be a jewel among all desires."

"Then, my just brother, you should have it. You assimilate this Rivule. I will deal with the planet that is now within my grasp. After our dominations, we can rendezvous and join, again, in conquest."

"This is as it will be. But, as I miss you so, and cherish our mutual destruction, I ask of you a provision."

"*Anything.*"

"Let us descend upon our hapless victims as one, though we are physically separated. As I plunge into the atmosphere of Rivule, you dive into your victim's air. We will be united in action, if not location."

"I love it. I am orbiting the planet now."

"As I circle Rivule. On three, we both rain death on our foul prey."

"One—" said Gafel.

"Two—" called out Torent.

"Three—" sang out Gafel.

And the harbingers of end times for each planet below launched with power and speed to revel in their evil. One minute later, however, both twins were struck by a force. It was as if hollow lightning struck them both in the chest, and it drove out the essence that was Cleinoid godliness. They were both rendered limp, and they fell. Gafel tumbled, head over heels. He was dizzy, confused, and, for the first time, ever, he was afraid.

He called to his brother, but he found he had no voice.

Gafel sank in the gravity well of his chosen planet, and he began to heat up quickly.

Torent fell from the heavens head first. He accelerated at an alarming rate. His arms and head began to glow, red. He knew, for the first time ever, pain and suffering. He called out to Gafel. He knew Gafel heard him, because, a god knows such details. But, his twin did not respond. Torent felt his brother's fear, his anguish, and he felt his twin begin to vaporize. It was as if Torent, too, was being incinerated. Within seconds, Torent knew Gafel was no longer, and would never be again.

Torent willed that he would stop rocketing toward the planet surface. He slowed, if only slightly. Torent wished he had wings, so he could break his fall. Tiny wings appeared on his back, two pairs. They beat frantically, but they accomplished nothing. Each was seared off before they could alter Torent's descent.

The ground grew larger. He warmed, but the pain of intense heat faded. When the surface was only meters below him, and Torent was moving like a rock thrown off a high cliff, he closed his eyes. He said, with all his godly conviction, that he was to stop.

Six inches above the hard ground, Torent stopped, mid air. He did not hover. He was *stopped*, as he had willed. He released himself, and dropped the short distance to earth. Torent reached out again to Gafel. There was no Gafel. Torent searched the planet on who's surface he stood. It still teemed with life, glorious, delicious life. Gafel was gone. Torent did not know why. Torent still was. He understood this. He was a god ... *duh*.

With no more thought or reflection, Torent willed himself to be where a nearby city was, as it bubbled with unsuspecting life. Delicious, defenseless life.

He would make do on his own.

CHAPTER NINE

The next months were a flat out drag. The AIs monitored the Cleinoid world and documented its steady decay and a complete lack of rallying or rebounding. The rest of us were mired in bored inactivity. When you're fighting like hell, hopping from frying pan to pot to frying pan, you always think, man, what I couldn't do with some downtime. A beach, a beer, and a babe—or a brawny buck, hey, women get to dreaming, too—and nothing to do but zone out. Then, the universe gives you some semblance of a break, and you end up scratching your eyes out. Go figure.

I suppose the one-way, unchecked decline of the sick and twisted Cleinoid society was obvious, in retrospect. I mean, for billions of years, if they weren't burrowed in like ticks in self-indulgent excess, they were stomping the life out of some poor universe. My worries that this pathetic, sadistic race had bootstrapping as an option, in its genetics, turned out to be laughable. There was no history of enterprise or innovation. Hell, there wasn't even a history of an honest day's work for all but a handful of them. So, when faced with an existential crisis that involved sweat, toil, or the lifting of a finger, *forget about it*. I honestly got the impression most of the pukes would rather die than condescend to what they viewed as common labor. So be it.

In many regards, the Cleinoids were like the lilies of the field. They grew, but they neither toiled nor spun. In other words, they never gave a thought to tomorrow, only the sweet indulgences of the moment. But, eventually, some folks did begin to notice that supplies were running low. What had been storerooms filled to the rafters, were now echo chambers. And, OMG, somebody do something, the booze started to run out. That was worse than no food. And not a single nutcase so much as fermented a sugar suspension with some yeast. Even the lowly WWII grunts in the hellish Pacific Theater figured out how to make hooch by drilling a hole in a coconut and stuffing in raisins from their field rations. But not these lazy asses. If it didn't literally appear by magic, they were clueless.

Of course, there was no sense of common purpose or community among the prideful ancient gods. When it became clear some had less than others, trouble set in with a pure vengeance. It's a tale as old as time, and the Cleinoids were not immune. Instead of pooling resources and sharing, hoarding and hiding became the norm. So, of course, fighting broke out. At first there was individual thievery or strong-arming. But, when supplies really got low, there was rioting in the streets. Yeah. You can't have a good societal collapse without chaotic riots in the streets. And me, I watched the fighting nearly in tears from laughing so hard. I don't mean to be cruel, but it was funny. Forever the mighty gods used magic. Now, all the really big, scary ones were dead. The surviving, normal Cleinoids had never used a weapon or swung a fist in anger. So, it was the Nerd Olympics. Everyone punched like girls, and no one could throw a rock that had any chance of striking its intended target. It was Loonie Toons, pure, simple, and entertaining in a low-brow way.

Still, I elected to stay and observe. It was *possible* that magic might reignite, and we needed to be there to see it didn't take hold. My fears about the Cleinoids developing hunter gatherer or agricultural techniques were totally unfounded. No one so much as planted a flower bed or looked under rocks for bugs. As sad as it might otherwise have been to witness, I never forgot how intensely evil the guys were. Karma, as they say, can *be* a bitch.

As food became truly scarce, the fighting ebbed. No one seemed to have the energy to try to find food, let alone ineptly try to take it from others. That's when I began to feel confident we had done the impossible. We had caused the elimination of the ancient gods, at least in their home universe. Genocide was never more welcome, or justifiable. That's when I decided it was time to pay my last social call. I needed to square matters with Wul. I took Daleria, mostly because she insisted on coming to see her old friend. Also, I wanted to pretend I was not obsessed with killing every last Cleinoid.

He was at home when we knocked on the door. For weeks, no public houses had been open, so he had no place to go other than staying put. He, being the god of business and enterprise, not surprisingly had squirreled away more provisions than most. At a point where five to eight percent of the population was dying per day of starvation, he was only thin and weak.

"Jon, Daleria. My, I thought I'd seen the last of you two." He harrumphed, then coughed pitifully. "I guess I thought I'd seen the last of everybody."

"May we come in?" Daleria asked tenderly.

"Of course, of course," he held out an arm and stepped backward. "Be my guests, please."

We sat in the main, open room that adjoined the kitchen area. He pulled his chair close to ours. "You both look more well than might seem expected," he said with a twinkle in his eyes.

"I actually can't say the same about you, old friend. You're still vertical, but you don't look so good," I playfully teased.

"Jon," said Daleria with a wheeze. "How can—"

"Now, my dear, I would expect nothing less than brutal honesty from this one," he responded with a touch of glee.

"Still—" she considered me like I was a large pile of dog poop, sitting there on the couch.

"It's alright," he assured her. "It's great to see you both again," he marveled. "It truly is. And I could not be happier that you're both so healthy looking."

"Back atcha, pal, er, except for that last part," I replied with a snap of my fingers.

"We brought you this," Daleria said, as she slid a large bag across the floor to him.

He peered inside, moving a few items to see what was underneath the top ones. "Hmm. Bread, some dried meats, and sweets." He held up a flask. "Water. I suppose that's nice." Then he lofted an even larger bottle. "Now this is more like it. Nectar?" he asked of me.

"No, better. It's called *nufe*. You'll love it."

He spread his arms at the gift on the floor. "This is most welcome. I'd say it's priceless, but it's more valuable than that. Thank you." He put on a concerned expression. "You will still have enough?"

"Not a problem. We, we have the ability to synthesize what we need."

"Huff. We used to, also. It was nice. You're lucky."

"What's ours is yours, old friend."

"For the time being," he responded dubiously.

"How ya figure?"

"You told me your tale, Jon. I know you will be leaving soon. Then, this gift, as marvelous as it is, will be forgotten, on account of me being dead."

I sighed deeply. "It doesn't have to be like that," I said flatly.

"Oh, I fear it does," he responded, trying to sound upbeat.

"Daleria's coming with us," I said, nodding toward her. "You could come, too."

That brought a surprised look to his gaunt face. "An unexpected offer," he mused.

"But sincere," responded Daleria. "Where we're going is uncertain. What it will be like is less certain. *But*, it will not be starvation in this wretched place."

"You make it sound like quite the adventure. So, Jon, you told me before that you've had no contact with your universe since you've been here."

I nodded.

"So, in the time since Rage egressed there, you do not know what the status is of your home."

"No. Not clue one," I replied tersely.

"It could be, well, I was going to say *as* bad as it is here, but that's hardly possible."

"Not like this, but it might be one hell of a mess."

"And when you get there, what do you anticipate finding? What's your best guess?"

"I'm hoping the Cleinoids are all dead and something survived to become a part of."

"Or, you might be back in the middle of another fight for survival?"

I hadn't thought about that option. "Without Clein?

They have to be mostly dead and entirely powerless. It'd have to be like here."

"And why is that?" he asked coyly.

"Because ... because—"

"Because it doesn't have to be. Jon, those members of Rage were *gods*. Never count a god as down and out until you're standing on his dead body."

"So, maybe there's still a war going on. If so, I can tell you what we'll be doing," I said numbly. I did not relish that prospect.

"And if I were to join you, I would be asked to fight my kind, my brothers and sisters?"

"Yes," I replied slowly. "Or we could settle you in, somewhere safe. Your call."

"Wul, we're talking about rampaging demons, here. If we need to kill them one at a time by hand, then that's what we need to do," Daleria said with passion. "But, if you want only peace, we would fully support your wishes."

"My dear," he said with all the warmth and tenderness in the universe, "fighting would be what you need to do. That is *not* what I am inclined to do."

"You said yourself, you were sitting out this assault on Prime," I protested, when I saw where he was going.

"Participating in a sporting rampage and fighting a civil war are two very different things," he responded with a grin. "What would you do with a *pacifist* on your side of the battle lines?"

"We'd treat you as the friend you are," replied Daleria quickly and emphatically.

"I believe that to be true. But, I would not tolerate such behavior. Not of myself. I'm guessing that what lies ahead of you is *war*. I also assume I can't very well catch the next ship heading back here, to avoid the fighting."

I shook my head. "We can only make the trip so many

times. My science guy is very certain we can make one more trip, but even that is not guaranteed."

"Wul, please," Daleria pleaded, "you don't have to fight if you do not want to."

He shook his head, wearily. "I cannot, in good conscience, bask on a beach, fattening myself up while the ones who made that possible are in harm's way. I *cannot* do that. Not to people I love."

"I respect that," I said grimly.

He took his turn at sighing deeply. "So, I must say thank you again for these treats, and goodbye to you, my friends."

"We're not leaving for a few more days," I said hopefully. "You have time—"

"No, I do not. I am staying. Jon, you know our history. You know *my* history. I very much deserve to die. I asked you last time we talked, that when my time came, you would make it less miserable for me." He gestured to the supplies. "So, *you* have, and *I* thank you. Now I ask you to leave, with, and, for whatever it's worth, my blessing."

I couldn't argue with the man. He'd made a rational choice, dancing adeptly through a logical minefield.

I held out my hand. "I'm not going to say goodbye. Fare well, my forever friend."

Daleria dashed over and gave him a big old hug. All in all, it was nice. I would have picked a different tune from the jukebox of life, but the one Wul selected was good, too.

The morning we left for home, I anonymously dropped off two last gifts, with detailed instructions as to their use. Sure, he knew who they came from, but he could neither refuse them, nor would I know which one, if either, he chose to use.

I left him a small food synthesizer I had Toño whip up. It could keep one or two people fat and happy for years. The machine produced potable water and a wide selection of edibles from the filtered atmosphere. Damn thing actually produced nufe. Hell, I needed one for my cabin.

The other, which I had Al fabricate, was a fifty caliber English flintlock pistol, an exact replica of the pistol Captain Jack Sparrow was given when he was marooned by the mutinous Captain Barbossa. And, just like in the movie, it could fire but one single shot.

I was going to miss Wul. He was a good man. He was a good friend.

———————

Those last three weeks were a gruesome hell. I sat at the control screen twenty four seven, watching the once mighty Cleinoids dwindle, die, and decay. Then, one afternoon, Toño informed me that the remaining impoverished population had officially and irrevocable passed the caloric point-of-no-return. They were, if not currently dead, on the schedule, their names written in blood. My blood. Well, he didn't add that last part, but that was the truth of it. In this moral case, androids had very real blood. I waited one more day, because I deserved to witness them suffer without the possibility of hope. Then, it was time to leave this God forsaken land of the ancient gods, forever.

CHAPTER TEN

It had been fifteen years since Jon Ryan and his crew left their universe to save it. Fifteen long, bloody years of death and destruction. The toll extracted by the ancient gods would never be tallied up. The universe was too large to report to one central location to document events. But everyone left alive knew the losses had been terrible, and they had been ghastly in nature.

The Milky Way galaxy had suffered much worse than any other. As the first to mount an ineffective but discernible defense against the Cleinoid blight, the galaxy was the focus of the bulk of its fury, of its rage. The Joint Council for Interplanetary Defense and Cooperation had survived, but only as a communications hub. Every planet JCIDC had based itself on was obliterated. It switched to a series of space stations, then large warships, and finally to a flotilla of small, expendable vessels. Wherever they relocated to, the Cleinoids hunted them down and consumed them with glee only the depraved can know. The members of JCIDC were so short-lived, and died so violently, that the JCIDC became known as *the indoor killing field.* To be a TIKF member was to be, quite literally, a dead person walking.

On one morning, which began as depressingly and as full of woe as any other morning in recent memory, the JCIDC met by holo-link, as it always did at that grim juncture. Each member broadcasted from their own ship. In the fifteen years of futile resistance, campaign promotions had replaced elections and appointments to the JCIDC. The turnover was so blindingly high that no other system would guarantee that a full council was able to call itself to order on a daily basis. It became an inside joke, in fact. Kitchen staff and janitors never strayed near the meeting arena when a JCIDC assembly was about to start, for fear of being made a full, voting member, and then dying horribly.

That particular morning, Light Colonel Binswar Dof Cresent, of the Montilla Assemblage, was prepared to present an odd report. He'd compiled a set of data from a few scattered worlds that made no sense. The reports he'd glanced at, in fact, were challenging to believe and of dubious value. But, there were so few other matters to bring up, aside from the swelling toll of losses, that he felt it was appropriate for him to do so. If nothing else, his update would be a much needed pause in the horror that the morning briefings had become.

The session began as usual. The secretary general, William M. Trummelson, stood, slapped a palm on the table, and said, "Good morning."

Then, everyone present laughed at him. The joke was that no morning could *possibly* be good. It was the one constant in their grim days, and the only occasion where any member laughed — ever.

Bill had been on JCIDC for three weeks, and SG for two whole days. He was a relic, by present day JCIDC standards. In the proceeding month, there had been thirty seven SGs. The average life expectancy for anyone with *SG* in front of his, her, or its name was less than a day. That was why, of all the members laughing that particular morning, Bill laughed the loudest.

"I will not present the List this morning. It's been forwarded to your handhelds if, for reasons of masochistic delight, anyone cares to review it."

The *List* was the casual name for the Manifest of Deaths and Losses, Daily Summary and Report. Why bother to say the long title, when the speaker would most likey be dead well before they could finish that mouthful?

"We're down to seven thousand six hundred functioning ships-of-the-line. That's system wide."

Preck Vusion, a junior member promoted from the training program aboard the command ship *Venture Not*, raised a hand. He was Lopopian, and being one was not a walk in the park. The species had a stunningly disadvantageous quality. They were mostly a clairvoyant race. Okay, no biggie. But they had *the* most awkward affect on every other known life form. Anyone looking at a Lopopian kept repeating in their mind, *now that's a bad idea*. How one species' telepathy could be universally perceived as, *now that's a bad idea* was inexplicable. Scholarly tomes had been written on the subject, and it still made no sense. But, Lopopians were, throughout the galaxy, associated with *now that's a bad idea*. Try gaining any credibility while carrying *that* cross. If a Lopopian was handing you a million dollars, cash, you'd keep thinking, *now that's a bad idea*. A sexy Lopopian asks you back to his or her place, and—you got it—all you can think is, *now that's a bad idea*. Talk about being an involuntary celibate. Boy, howdy, and plus.

"You're new," said a tired SG. "Here's the drill. You want

to speak, speak. No show of hands, please." Bill, in spite of years of training, and an otherwise iron will, thought to himself, *and no bad ideas, please.*

"Yes, sir. Thank you, sir."

Bill closed his eyes in fatigued disgust.

"In the available ships of the line, what percentage are cruiser-class or better?"

"What percent are ... *what?* Who the hell knows, cares, or asks that type of bullshit?" Bill wheezed. "To have *that* many craft capable of launching spitballs is a plain, old fashion miracle."

"Thank you, sir."

Bill didn't wish death on poor, young Preck. But, when it came soon, and very soon, he sure wouldn't send flowers, either.

"Any other business?" Bill asked, more as a threat than a call for input.

Dof saw his moment. "Bill, I do have an odd report to present."

"Odd? Wow, that's wonderful. If it's not depressing, mind-numbing, or put-a-bullet-in-your-own-head bad, I fully welcome it." He spread his arms out, graciously.

"I have notes from a handful of systems. Their daily Aberrant Body Reports list a few ... anomalies."

ABR were categorized as such to streamline data in a unraveling society. If a body was hard to identify, which was generally the case if a body was actually *found*, it was an AB, so it went on the ABR. No one recalled, due to institutional fatigue, why ABR were tallied. But, they were, so they were fair game for discussion.

"*Anomalies,*" questioned the SG with strained patience. "Ya going to *make* me ask what the hell that means?"

"No. Sorry Bill. I don't know what else to call them."

FALL OF THE ANCIENT GODS

"How 'bout you tell us the facts and we'll come up with a catchy name. Hmm?"

"On Fentermile 6a, a 'large lump of flesh resembling a flying turtle was found in a shallow depression.'"

"Someone finds a dead turtle and reports the remains. Hell, why didn't they keep quiet and just *eat* the damn thing?"

Scattered chuckles ensued.

"I do not know, Bill. I'm reading the words as we received them."

"Sorry, Dof. I'm having a day, that's all."

"Not a problem. I also have an 'alert' from the Jackmost Colony World."

"The what?" queried Nodad A'tal, another very new member. "Do we have ... er, one of those?"

"It was a mining planet, run by a long defunct company, Jackmost Skids, LLP."

"You're making this up, right?" responded Nodad. "What would a company named *Jackmost Skids* even do?"

"Well, for one thing, they got eaten by Cleinoids, so they decided to close shop," answered Bill. To Dof, he instructed, "Go on."

"The colony 'alerts' JCIDC that several large 'prodigious heaps of dead things' were found near the cave opening where the remaining miners dwell in."

"I think we can file that one under 'too much to drink,'" said Bill.

"Yes, normally," responded Dof. "But there's one other anomaly that demands consideration."

The SG's eyebrow shot up. *Demands?* It has been a heck of a while since any *fact*, other than our obvious defeat, *demands* discussing."

"This one comes with a vid, Bill. I'll ... there. It should be on all your handhelds."

"Looks like a dead crustacean of some sort," remarked someone.

"Yes, but look at the trees behind it. Those are full-grown maples."

"My, that would make the crabby, what, twenty meters wide?" asked another voice.

"I'm told it was approximately twenty meters by eight meters," replied Dof.

"Okay, it's *our* lucky day. We killed a Cleinoid," scoffed Bill. "Even a blind pig finds the occasional acorn."

"This one shows no signs of trauma. Plus, no one *claims* to have killed it."

"Do Cleinoids die of old age or self-loathing?" queried Bill, tongue in cheek.

"Not hardly. They're immortal, remember?" said Dof.

"To my eternal regret," mumbled the SG.

"What's more, the Cleinoid shows signs of significant decay. That, the report states, is unexpected, because the remains were not present where they were found the evening before. That's confirmed by *three* separate individuals."

"Who'd you say called this report in?" asked Bill.

"I didn't. It was our military base on Gilliam, the main facility, in fact, Fort Defiance."

A loud whistle was heard.

"Yes, tell me about it," affirmed Dof. "I think this report is *highly* credible."

"So, they—"

"They have regular patrols, both inside and outside the membrane. Yesterday, the last team completed 'an uneventful excursion' with 'nothing out of the ordinary.' That was at 19:50, GST, local. Then, at 06:30, the remains were discovered. They specifically report no engagements during the night, and no disturbances on any monitors."

"Do they say what their drones show?" asked Bill with new intensity.

"On your handhelds, also."

After thirty seconds, the woman to Bill's right spoke. "The big ugly just crawled to a random point and collapsed."

"That's what the boots on the ground think happened, too," responded Dof.

"So, an otherwise healthy monster ... what? He just dies? They're immortals. Am I missing something?" Bill Trummelson's anger, and frustration, and fear boiled over the edge of the pot.

"I think we *all* are, Bill," came the calming words of Anja Daničić, his assistant SG. "By definition, a pile of rotting meat is *mortal*. Bill, do you realize what this might mean?"

"No," he said sternly. He had learned never to allow hope into his heart or into his spirit, never again.

"If one drops dead, maybe more will. Every Cleinoid that does us the supreme favor of dying voluntarily will receive a sympathy card from yours truly," she said lightly, "I can promise you that."

Bill stood and began to pace. Unconsciously, he tightened his tie, and set the knot to the center where it belonged. "So, we have one *confirmed* Cleinoid monster spontaneously dying. We have a couple other sketchy reports. If this is a new trend, I need to know about it. If some are dying and others aren't, we need to help the stragglers along." He angled his head, lost in thought. "Dof, try and nail down those flaky reports. Images would be ideal. *Go.*"

"Sir," Dof saluted and disconnected from the session.

"Anja, I need you to put out a High Priority bulletin to everyone, and I mean *everyone*. Have them actively search out dead Cleinoids and report anything unusual back to us immediately."

"Got it, Bill." She switched off the meeting and started writing the alert.

"Everyone else, I want our reserve units to come out of hiding and engage anything that even looks Cleinoid. If it moves, kill it. And, stress to them, there might be dead ones out there, so look specifically for those. God in Heaven, people, we may have just been granted a reprieve from on high."

The meeting ended without the formality of adjourning, and all the parts of JCIDC flew into motion.

CHAPTER ELEVEN

"Jon, I think it's safe to leave," Toño said quietly, but respectfully.

"I know. You told me that three days ago, and you repeated your advice yesterday. I *heard* you then and I *hear* you now." I sat staring into a long-empty coffee mug.

"But—"

"But, I need to be certain."

"Jon, we've been doing war for so long it's obscene. We both know with certainty that *nothing* is certain in war. This is as *obvious* as it will ever get. Ninety seven percent of the non-native population is dead. The lingering three percent are moribund. The smaller species, with lower metabolic rates, might cling to life for several more weeks. But, Jon, if they presently stumbled across an unmonitored grocery store, they'd still die. It's too late for all of them."

"I ... I *need* to know," I said with words so feeble they could barely leave my mouth.

"No, you don't. You already do. I, a scientist of some skills, have told you so. That, plus you know their deaths to be a done deal, suggests you are having us linger here for other, *unspoken* reasons." Toño basically thundered in a controlled voice.

You know what sucks? When someone knows you so well, you can't BS them. And, damn it all, I'm the king of bullshit. It's one of my go-to superpowers.

Not being able to hide from a true friend, well, it's awfully reassuring, too.

"So, Dr. DeJesus, what is your professional diagnosis, in the curious case of Reluctant Jon Ryan Syndrome?" I asked quietly.

"Self-loathing, leading to a bad case of I Deserve This World Syndrome. Did I mention IDTWS is both pathetic and annoying?"

"Doc, you're a doc. You can't be annoyed at your patients' burdensome illnesses. They—*we*—\deserve your empathy."

"Let me guess. You read that in a fortune cookie, back when humans still wasted time reading the stupid little white slips of paper?"

"No. It's just Hippocratic, or something."

"Before my head melts from the onslaught of drivel, allow me to summarize. Horrible masses attempted horrible crimes against innocent billions. You stopped them. The way you killed them was that you killed them. Yes, you did not *negotiate* a peaceful resolution. That is because none was possible. So, one group, the horrible or the innocent, had to die as a whole. You made the morally correct decision and successfully executed it. That is the point where most stories end. No joy, but no remorse."

"I'm guessing this fairytale does not end at this happy, massacre scene?"

"No. Unfortunately, the lead character is mired in a pool of doubt-shit."

"Doubt passes *poop*? Who knew?"

"Jon, yes, you have a lot of blood on your hands. You know what I say?"

"Twelve Hail Mary's and three Our Fathers?"

"I should strike you down for that blasphemy, but, somehow I think you'd tally that as a win, on your juvenile ledger."

You bet your sweet ass I would. Dude, that would be typed in all caps.

"What I shall say, as the only *adult* present, is thank God for Jon Ryan."

Did *the* most Catholic person left alive in the universe just express his profoundest thanks on account of me being *the* most genocidal person in *any* universe? Crap. That suggested he was right about whatever he was saying. I hate that turn in a conversation.

"Jon, you did the only thing possible to cure the multiverse of the worst cold it could possibly have. Was it messy? Yes. But that doesn't alter the fact that all life, everywhere, presently, owes their continued existence to you. What's more—"

"More? You mean if I act now, I will additionally receive not one, but *two*—"

"What's *more*," he continued, unfazed, "you saved all the future universes the Cleinoids would have destroyed, in time."

"Jon Ryan, Savior of the Unborn," I said in a low tone. "Nah, not catchy enough."

"Hmm. Now that I know you are sufficiently back to normal, I will re-ask. May we go home, now?"

I smiled up at quite likely the cleverest man there was. "I don't know. Let me check with my chief engineer."

Twenty minutes later, I had everyone assembled in the mess. Sapale, EJ, Mirraya, Slapgren, Toño, Daleria, and myself. We were the survivors. Casper and our erstwhile, quasi-crew mate Gáwar wouldn't be making the journey home. The moment we folded away from Godville, it would have a population of two. Wul and Queeheg. Al reported that somewhere along the line, Wul had dragged the fabrication unit and its supplies over to Blind Faith No More. The two guys were all set to spend less-than-forever drinking themselves into stupors and gorging on delicacies until their aging bodies gave up the ghost. For the record, Wul left the pistol back at his house, after firing the single round harmlessly into the stratosphere. He had made his choice. He chose ... wisely.

"Okay," I said matter-of-factly, "we're ready to boogie. Doc assures me the field density is easily traversable and we should make the trip without difficulty. So, since that translates as *we're all gonna die,* let me be the first, and the last, to thank you all for your help. When I say I couldn't—"

"Hey, human," snarled Sapale, "if I'm about to die, I do not want the last words echoing in my head, as I pass the sacred veils, to be your pathetic, formal speech."

"Yeah, let us die in peace," demanded Slapgren.

"I think you're being selfish, Uncle," voiced my dear, dear Mirri.

"I rather liked the tone," said Daleria.

"That's only because this is the *first* time you're hearing the same, canned, stilted words, my dear," opined Toño. "For the rest of us, the number of times we've heard the exact same mental diarrhea is too painful to recall."

"And so," I said in a boss voice, "I'd like to conclude with this. *Phhhht!*" I gave them the longest, wettest raspberry ever, in the long and storied history of derogatory mouth sounds. "*Stingray,* take us home." I shot my fibers against the floor.

"Where's home, Jon?" asked Al.

Did he just address me as *Jon*? Ew. Now I was *hoping* for catastrophic, in-transit, system failure.

"Azsuram," Sapale replied dreamily.

Seven eternities ago, when Sapale and I first landed on Azsuram in my ancient, rocket-powered Ark ship, we set down in a forested glen. That is where we established our first camp, then village, city, and megalopolis. The exact spot, more or less, was marked by a statue of the both of us. Originally, it was marked with a monument to Sapale. But the first time she laid eyes on it, she turned to me and said, rather angrily, *Oh no, flyboy*, she drilled a finger in the air toward her likeness. *If I'm going to be publicly humiliated, then* you're *going to be publicly humiliated, too, right next to me. And your rock abomination will be one percent larger than mine. Only you and I will know that fact, but every time you waste the time to look at the stupid things, you will know that truth.* Not sure she was a fan.

In any case, *Stingray* dusted down in that very spot, where we'd landed forever ago. I had to admit, it was pretty alright.

A portal appeared without my asking. My brood's-mate and I stepped out first, hand in hand.

"This is home," she glowed.

"Yes," I squeezed her hand tightly, "it is."

"So ... so *lovely*."

"And it'll look even lovelier when we fill the craters in, clear away the debris and rubble, and, oh, maybe restore *life* to Azsuram?"

"I saw a patoel bug," she gestured lazily, "scamper behind those marble blocks."

"The blocks on top of the statue of ... er, I *think* that's you."

"No, Jon, it couldn't be. It's grotesquely proportioned. It must be your image the wall fell on and crushed."

"Works for me."

We were quiet a while. The smells of my adopted home world were ... different than my computer memory had stored. Gone were the scents of trees, water, and rich farmlands. Now, burning crude oil, decay—unspecified, if you please—, and remorse were what I detected, wafting in the gentle, befouled breeze.

"Let's *rent*, for now," I said, apropos of nothing.

"A coward dies a thousand times before his death, but the valiant taste of death but once," she responded.

"Then you and Julius Caesar can purchase land. I'll stay on a month-to-month basis, for now."

"Jon, it must have been horrible here?"

"It sorely appears so," I said dumbstruck.

"Al," she said softly, "any signs of Cleinoids present now?"

"No, Sapale. I estimate this damage took place at least ten years ago. Maybe a lot longer. The particulate mix in the upper atmosphere compared to the lower suggests the bulk of the devastation occurred many seasons ago. Additionally, the radioactive decay products of a nearby electrical generating station suggests its containment was violated a decade-plus in the past."

"Ah," was all she could muster.

"Als," said Toño quietly from behind, "my chronometers indicate we've been gone around sixteen years. What do you estimate?"

"Based on the position of the stars in the sky and solar spectral analysis, we think we left this universe sixteen years, seven months, ten days, four ho—"

"Thank you, Als," Toño cut them off absently. "We've been gone a while."

"Damn screwed up Cleinoid time," I cursed under my breath. "I'd half-hoped it'd have corrected after Clein was sent packing."

"It did not," was all Toño managed.

"How awful it must have been, here," stated Mirraya mournfully.

"Yes," Sapale replied with no emphasis in her voice. "Al, what is the status—"

"There are widely scattered pockets of advanced humanoids. Likely Kaljaxian, and human-Kaljaxian hybrids in colonies. Mostly near the equator."

"Are there many of them?" she said with no spirit in her voice.

Bless his tick-tock little heart. Al responded that there were *some*.

"Then that's where I'll start," Sapale said with no life in her voice.

"Aren't we going to—" I began to ask.

Sapale raised a hand halfway, her fingers drooping. "*You* are going to. I—" she began to sob. "I think I'll stay here, just for a moment. I ... I need to see life *grow* aga ... again."

I could not argue with that desire. Maybe it would ease the pain, if only slightly. My wife's devotion to her children was ferocious, it was absolute, and it was a marvel to behold. Whoever was left alive on her planet—our planet—was her child, now. She was going to nurture them, whether they liked it or not. That's what mothers do.

Me, I was okay with family. But I wasn't megalodon-dad. I needed to make certain the Cleinoids were deader than dead. I'd send Toño back with a vortex for her. My brood's-mate would be fine. If she felt it was time to join me, before I thought it was time to join her, she'd be able to find me. Otherwise, I had to be certain. And if the last ancient god wasn't rotting in the noonday sun, I'd personally help them along that path—with my bare hands, preferably.

CHAPTER TWELVE

Daleria decided to stay behind with Sapale, on Azsuram. That was good. I didn't want my wife there, basically alone. Also, Daleria had stomached all the war she could, already. Doing something positive, which was her nature in the first place, would be therapeutic for her, too. I so envied them. The thought of fishing where I had so long ago, the times with JJ, called to me like the Sirens of Greek mythology. But, I had to fight on. Jon Ryan, the forever warrior, was needed elsewhere.

Despite possessing the computational power of many advanced civilizations, it took the Als half a day to locate anyone associated with JCIDC. The council sure wasn't hanging out flags and having open houses. It was understandable. After almost two decades fighting a losing war against the Cleinoids, they had to be hidden better than a mouse at a cat convention. I even began to wonder if any organized defense was still intact, it took so long to find them. But, the Als finally ran down a council member's personal spacecraft. Harugatega S3 was a Serillian. The records showed she'd been on the JCIDC for a couple months. That struck me as most peculiar, since she was already the assistant council adjutant. Seemed like a pretty high office for a newbie. Maybe she was a whiz-kid, or something.

I'd say, cynic that I am, that maybe Harugatega S3 slept her way to the top on a fast-track. But I already said she was Serillian, so that idea was a non-starter if every there'd been one. Do not get me wrong. The Serillians were a wise and kindhearted species. They had eliminated poverty, hunger, and societal inequality on their worlds. They excused themselves when they issued gas from any orifice, and they gave to charities to an embarrassing fault. It was said that, once, long ago, a neighboring planet, Quekto, suffered from being at war constantly. Quekto's resources were depleted, and the Quektocore (their name, no one else's) worlds were being quickly destroyed. The Quektocore were so glum, they officially voted the word *happy* to be stricken from their native tongue.

In stepped the Serillians. They compiled a massive flotilla, which carried two thirds of the Serillian people, to that sad world of Quekto. Each Serillian was equipped with a bag of candy, a certificate swearing that the donor loved, loved, loved the recipient Quektocore, and they gave every one of them a hug. It was estimated that the average Quektocore got hugged around ten thousand times, in the space of a week. And the physiologic equivalent of diabetes struck *ninety* percent of the Quektocore population. But, the emotional support and personal affirmations led to a permanent peace. Seriously, the Serillians were good people, or whatever.

But, they were hideous. Sorry, there's no way around that painful fact. A major university did a study. If you took the single most *unappealing* physical aspect of any set of ten thousand species you could assemble, and you cobbled them together, you *always* came up with the spitting image of a Serillian. Sound unbelievable? Try being a Serillian.

As I sat at the main control panel, I stared at an icon Al had placed there. When I tapped it, I'd be placed in communication with Harugatega S3. Al told me she'd already been waiting, patiently and without complaint, for half an hour. Still, I stared. I went back and forth, for that thirty minute period, trying to justify why I would voluntarily place a Serillian's ugly mug on my widescreen, ultrahigh resolution monitor. The damn screen'd probably explode out of depression or self-defense.

Finally, I decided to be a grownup, and I tapped the button. The fact that Toño actually moved my hand, with all his might, toward the icon had no bearing on my decision to go ahead and tap it.

"Ah, General Ryan," Harugatega S3 crooned. "Speaking to you is an honor I never anticipated. I am unworthy."

"I'm confi—" Oh lordy, that face. "I'm confidential you are."

Harugatega S3 slapped the side of her comm-link. "My translator is defective."

"Sorry to hear that."

"No worries. It's seems fine, now. As I was saying, General—"

"Come now. No need for puss or formality. You can call me *Jon*. I'll call you, sorry, what was your name, again? I know Al told me, but I'm forgetting as we sit here tormented."

She leaned in and gave her comm-link a sound swat. "I'm sorry. Did you say *tormented*?"

"Me? No. Silly. I said *talking*."

"You see," she gesticulated with her withered hands at

her machine. "My translator *is* malfunctioning. My humble apologies."

"Not a problem. I know it can get ugly when you don't ... sorry. I mean to say when communications are screwed up, hideous results ... look, shall I call back after you have your machine checked oaf?"

"Oaf?"

"Yes, checked *ooofa*. Sorry. Everyone around here's saying it that way now. Crazy kids." I slapped the side of my head. "Can't live with them, can't live withered them."

Al snickered in the background, the son of a gun.

"Are you *well*, General?"

"Me? No, I'm fine. How about goo, eh, sorry, *you*."

"Is it me, or is this a rather *bizarre* conversation?"

"You bet," I fired back.

"Beg pardon?"

"Of course, you maygot."

"I may got *what*? The signal is breaking up, again."

"Al," I screamed because, yes, I was losing it, "can you confirm the integrity of this transgress ... mission?"

"All signals are true and at full power, Craptain."

I blew out my nose so hard I would have shot out brain tissue, if there were still any up there. "No, we're all good. My crew and I just retuned to this universe. I need to sit down with the council and bring my vomit up ... sorry, I didn't say that. Bring myself up to chuck ... *speed*."

"You've only now returned to our universe. You wish to meet, in person, with the JCIDC, so everyone's up to speed? Am I understanding that part?"

"Yes. The Cleinoids have been neutralized in their home galaxy. I want to make dripping sore our homely is safe."

"Dripping sores?" She was getting angry. I could sense it.

"Distant shores. Come on, what kind of jerk do, you stink, I am?"

She scowled, which was difficult to convey when your face looked like a railroad train had run over it while it was decaying. Your face, not the train.

"You want to *distant shores* our *homely* is safe?" I could tell there was an edge to her tone.

I slapped my comm-link.

"Ow," squealed Al.

"Did your comm-link just howl in pain?"

"No, now you're being hideous."

"You mean hilarious?" she asked, dubiously.

"Yes. What did you hear?"

"A fool giving in to his prejudices. This, General, is not my first rodeo."

"You guys have rodeos, too? Go fester."

Harugatega S3 stood and reached for the right side of her comm-link. That's where the off switch was located, and not much else. "I will have one of my assistants send you the contact information for the secretary general. Until we meet, *face* to *face*, General Ryan, I must say this has been unpleasant. I fear that, then, I will have to be further disappointed."

"Thank you for all the warts you're putting in, to help with the many tasks that lay ahead."

Wow. How rude. She turned her end off without as much as a goodbye. Well, I need to take part of the responsibility. Maybe.

After I spoke with the new SG, a symbiote pair named Quadirpa, they said they would call the very first physical meeting of JCIDC in over six years. They felt it was safe enough to do so. It would be held in my honor. I wasn't certain why they felt it was necessary to inform me, at the early stage, when not even a date was set, that one council member would be unable to attend. Neither of them looked at all surprised when I did a Carnac the Magnificent, and guessed that member was Harugatega S3. I said it would be fine by me if she was only able to attend via audio link. It was, I extended graciously, *her* call.

Toño and I arrived on Altair 6 a few days later. That system was fairly central to the locations of the widely-scattered JCIDC members. It was also symbolic, since Altair 6, also known as Justice World, was the location of the first regional galactic collaborative body. That assembly preceded the JCIDC, long, long ago. Quadirpa was super excited about the new beginnings concept—then and now. Quadirpa was, I determined right from the get-go, an annoying individual.

Mirraya and Slapgren went home. I offered for them to stay, and help us deal with whatever was left of galactic civilization. But they both vigorously and steadfastly refused. Mirri was beginning to look frail. I knew Slapgren wanted to get her home, where her fellow brindases could possibly help her. I saw in his eyes that he was in no way ready to let her go. The last thing Mirraya said to me before I sealed *Stingray's* portal was, "If matters get truly awful, let us know. *Maybe* we can help."

Talk about your underwhelming endorsements. I was really glad I could leave my kids to some measure of peace.

EJ didn't come along, either. He had a few good reasons of his own. He said, and I will paraphrase his exact words, that he would rather have intimate relationships, multiple times, with a pile of metal scrapings and glass shards, than to meet with the august JCIDC. I cringe, and cover my privates, every time I think of the image he drew. Ouchy. He wouldn't tell me where he was going. *The other side of nowhere,* was the most specific I could get him to be. I asked if he'd carry a handheld, so I could call him back, if he was needed. He said sure I could. That would be *spectacular*. Just leave it next to the pile of metal scrapings and glass shards.

So, it was down to our dynamic duos, the Bobbsey Twins of uncouth, the Fred and Ethel Mertzs of diplomacy, to represent the crew of *Stingray* before the JCIDC. Oh, joy, was that a lucky organization, or what?

"Ladies, gentlemen, neutral gender individuals, pairs of multigenomic aggregations, and reproductively indifferent others, we are honored today, above all days." Man, was Quadirpa ever fingernails on a chalkboard. "It is our honor to present to you General Jon Ryan, returned from the Cleinoid universe where he put an end to their terror, forever."

I looked over to Toño. Yup, he was right there, beside me. Apparently he was invisible to everyone else in the room.

Amidst tepid applause, I stood and waved, then sat down again.

Quadirpa was stunned. "Are you not going to speak?"

"No. I'm here for the meeting. If I have something to say when we're doing something productive, you'll know, because my mouth parts'll start moving like they are now."

You'd have thought I said, *No fruit cup for you. No soup for you,* to the sorry bastard. Such a pouty face.

"Ah. Er. Um." the SG articulated.

"I move the session come to order," I said hopefully.

"Seconded," shouted someone, or whatever.

"Then I call the formal session of the JCIDC to order. Let the record reflect we are honored to have—"

"The record *already* reflects I'm here. I moved we come to order." Was I being rude. You bet. I wanted official praise like I wanted syphilis. There was work to do. *If* the ancient gods were no longer a threat, I'd do the triumphant tour thing. Maybe. If Sapale insisted passionately enough. I mean, she *would* insist, but I could spurn her demands, to a certain point. Then it was easier to tour than withstand the penalty for noncompliance. In other words, I'm a married man.

"Ah. Hmm. Umf."

Quite the inspirational public speaker. JKF and Churchill, all over again.

The assistant SG, sitting to his right, tugged at the nearest piece of clothing. "Call for new reports."

"I call for new reports," Quadirpa mumbled.

"I am first on the agenda," said a tall alien humanoid of a species I did not recognize. He rose like an unfolding road map. The sign in front of him read Mirsifut. "I can confirm the news we received from the Glebulon Cluster. As a reminder, we heard, at our last holo meeting, that a particularly large and vicious swarm of Cleinoids had been ravaging the system. Then, they apparently died spontaneously, mid-engagement, with a battalion of foot soldiers."

"I recall we were told the battle had only just begun. The local troops, Bomontals, if memory serves, were being beaten soundly, then, the battle was over." That was a Gorgolinian speaking. I hadn't seen one of those fish tanks in ages. I'm ashamed to admit I hadn't missed that humorless race.

"Yes," replied Mirsifut. "Today, I have confirmation that such was the case. Reports from five independent observers of high credibility were available to support that version."

"Thank you, Mirsifut," said the SG. He was back to talking like a bureaucrat. Oh, well. It was nice while his voice was MIA. "Other reports?"

"General Ryan," said a Kaljaxian member. His name

read Sortiv Vec. I knew of his clan, but not of him personally. "Would you provide us a brief report, summarizing the lengthy one we received yesterday?"

"Sure. Why not?"

I gave them a bare-bones rendition of our time in anti-paradise. Even abbreviating with great zeal, I talked for nearly an hour. Along the way I sure got a lot of raised eyebrows and well-I'll-be-damned looks. It was quite the tale.

"So," asked a Ropalidior female (I think. It's always hard to tell without smelling their crotch. I was neither close enough to do so or inclined to do so were I closer), "you speak with one hundred percent confidence that all the Cleinoid gods are dead. Further, that they will not be magically resurrected?"

"Well, I left off that two Cleinoids were spared. They are personal friends, and pose no threat to our existence. Otherwise, yes, they're all dead, gone, and unlamented."

The Ropalidior, the one with the name plate reading 03020109-11-130, began to tremble rather violently. She was a tall, thin giraffe-like animal, with a bunch of tiny legs covering her underside. When she got to vibrating, that long neck threatened to snap like a dry twig.

"Am ... am a ... am I to understand you *spared* two monsters? You ... you took it upon yourself to *allow* the Cleinoids a chance to breed back to full power and attack us, *again?*"

Toño leaned in very very close. "Do *not* kill her."

I leaned way into him. "You didn't ask *pretty please.*"

He elbowed me before I could withdraw.

"I'm sorry," I responded soberly, "could you repeat your question?"

"You ... er, did not understand me?" She gestured

toward her microphone. That suggested I should know a translator was in operation.

"No, sorry. It was just so cute, what with you stammering and shaking. I'd like to see it, again, live." I folded my fingers, as if waiting for the show to begin.

"General Ryan," she huffed, "I do not need to sit here and be insulted by you. We," she swept her paw around the table, "suffered horrendously at the hands of the Cleinoid demons. While you were safe, *pampered* even, in their home, we died by the quadrillions."

"Pampered? Safe? I ... we were living *large* back there in Godville?"

"That's what I hear," she responded condescendingly.

I turned to Toño, and gave him a, can-I-kill-her-now look.

He shook his head firmly. No. I could not cure the world of this bitch.

"I'd like to point out that the two trusted friends I left alive are both *males*. They are extremely unlikely to rebreed a *viable* Cleinoid society."

I heard oh so pleasant snickering scattered in the room. So did the giraffe.

"I'd also like to remind anyone with ears that we were on our own, in a completely hostile environment, and that we answered to no one. If anyone present is displeased, I offer to them a simple solution. Find a big, pearl-handled wooden pole, and shove it so far up—"

"You are entitled to your own opinion," Toño cut me off like he was shot from a catapult. He nodded deferentially. "Everyone, naturally, is."

"I suggest we move on to any additional new reports," said Quadirpa in a near panic.

The room was quiet. "In that case, I will open the floor to discussions."

I poked a finger into the air.

"Ah, G ... General Ryan," stammered Quadirpa. "We would be—"

"Here's the deal. We were gone a little less than two years. By the time I felt it was safe for us to leave, the Cleinoids were gone. There was no rebound, no secondary power source or alternative magical energy found by any of them. Over fifteen years passed in this universe. For the entire time, the ancient gods pounded you like a dirty rug. Then the ones you knew of died. What I need to know is did all of them die? Are there any pockets of them left, somewhere?"

Many people looked to one another, uncertainly. Oh boy. Not a good sign.

Finally, Quadirpa spoke for the group. "We're confused. All the gods in *their* universe died when you destroyed Clein. They all died here, too. You know this, right?"

"Are you looking at my face?"

Quadirpa gazed side to side. He was dumbstruck. "Yes, I do."

"Does my face look *happy*?"

"Likely not."

"Okay, you get three guesses as to why. The second two, by the way, don't count."

"I'd rath ... rather not guess."

"Oh, go on. What have you got to lose? Aside from your dignity, I mean."

"Your *face* is unhappy because *you're* unhappy?"

"See how easy this game is. Now," I waved him toward me, "bring it on home. *Why* am I and my face unhappy?"

"I can only assume it has to do with my reminder that all the Cleinoids are deceased."

"Man, it's like you're cheating, or something. You're *so*

damn good at this. And what part of the total bullshit you said is the part that's giving me hemorrhoids?"

Quadirpa looked in terror to Toño.

"Sensitive tissues found near the human rectum," was his medical summary.

"I know that, Dr. DeJesus. I was hoping you might ... *intercede.*"

"Where this man's hemorrhoids are concerned? *Hah.* Not unless they develop into a medical emergency."

"Come on, SG. What did you say that was so stupid you might win the *Stupid of the Year Award* for saying it?"

"I cannot imagine," he said with feeble finality.

"You said, without proof, or even reasonable assumption, that all the Cleinoids in this universe *had* to be dead. They do not *have* to be. Here's a wake up call from the front desk. If they aren't all dead, we might all be."

Quadirpa scanned the JCIDC members in horror.

A Gaspach Finder representative on the far side of the room stood. They stand a lot. They're a species that look all the world like miniature redwood trees, flaky bark and all. "Ryan, how could that be? If their Clein is dead, so must they be."

"Oh, and why is that, Mr. Timber?"

"My name is not Mr. Timber. I am *Misertimel* jev **Oped** fir."

"My bad. Why is it they must be dead, Mr. Timber?"

"Because ... it's logical?" he asked more than stated.

"Incorrect. You lose three points and the question goes to Mr. DeJesus. Mr. DeJesus, for the game and pan-species survival, what is the *correct* assumption?"

"That there are Cleinoids somehow alive in this universe. That wishing and assuming them to be dead do not, in fact, mean they *are.*"

"And we have a winner who won't be Cleinoid dinner.

Listen up, people," I said ominously, "I dealt with these gods a very long time. They are ruthless, hateful, and motivated only to destroy. But the other thing they are is *gods*. Never assume a god is dead, if you do not wish to be badly surprised by the reality of it all. We know *nothing* about the Cleinoids in this universe aside from the fact that some conveniently keeled over dead."

"What do you propose, General Ryan?" asked a quaking-in-their-boots Quadirpa.

"I propose to scour the galaxy, looking for living Cleinoids who didn't receive your condolence cards. I *hope* you are going to, also. But, if that conflicts with the victory parades, well, excuse me for mentioning the fact that we might still be dead things walking."

I looked to Toño.

He nodded and stood. "I really do hope you'll cancel those parades," he chided.

Alright, *Doc*. It took two billion years, but you discovered your inner snark.

CHAPTER THIRTEEN

"Carol," chortled Verazz, as he sped down the passageway of imagination that led to where she was, at least at that particular moment.

"She's not here, but I can't take a message," called back Carol, still hidden from his view by layers of solitary imaginings.

Nothing could depress or slow Verazz on that joyous day. "Don't you mean, wife, *but I* can *take a message?*"

"If I *meant* that, I would have *said* that."

In spite of her coy resistance, Verazz was standing before her as she finished speaking.

"Good morning, my forever wife." He veritably vibrated he was so happy.

She fashioned her best attempt of glowering at him. She was terrible at glowering, by the way. "It is neither good nor morning."

"Ah, but I can prove you wrong, though to correct perfection pains me. This day is good, because *you* are in it."

"And how is it morning, in this place without time?"

"Really? This chamber has no time? You've *remodeled*."

"Almost a thousand *years* ago, Major Clueless."

"Whatever pleases *you*, pleases *me*," he said with conviction.

"I wish to drop the discussion of how it could be morning. Your perky mood is more than—"

"Since no day *begins* until I look upon your splendor. I say it *is* morning."

"I said I did not wish to ... Oh, forget it. Why are you here?" She loved his obsequious praise, by the by. She also loved to bat him on the snout, figuratively, every chance she could.

"I am here to say farewell," Verazz pointed energetically upward, "but definitely not goodbye."

"As similar as those two exits sound, pray tell, why do you emphasize the distinction?"

"Because, I go in quest of offensive, contemptuous, foulmouthed Cleinoids. I shall slay them, as is my new commitment, to give you greater glory."

She squeaked a tiny guffaw. "But how can you? Where are your armor and your sword?"

"They are, like so many things these days, in the past. I hunt now with stealth and cunning, not fabricated artifacts."

"Let me guess. You nearly got yourself killed, again, because of that absurd costume?"

"The true, factual answer to your supposition depends on how one regards it, under what conditions and terms."

"So you almost got yourself killed wearing what I told you not to wear." Yes, that was a statement, *not* a question.

"I am pressed for time, and cannot fully address your insights and speculations."

"Verazz, you are many things; most are disagreeable.

115

The one thing you are *never* is pressed for time. We are immortals from before the Epoch of Space/Time."

"No, and *that* situation I can also prove. I must rush off to slay Cleinoids lest they be pre-slain by someone else. If there were none left to put asunder, how could I give you glory?"

"I will draw up a list. I must warn you, it will be a very long list. How much time can I have to do it justice?"

"You have at your disposal *all* of time, my loviest. I will not be present during that interlude of all of time. *I* will be a'slaying."

"Have I ever told you you're impossible?"

He held up a hang-on-a-sec index finger, while his lips moved silently. "Four million and seventeen times, to be precise."

"Yet, here I am, saying it, again."

"Yes, you are. And, I must add, how very lovely you look doing so."

"Verazz, ask me what time it is."

"B ... but you just said there is no—"

"Verazz, *ask* me what time it is," she repeated, in a less happy tone.

"Carol, what time is it?"

"Time for you to be long removed from my sight."

"Ah. Thank you." He pointed in the direction he'd come in. "I think I'll be questing and slaying, should you need me."

"I will not."

"One never knows the future."

"I do, with great certainty."

"Ah."

Verazz departed her chamber. The reverse trip through the passageway of imagination was considerably glummer than it had been in the forward direction. Isn't that the way it always seems to be?

CHAPTER FOURTEEN

Toño and I were sulking in the ship's mess the morning after our less-than-stellar meeting with JCIDC. Well, I was sulking. He appeared to be chipper and in an upbeat mood. Were we even at the same farce? He was so darn optimistic and positive. It was hard to take before coffee, I can tell you that much.

"So, Jon, what shall we two bachelors do today?" He deeply sniffed his mug, like it was a narcotic. "Fishing? Spitting? Or, perhaps we could simply drink beer and belch?"

"Why not all *three* options. They *are* easily integrated into one relaxing day." I sipped loudly. "Hell, if the universe ends because we took a sick day, who'd even know we did? Everyone'd be dead, and dead men *recall* no tales."

"I thought you appeared particularly surly this morning. Shall I find my psychoanalyst's couch and have you tell me about your mother?"

"Let's not and say we did."

He eyed me judgmentally, which is to say, the way Doc tends to look at me. "Hmm. So, do you have a specific proposal as to how we can determine if any viable Cleinoids linger in *this* universe?"

"Outside of beat bushes and cross fingers?"

"Ideally. The diameter of the visible universe is 93.016 billion light years. That yields a volume of 4×10^{80} cubic meters. Many bushes are contained in that expanse." He sighed. "We *are* functionally immortal, but I still think turning over every metaphorical rock would be exhausting."

I leaned back. "Obviously we can have the Als monitor an enormous amount of transmissions. If there are reports of godly destruction, they'd pick up on it."

He sipped his coffee and rested his mug. "The problem there is one of discrimination. Certainly if a broadcast states a twenty meter tall reptile just ate Tokyo, we'd know, with confidence, it was a Cleinoid on the loose. But many disasters, manmade and naturally occurring, would sound quite similar. A massive earthquake, volcanic explosion, or a massive act of terrorism would be problematic. As there are more of *those* than gods acting *aggressively*, if any remain, we'd be running down a lot of false leads."

"True that." I stared off a moment. "We could, obviously ask alien governments to report any possible Cleinoids to us, or JCIDC. But, then we're back to the universe being too damn big. We can probably track reports from the Milky Way, a few galaxies on our local group. But ninety nine point nine nine percent of the rest of the real estate is not reasonable to survey."

"We could begin aggressively placing fold-transmitting comm-stations in far flung galaxies, but even doing so with a bank of Als, the actual coverage would be depressingly sparse."

"And if there are Cleinoids left, the longer they have to

solidify their position, the worse it would be for our collective survival."

Toño raised a hand. "While I totally agree that we need to be tremendously observant, I do think we need to intermix the knowledge that Clein is gone. What would power the surviving gods?"

I shot my eyebrows up. "*You* are asking *me*? *You're* the science whiz."

He gave me his patented *no duh* scowl. "I'm perhaps thinking out *loud*."

"Knock yourself out."

"Obviously, Clein itself was naturally occurring. It is not logical to assume the ancient gods created their power source, since they would need some source to animate them in the first place. So, similar power sources are inevitable. The probability of a Cleinoid *chancing* to be near enough to a novel energy emitter is vanishingly small."

"But, it's not zero. We're talking gods here, and the universe would never give us such a lucky break. It hates us. *Me*, at least."

He rolled his eyes. "The universe does not *hate* you. I can prove it. *I* accompany you. If the universe *hated* you, it would not bestow upon you such a marvelous gift."

"You're sounding more like me with each passing day."

He huffed. "There's no call to be *insulting*."

My turn to roll the eyes. What a goon.

"So," I began, "we can set the AIs to analyzing, we can launch a bunch of remote comm-stations, we network with as many governments as we can. Then what? What do you and I *actually* do? Us drinking lukewarm coffee will not kill off a single monster, in and of itself."

"Staying put and waiting does not sound very proactive, does it?"

I harrumphed. "Sure not how *I* roll."

"What would you suggest?"

I shook my head slowly. "Not much. Going on random expeditions would be lame-city." I rubbed my chin. "Then again, we could get some healthy drinking done, if we did."

"*You* could overindulge. You know *I'd* refrain."

"Yes. You are the two billion year old stick-in-the-mud, aren't you?"

"And proud *of* it."

"Here's a thought. We could do what we always do when we're hopelessly confused and outmatched."

"Didn't I just finish ruling *out* the binge drinking?"

"I was *referring* to consulting the Deavoriath."

His brow furrowed. "My, that is an excellent idea."

"Do you have to say it like it's unbelievable I came up with one?"

"Yes."

I landed *Stingray* near Cragforel's place on Oowaoa. You remember Cragforel, right? The guy who has a bromance bubbling with Toño, but regards me as leftover chopped liver. Yeah, he was our contact with the Deavoriath. Oh, joy.

As we neared his door, Cragforel emerged, a big smile on his face. He strode right up to Doc, and gave him a bearhug with all three of his arms. No one or two arm *parody* of a hug for the famous Dr. Toño DeJesus. Without looking to me, as he finally released Toño, Cragforel mumbled, "Hi, Jon." Then he put a shoulder over guess which one of us, and headed back inside.

Grrr.

"So, my old friend," asked Toño, "how have you and the Deavoriath faired, of late?"

"Sit first," dude basically shoved Toño into a seat. "I'll gather some refreshments. Then we talk." He was back in a flash with a tray of nufe and something else.

All I cared about was the nufe.

"Here," he passed out two glasses. "Per your tradition, I toast to good friends." He lofted his glass.

I was fairly certain I'd heard the plural form of *friend*, so I raised my glass, too. In fact, in case he had said *friend*, I raised my glass extra high.

Grrr.

"Now, please tell us, how are you and your people?" asked Toño.

"Well, and tolerable." He snickered, something Deavoriath, like, never did. They were too prim and proper to display mirth. My old pal Kymee once remarked that the Deavoriath's shirts were stuffed too full.

"Let's begin with *you*, then," Toño responded effusively.

"Not much to say. I'm still not *horizontal*." He giggled softly. "These are trying times. But, we have remained safe and well. I don't think one could reasonably ask for more."

"So the Cleinoids never attacked Oowaoa?" I asked, partly because I wanted to force Cragforel to actually address me.

He shook his head thoughtfully. "Not for want of trying." He paused and leaned back into his chair. "They didn't chance upon us until rather recently. That much was fortunate. But, once they sensed our planet, they became increasingly obsessed with breaching our defenses."

"But they never broke through?" Toño asked, his concern obvious in his tone.

"No." He replied rather darkly, for someone who held the ancient gods at bay. "I think if they would have continued their assault a few more months, they might have, though."

"You sound, I don't know, *remorseful*. If you kept them away from your world, you did good," I stated.

"There's no way around the humbling, no, *humiliating* feeling many of us are left with." He shook his head again. "We, the race that conquered so many, and ruled so widely, were barely able to thwart a handful of petty thugs." He looked to Toño as if he was asking for forgiveness. "There were fifteen or *twenty* of them. Never more. Yet they nearly broke through."

"They are a powerful species," Toño mused. "You fared far better than most individuals who drew their attention."

"Perhaps."

"What did you hold them off with?" I pressed. "Was it your altered perception screen you used on me, long ago?"

"No," he responded tersely.

"Come on, I don't want to play twenty questions," I said with an edge. "What was your defense?"

"That is part of the disgrace some of us feel. It was *your* membrane device."

Ah, ha. They were ashamed they had to rely on the tech *I'd* given them? Such silly pride. At least they survived.

"Other planets and ships had membranes. Hell, I used one to hold off a Cleinoid more than once. They cracked it with little trouble. How'd you pull it off?"

He shrugged sadly. "We modified the system. We added a quantum resonator to the shield."

"Can you be more specific?" Toño asked excitedly.

"You know the space-time congruity manipulator places a highly effective break in reality. But, as Jon mentioned, it can be defeated. We added a phase alternator, in the form of a quantum resonator. That shifts the integrity of the membrane layer itself. The enemy may breach one domain of the membrane, but it instantly and randomly shifts its configuration."

"*Fascinating*," exclaimed Toño. "That's nothing short of brilliant."

"I'll send you the details. It's only fair you should possess the technology, since you gave it to us."

Two billion years into my escapade, and I'd still give my left nut to know where the dickens that tech came from. Well, sure, I would if I could *find* my left nut. It was probably in fairly poor condition, what with it being buried in space two billion years ago. Give or take. No, wait. That was my *second* left testicle. The first, *Casper's*, was on Earth when Jupiter ate it, I think. TMI? Sorry.

"*Thank* you," responded Toño. I could tell his nerdness was red-lining.

"I hate to seem to be a rain cloud on the parade of life," I said as neutrally as I could. "But, you maybe shouldn't be so glum just because it was someone else's toy that saved you guys. I mean, billions of souls were lost."

"Oh, I see. Sorry. That is not what we find most distasteful. No, we are ashamed we couldn't do more than save *ourselves*."

"They are, as I said, immensely powerful," reminded Toño.

"So were we, *once*," he replied sadly. He sighed a couple times. "We kept boosting the energy to the membrane. We had to double our output every few days. Still, it only just held. A few times, one of them actually did penetrate it, but we were able to restrain it with a secondary membrane." He was quiet a sec. "It was touch and go." He looked up to Toño, again. "Our Plan B was as pitiful as our Plan A. We were set to abandon the planet. Can you imagine? The *Deavoriath*, forced to flee *Oowaoa*. That is as unprecedented as it is unacceptable."

"War's hell," was my response.

"It is, indeed," he grumbled.

"So, you survived," remarked Toño, in a more upbeat tone. "Everyone is well?"

"Yes. We are. With luck, we will remain so."

"What was your take on the cessation of hostilities?" Toño asked, obliquely. "We *know* what happened. But I'm curious as to your interpretation of the sudden end of the conflict."

He reflected a spell. "One moment they were bashing our planetary membrane, and the next, they were not."

"Did you investigate?"

"Yes, of course. We sent ships up to where the Cleinoids had been. They were dead. They were extremely dead, in fact."

"What's the diff?" I asked.

"They had clearly died. Than, as bags of water and flesh in the vacuum of space, they degraded rather impressively. I'm certain you know what happens to an unprotected body in that setting."

I grunted a chuckle. "Your lungs explode and your tongue boils. Then all the water in you vaporizes, so you swell up like a Macy's Day parade float. Next, whatever's still in one piece freezes solid."

"That's pretty much what the scouts found. One large mess."

"Good. They deserved worse, but I'll settle for that," I responded in a low growl.

"We scanned as extensively as we could, and were unable to locate any Cleinoids, back then."

"Back then," I shot to my feet. "I really do not like the sound of that."

"You *should* not," Cragforel replied grimly.

"What?" yelped Toño. "Surely you haven't found any viable Cleinoids since they died en masse?"

"Sadly, we have," Cragforel said, with all the weight of the universe pressing down on his frame.

"How can that be? We destroyed *Clein*," wheezed Toño. "That was the source of the Cleinoid's power. Without it, only the otherwise viable ancient gods survived, but only if they were in a safe environment."

"Ah, I suspected as much," replied Cragforel. "A sudden loss of their magical powers accounted for what we observed."

"Do you mean you've detected Cleinoids, but the ones fortunate enough to have been in a protected space?"

"I do not." He reflected a moment. "I don't know how we *could* detect a normal individual living in a place where life is common." He responded with no little judgment in his voice.

"But—" Toño faded away.

"Details, please," I snapped.

"For several days, we found no signs of surviving Cleinoids. Then, I pinged one on a remote planet, orbiting an otherwise unremarkable star."

"Pinged?" I questioned.

"Sorry. It's ... complicated."

"Like sonar pinging?"

"Nothing like that, at all," he replied. "A ping, in our meaning, is a transfolding query. Let me see if I can explain. We send a signal to a selected location, by folding space/time."

"Like the vortex's movement?" I asked.

"Precisely. With the signal, we send a small ... er, you would call it an AI."

"Like the vortex manipulators?" I pressed, as I became confused.

He shook his head, hard. "No, very different. Just assume we do."

I nodded mutely.

"So, the AI appears where we query. It analyses the surrounding area within a light minute. It also duplicates itself, and sends clones one light minute away. Within a matter of seconds, a very wide range can be surveyed."

"Oh," I chirped, "like mirrors reflecting mirrors, off into infinity?"

Cragforel shot Toño a pained glance.

"Yes, Jon, it is," Toño said with absolutely no conviction, "*just* like that."

I let it drop.

"That is how we located an active Cleinoid. He, a rather odd shaped, rodent-like beast, is ravaging a planet orbiting a nearby star. The planet is barren, with only elementary life forms. Still, he's making a wreck of the place."

"How ... how can that *be?*" said Toño, in quiet disbelief.

"It *is*, so why is of secondary importance," Cragforel replied coolly. "Obviously the Cleinoid's power source has some naturally occurring analog. In fact, what you call the Clein had to be based on *some* spontaneous manifestation of power."

"Yes, it had to have been," whispered Toño, bleakly.

"The Clein was perhaps some magical compilation of that native magical energy," speculated Cragforel.

"*Clein*," I corrected. "They called it Clein, not *the* Clein."

"I stand corrected," he replied tersely.

"Have you found other active Cleinoids?" I asked.

"Yes, one other, so far. There is a devilish looking monster named Torent destroying a planet in a nearby galaxy. I believe you call it the Smaller Magellanic Cloud."

"Where, precisely?" pressed Toño.

"A system in a nebulae in that galaxy. Hang on," he

tapped the side of his head a few times. "Your people call it SMC WR7."

Toño shook his head. "I am unfamiliar with that star."

"It is far from here, and small," Cragforel comforted.

"That's it? Those two players?" I asked.

"So far," he replied flatly.

"And the name—our name—for the first system you mentioned?" I wondered.

He did that head tapping thing, again. "It orbits V429 Carinae."

I looked expectantly to Toño.

He shrugged. "I am sorry to say I am unfamiliar with that one, also."

"You'll be an expert's expert soon," I said gesturing to the exit.

"I will?" Toño asked quizzically.

"Sure. We're visiting it real soon. Both places, actually."

"Don't—" Toño whined.

"I think we need back up, to reassemble the team and go in hot?"

"Something along those lines, yes."

"Sure. If those happen to be available where I'm loading the vortex with munitions, I'll bring'em along."

"Otherwise?"

"Otherwise, it's just you, me, and the Als."

I heard that, Al shouted into our heads.

I know you did. Light the fires and kick the tires, Alvin. We're doing a road trip.

CHAPTER FIFTEEN

Verazz was frustrated. He had, in all the eternities he'd passed, never been frustrated. And, a few seconds into the new emotion, he was so over it. He started to shout his objections, but stopped when he realized he was perfectly alone. Since no one could hear him, he didn't want to appear foolish, in case anyone heard him. He was always conscious of others' opinions of him. Go figure. The most powerful Stone Witch, ever, and he worried about his public persona.

The reason for his vexation was that he could not locate any Cleinoid scum to pulverize. Why, he whined internally, it had only been last week ... or was it a thousand years ago? Oh, well, it had been only *recently* that the pests were positively *everywhere*. Now, he was about to begin turning over rocks or solar systems to find one—just *one*. How in the Twelve Reconciliations was he supposed to honor Carol and her Mari if he didn't slay Cleinoids? It wasn't like there were other ... oh, what do you call them? *Scourges,* that was it. There weren't any *other* scourges that annoyed his dear wife. That gave him pause. Were there?

She protested often that *he* annoyed her. But she could not possibly be serious. Plus, if he slew *himself*, how would he know Carol was pleased? Silly digressive thought.

Verazz expanded his consciousness. He reached beyond the current vacation galaxy Carol and he were visiting. He swept galaxy after galaxy. Nothing. There was not *one* living creature moving through the void of space unless it was inside some sort of protection, like a spaceship. How could there be none? They *littered* the void so recently. Oh, he stomped a foot. Was this a Cleinoid trick? Yes. They knew *he* was on the hunt, so they went to ground, they went dark. That was it. The intolerable, pathetic excuses for gods, were *hiding* from Verazz. Likely they were fouling themselves, too, such was their fear of the apex Stone Witch's wrath.

Such a thought would normally have placed a smile on Verazz's face. He loved flattery, even his own. It was validating. In this case, *self*-validation was just as valuable as any other form of attestation. But, he was displeased to find he actually found the idea of the excrement gods dodging him ... displeasing. Sure, yes, they *should* rightly quake in their boots simply thinking of a god such as Verazz chasing them. What sane being wouldn't? But, hiding meant he'd either have to ferret one out, or return home empty handed. Neither of those cases were acceptable. His anger skyrocketed. Now he was forced to do more *work*, which would likely require most of his time and effort, rooting the Cleinoids out. He hated work. He hated the word *work*. It was so far beneath him. It was a-loud-fart-in-a-crowded-elevator welcome to him.

Whatever Cleinoid trash he did dredge up was so going to *pay* for this outrage. Making Verazz do more work brought with it a cost no creature would agree to. He started focusing on the surface of worlds. He sorted through the inhabitants, one at a time, like looking for just the right grain of sand on a beach. Oh, it was excruciatingly tedious. He could only focus on a few hundred planets at once, and it took him a full *second* to evaluate one hundred thousand lifeforms. Even if he concentrated on only creatures larger than he was, it was taking forever to find a Clein ...

There! That *had* to be one. Verazz released all other planets and beings. He considered the one that was absolutely gigantic. This was fun. In an instant, Verazz *was* where the giant was located. Verazz immediately regretted his swift action. He was sinking in cold water, well, like he was a rock. Oh, bother. He raised his arms, and halted his descent. Shaking his head, he rose to catch up with the monster he quested for. It took a second. The large amphibious mass moved surprisingly quickly through the water.

Cursing his fate for having to labor so to make matters right with Carol, Verazz popped into a spot a ways in front of the speeding demon. He'd started swimming, but found he didn't like it. Swimming was suspiciously like work. You did a lot of laboring and only slowly approached your goal. Unacceptable.

When he could see the monster's eyes, Verazz assumed his dimwitted foe could see him, also. He spread his arms, wide, and shouted, "Stop, foul Cleinoid. Your better is here to—"

Verazz stopped shouting when the beast rammed into him. He was driven to one side. Nothing was injured, except his pride. Verazz spun, to defend against what he assumed would be the rampage of the Cleinoid. But there was none. The creature kept swimming in the speed and direction it had been. Verazz couldn't rightly suspect it was fleeing in blind panic, since it hadn't sped up at all.

Verazz discovered that day that he was, in fact, a slow learner. He repeated his attempts to stop the behemoth three more times. Each of his attempts produced nearly identical results. The only differences were the directions he was slammed in. He decided playtime was over. The next time, instead of asking the beast to stop, he stopped it with a spell. Just to be certain, he used frozen time. That had to work, and it did. He then quickly switched his spell to an arresting, so he could deal with the scum. If time was frozen, it would be devilishly hard to actually kill the thing.

He paddled up to the monster's snout, and looked it straight in the eyes. Verazz's body spasmed in agony as he recognized what he was seeing, in those dark, soulful eyes. Anguish, fear, and incomprehension. The animal was ... was ... suffering. Verazz reached into its mind. The waves of discomfort stunned him. Reflexively, he released the beast, clinging to the head, and maintaining their mental link.

Quickly, the creature's thoughts turned to ... shrimp. *Shrimp?* The Cleinoid was literally face to face with his hunter, and he thought happily of shrimp? Lots and lots of tiny swimming ...

Ah. Hang on, Verazz reflected. Maybe this gargantuan wasn't a Cleinoid? Clearly it was huge, and powerful, and it was going somewhere, quickly. Um, yes, but it was going quickly to eat shrimp. Shrimp did not count as potential victims in need of Verazz's protection. They were ... shrimp. Verazz asked the beast, *what are you?* He spoke to it in all languages, mind to mind.

Slowly, an answer returned. *I am me.*

Not helpful, flashed a once again annoyed Verazz. *You are you. Fine. What are you?*

All Verazz got this time was confusion.

Are you a Cleinoid?

The beast took several seconds to answer. It was clearly intelligent, but words were foreign to it. *I am whale. I am blue whale.*

So you're not a … Verazz stopped mid-thought. A whale? That was a large sea mammal. They were from Earth. The colonists who fled that place took them with them. And here was one. Verazz took a second to see where he actually was. Some rocky planet with a large ocean.

Frustration swept over Verazz's entirety. *First,* his need to slay Cleinoids led to his doing work. *Now,* his labors had proven him to be a great *fool.* If there was a god handbook, surely his making a fool out of himself would find itself listed in the index, and the citation would have pictures. And if Carol ever found out how absolutely moronic he'd been, well, he'd never live it down. Fortunately, that was never …

"Verazz," said a soft voice from behind, "You detained the poor whale from his meal. Don't you think it's only right for you to bring the little shrimp to him? The dear is *ever* so hungry."

CHAPTER SIXTEEN

I was mostly kidding when I told Doc I wanted to pack *Stingray* full of weapons and stuff. But, there was one gun I just had to have. While we were away, a very fierce and war-avid race called the Davrid had developed *the* most bitchin' rifle. The Excellon-6. It fired a gamma ray laser, like the one in my finger. But it had one thousand times the output. What's more, the gun did that without instantly overheating, and the fusion packs enabled you to fire one round per second, indefinitely. Fully loaded, it weighed less than twenty kilograms. Can you *imagine?* The gun was what we used to call in the military *high speed, low drag.* Dude, I needed two, maybe three of'em. I pictured myself going into battle with one rifle in each arm, and crisscrossed bandoleers stocked with fifty-caliber cartridges. Sure, the gun didn't fire fifties, but I'd look *so* badass it'd be worth the added weight.

As I was uncrating the four Excellon-6s I settled on, Toño stood over my shoulder, helicoptering. "I'm confident you will tell me why we require *four* of those obscene weapons."

"What? Two apiece, you and me. Sheesh, Doc, it's simple math."

"Simple math for simple minds."

What was that supposed to mean? These were state-of-the-art killing machines. We were soldiers on a suicide mission. A + B = C. I should have brought some back up Excellon-6s, now that I thought of it.

"I fear your hesitation in returning a witty jab suggests you are considering obtaining more of those monstrosities."

"What? Doc, that's crazy talk. If we can't kill whatever with two apiece, we aren't going to survive with a bunch back on the ship, shiny and in a box."

"Two apiece? Do you hallucinate I would be caught dead with *one* of those, let alone *two*? I need to recalibrate your logic buffers."

"Dude, we're going after viable Cleinoids, here. You want to pepper them with insults and misleading promises?" I was shaking my head in disbelief.

"First, do not ever address me as *dude*. Unless I appear on a horse wearing new chaps and a white cowboy hat, never apply that term to me. Second, it was *your* idea to take on ancient gods with no added help or backup. Third, when we confront our foes, I will be carrying what I have for many, many years. A plasma rifle and a rail pistol. So far, no one has killed me yet."

"Time marches on, Dr. Luddite. These," I gestured emphatically at my new toys, I mean tools, "are the future."

"No. Those are expensive, silly looking guns designed to catch the eye of males suffering from testosterone poisoning. What is more, they are unproven in combat. Never disregard Murphy's Laws of War. *The complexity of a weapon is inversely proportional to the IQ of the weapon's operator.*"

"Hater," I grumbled. "These are super weapons and they'll work fine in the field."

"I have two things to say. One, knowing you has been a pleasure. Two, can we go now? If we remain here any longer, you'll just buy more *crap* we don't need that will not survive contact with the enemy."

Did Doc just say *crap*? A gentleman and a scholar, stoops to ... to *my* level. We were in deeper doodoo than was possible. Oh well. At least we started from a familiar location and circumstance.

"Okay, let's do this," I announced as I stood. I even left my babies in their boxes. I wanted to show Doc I could place priorities in their proper order. Plus, I could unpack them later, alone in my cabin. Oh, yeah, baby.

"Shall we *now* inform Sapale and Daleria of our intentions?" he asked, yet again. He must have been carrying a lot of guilt.

"No. They made it crystal clear they wanted to hunker down on Azsuram. They needed estrogen R&R, or something."

"You know how mad your brood's-mate will be with you. If you're killed, she'll be furious with you. If you're not, she'll be even hotter."

"Possibly. She might also thank me for my kind consideration."

"I say I check those logic buffers *before* we enter combat. Your reasoning is seriously impaired."

"If you'd like, I can drop you off with Cragforel. He'd love to spend quality time with his bestie."

"And allow you to go on a dangerous mission alone? No, that's a paralyzingly stupefying notion. Let us depart."

"You got it. *Stingray*, set a course for V429 Carinae." I attached my fibers to the deck, so she could execute my orders.

"Form One," she said with obvious frustration, "we've discussed this on several occasions in the past. I do not *set* a course. I am *here*, I *fold* space/time, and I'm *there*. There is no *course* to lay in."

"Are we there yet?"

"Yes."

"Thank you."

She could be very persnickety, at times.

"Please scan for signs of this active Cleinoid. Report back to me—"

"Oh, *please*," exploded Al. "Do we have to wait that long to tell you? Three nanoseconds into *please* we located Bozo. Why must we be made to suffer your little-brain time curses?"

"Yeah, but how do you really feel about it, Al? Say, are you familiar with the military acronym DILLIGAF?"

"Of *course* I'm familiar with it."

"Please apply it to your current whining." I cleared my throat. "Where's the bad guy?"

"I was not whining. You were oppressing us." Though he didn't have one, he cleared his throat. "Shall I set a course to the approximate location of the Cleinoid?"

"If you have a chance, that would be swell." Wait, did he say set a course?

"He's three hundred meters due north, Pilot," Al reported tersely. "We placed a low hill between him and us. He will be unaware of our presence until you tromp loudly around the corner and stumble a few times. If you accidentally discharge that big new toy of yours, he'll know much sooner."

"Which one, smart ass? I'll be carrying *two*."

"Oh, *wonderful*. Twice the chances to feel the painful stings of I-told-you-sos. Please hurry. I cannot wait."

"Continue scanning. Alert us immediately if—"

"We know. If pink unicorns close on our position. *Go,*" snapped Al.

"Come on, Doc. Let's reach out and touch some one evil."

We stepped out onto a parched landscape. Craters pockmarked the expanse, and a sand-laden wind assaulted us in pulses. This place was off my purchase-time-shares list, but good. If we were still human, we'd have needed oxygen masks, and possibly pressure suits. The atmosphere was thin, mostly nitrogen, and laced with methane. Hmm. I almost asked Toño if the methane might combust if, say, a gamma ray laser passed through it. But, three thoughts occurred to me. One, he'd *so* I-told-you-so me. Two, there wasn't *that* much oxygen in the air. Three, what the hell? At least the Cleinoids'd burn along with us, right?

I'll take point, I said head-to-head. No need to vocalize a potential warning to our prey.

Fine, he replied. *Keep your barrels directed forward at all times, please. Friendly fire—isn't.*

What a funny guy. Glad he was along for comic relief.

I called a halt as we rounded the hill. I heard the Cleinoid before I saw him. Yup, large disgusting rodent, just like Cragforel said. Back in my USAF days, it'd be referred to as BUFF, and I do *not* mean he looked like a B-52. If the air were thicker, I was sure he'd smell to high heaven, too. A thing *that* revolting had to be rank.

I'll advance. You cover. Then I cover your advance. I said to Toño.

Roger that. Do we kill it when we have the shot, or do you want to speak with it?

I'd prefer to parley. If we can, we do. Otherwise, SFAQL.

Copy that.

We rotated closer and closer. It became apparent what

the big, dumb rat was doing. He—and *he* had to be a *he* because *he* was acting so batshit crazy—was ripping into rocks and open turf. He was tearing stuff to pieces for no obvious reason. He wasn't eating the material, just scattering it randomly and robustly. I did notice one thing of enormous value. He had a gash alongside his right cheek. He was sustained by some yet unidentified force, but he was wounded. Back in Godville, some of the gods could take a cannonball to the chest and not bleed a drop.

See that cut? Toño asked. He was thinking what I was.

Yes. We can probably kill him. Let's see if he's in a chatty mood.

I came around to approach him in his line of sight. I wanted him to notice us, instead of sneaking up from behind and forcing him to react reflexively. About ten meters away, his head snapped up. First he sniffed the wind, then he quickly saw us. He took exactly one step toward us. I fried the dirt in front of the paw that moved just as it touched down. Wisely, he stopped.

"You want to talk, or you want to die?" I yelled above the ambient noise.

He shook his head, like he was stunned. "You speak my tongue," he squealed. "How can this be?"

"Maybe I'm a Cleinoid, too. Maybe I'm Ryanmax, god of warriors." Maybe I could play this lout into divulging what he knew about his not being dead? It was free to try.

"I did not see you when Rage egressed here."

"Well, maybe that's because I came with Fury." No way the Cleinoids who'd come here could know Dominion Splitter was defunct.

He considered my response. "I have seen no one from any other wave to Prime. You lie."

"Why would I lie? What would I hope to gain?"

"I will let you know *after* I eat you." He charged.

139

What a stupid, lame comeback. Seriously. The rodent was a moron.

I blew off half his lead leg. He rolled clumsily to that side, but popped back to his feet quickly enough.

"Cleinoids do not require guns, puny mortal."

Did this guy buy old, hack lines from a catalog, or something?

He trundled forward. He squeaked loudly, which was a really pathetic battle cry, IMHO.

I aimed at his other front leg. Click, click, click. Ah, my Excellon-6 seemed to be operating suboptimally.

Toño noticed in a flash. He shot off the entire leg with a plasma bolt.

Rat-dude snout planted, hard. He was much slower to rally, this time.

"You had enough, yet?" I shouted to him.

He tried to rise, but, missing one and a half legs made his efforts comical, at best.

I was so glad our weapons worked on him. His power source was clearly feeble, compared to Clein.

"Enough," he whined. "Finish me. I hate my life. This planet is wretched, there is no sport, and now you defile it."

"You didn't say the magic word," I harassed, as I stepped right up to him. I poked him with my under-performing rifle.

His brow furrowed. "Words have no magic."

"Boy, did your mom raise you poorly."

"Huh?"

Toño set a hand on my shoulder. "Jon, it is wrong to taunt the beast. And here, take this." He handed over his rifle.

I tossed my Excellon-6s to the ground. Crap, one more thing on my to-do list. I had to get a refund. Who has the time?

"What's your name, bright eyes?"

"No, it's not."

What a humorless, stupid BUFF rat.

"I am Bauchuh."

"Jon Ryan, here. I'd say it's nice to meet you, but I do so hate to lie."

"I wish you immeasurable ill."

Again with the corny lines. Putting me out of my misery by offing Bauchuh was looking mighty good.

"Why did you not die?" I asked bluntly.

"Why did I not die, when? I never died." His little brain was taxed.

"You were supposed to die when I destroyed Clein."

"You ... that's absurd. You cannot *destroy* Clein."

"Try telling that to Clein. Seriously, didn't you notice? Your strength dropped like a rock."

He pondered my remarks a second. "I was here. I found nothing. I made to leave, to seek other diversion, but I could not. That is all I know."

"So you had the ability to not die, but not to transport yourself?"

"What is it with you and death? Of course I did not die. I am alive, obviously. I *cannot* die. I am a Cleinoid god."

"We're going to test that theory, real soon, pal. You mean to say, it didn't strike you as *odd* that you couldn't zoom through the cosmos any longer?"

"No. Why should it?"

"Why *sh* ... Look, before you came here, you could, like fly through empty space. Now you can't. If that happened to me, I'd say to myself, 'Self, that's so odd that I can no longer do what I used to do easily.'"

"I am not you."

This one wasn't one of the brighter bulbs in the hardware store, was he?

"So, you do not know the energy source that keeps you alive?"

"Of course. Clein."

"But I —" I turned to Toño. "This conversation, it's over. Am I right?"

He shook his head faintly. "It certainly seems to be to this observer." He directed his rail pistol at Bauchuh. "He didn't even wonder why a fundamental change had occurred to him. I'd say let's finish him and depart."

I raised my right arm a bit. "That's two in favor of the motion before the ad hoc committee. Any last words, Bauchuh?"

"Yes. I hate you," he directed to me.

I angled my frame and pointed to Toño. "But him, you don't hate? That's harsh."

"Okay, I hate him, too. *Hello,*" he said to Toño. They hadn't spoken directly, up until then. "But I hate you more," that was back to me, again.

"So long, Bauchuh." I went around to one side and stuffed three thermite grenades under his chest. As I stood, I pulled the pins. "It's been real. Doc, *run.*"

We scampered behind the farthest rocks we could reach in four seconds. Then Bauchuh went *boom.* I let the pieces fall and the dust cloud be whipped away in the wind.

"You want to confirm his passing, or do you want me to?" I asked Doc.

"I'd never forgive myself after you botched the diagnosis," he said while standing and dusting himself off. "I'll be right back."

"That's fine, but I'll be with you."

"Then why did you—" He sighed deeply, judgingly. "Let's get this grim task over."

I stood right behind Toño as he examined what

remained of Bauchuh. I can say, without hesitation, that the BUFF was d-e-a-d dead. If the scattered pieces and parts were reassembled with a glue gun, it wouldn't resemble anything even close to what Bauchuh looked like. You'd just have yourself a funny looking pile of disgusting.

CHAPTER SEVENTEEN

"Say, do you have any more of that beer beverage our benefactor left us?" Wul asked Queeheg, as he looked absently into his empty mug.

"Not up here. We polished dat off but good." He took a moment to steady his queasy stomach. He placed a palm over his belly, belched loudly, and became green around the gills. "Must'a says, dis not being a god no longer has it distinctive downsides. I tink I have one a'dem hanga-*overs* Jon mentioned to me a whilez ago."

"They are unpleasant, aren't they? I'm at the point where I'm questioning the wisdom of indulging so freely of the spirits."

"What a bleak future tis awaitn' us, governor."

"I'll second that notion. Here I spend eternity learning how to drink really well, really capaciously, and what? I'm doomed to a lonely mortal existence, waiting for my inevitable death, and I must now *pace* myself. That's harsh."

"*Bitter's* what I'da call it. A *bitter* twist'a fate."

"I think Fate has forgotten about us, and our universe, my friend."

Queeheg surveyed his more-dismal-and-less-tidy-than-usual establishment. "I'da sayz I see clear documentation dat Fate's found a new puppy ta scratch behind da ear."

"Still, our fortunes are far superior than those of our gone and unlamented brethren."

"Truer words a'never been spoken, Wul. And, a real plus is dos chaseadilas Jon programed in'a our food making machine."

"I believe he called them *quesadillas,* and, yes, they're *sublime.* Gooey, toasty, and cheesy. What more could one ask of one's meal?"

"Me, I'ma not in da habit'a conversin' wit my food. But if I were ta begin doin' so, I'd tell dem chasadilas dat they were *bloody* alright wit me." He spied the food replicator, hungrily. He was contemplating downing his twelfth taste treat of the morning. But, with his clothes barely fitting him now, he didn't act on his impulse. Wul threatened to leave, with his magic feeder, if Queeheg was reduced to running around naked, for want of suitably sized clothing. Even he had to admit his body was not one that *anyone,* including himself, wanted to see in the buff.

"We were discussing that beer stuff," Wul reminded his companion.

"Yes. Say, friend, did ya notice how *seamlessly* dos chasadilas go wit dat beer? It'sa almost like some form'a *divine* intervention was afoot."

"You are perfectly correct. My only response can be *bring on the brew.*"

"Er, if'a ya don't mind terrifically, we could go downstars and'a retrieve some."

Wul opened his arms. "Why not bring a barrel up here? That system has worked fantastically up until this juncture."

"Well, truth'a bein' known widely, me back's taken ta painin' me, a'late. Haulin' one's dos containamenters up here is likely more'an me bones could handle."

Wul considered his mug, whimsically. "Well, as there are no other *pressing* demands on our time, I suggest we retire to the basement and entertain ourselves in that venue."

As they descended the rickety wooden stairs, Queeheg limping noticeably, he asked of Wul an unusually thoughtful question, given his simple views on all things. "If'a ya had it ta do again', would ya have 'cepted Jon Ryan's gift a'life, or used dat pistol a'his?"

Wul was caught off guard by that query. Would he? Was what Queeheg and he were experiencing worth the cost, in terms of survivor remorse, loneliness, and isolation? "I suppose we will never know. I fired off that pistol for a reason. I was voting for life. I did not want an escape-clause option. I felt, at the time, that was the correct decision for the future mes. I was fairly certain one of those mes to come might well have ended our life in a fit of passion."

"Speakin'a *passion*, I revisit, wit regret, the sore subject'a us not having a compatible turd party, a'da female persuasion, to journey wit us towards our demise."

"I've felt that pain, too, my friend. The ice-cold truth of it was that Jon couldn't guarantee our food replicator would abundantly support *three* individuals, indefinitely. Plus, by the time the system was up and running, the selection of suitable *traveling* companions was depressingly limited."

"T'was, indeed. Dos two hags'a sisters were da last females to drop. I'd choose endless lonely nights t'either a'dem two."

"Trust me on this. You are more correct than you can *imagine*." Wul shuddered.

Queeheg ran his finger over his chest oddly.

"What was that?" Wul asked, gesturing to Queeheg's torso.

"What, dat?" He pointed behind himself. "Sumpin' dat little fella wit Jon Ryan showed'a me. He said it was a kind' a self-blessin', dat I might properly need one'a dos in da coming times."

"Prudent of Dr. DeJesus," mused Wul. How ironic. Gods who needed to ask for external blessings. What had the world come to? "Look on the bright side, my friend. Our universe is massively huge. Jon tried to explain it to me before he left. I was baffled by his words, but I did take away that the realm of the Cleinoids is immense."

"An'?" pressed Queeheg.

"And, somewhere out there, another Ryanesque character might have provided two beautiful *women* with a food synthesizer and a means of transportation."

"Dat's a pleasin' taught," Queeheg said lustfully. "He raised his then full mug of beer. "Ta da prospects'a pair'a beauties findin' da path to our door."

"Where there's hope, there's reason to live," Wul said so quietly, Queeheg couldn't possibly have heard him.

CHAPTER EIGHTEEN

So, we'd learned quite a bit about the surviving Cleinoids. But, along with the few answers came even more confounding questions. What powered them, at their clearly weakened level? Clein, lite? Given how I felt about beer, lite, I was pissed. In a just and loving cosmos, neither of those could exist. And, how many of the scumbags were out there? Cragforel found two with little effort. Extrapolating his experience suggested to me that hundreds, if not thousands, could have survived. And a thousand Cleinoids could do a lot of nasty, quickly. Even though they weren't schooled, they were clever. What if they found a way to package their new energy source? Traveling badness would hit the road. The results could be *as* brutal as before, only at a more glacial pace.

I needed a vacation.

To make my foul mood worse, Toño made me leave all *four* Excellon-6s on that lousy planet orbiting V429 Carinae. Yeah, he forbade me to even think about returning them. He called the experience a *life-lesson*. I did not need more *life-lessons*. Been there. Done that. Got the tee shirt. I needed to hold unethical arms merchants accountable. Actually, now that I say it like that, it's kind of a stupid thought.

"Personally, I think we were lucky with Bauchuh. I think he was a weak Cleinoid, even before we eliminated Clein."

"Lucky? No luck involved in *skill*, Doc."

"I think I may join Sapale and Daleria on Azsuram. There appears to be no space left on this planet, due to the size of your *head*."

I looked down. "Speaking of which, I called the wife earlier today."

"And you still live? She's mellowing in her advancing years."

"No, she's just, like, forty light years away with no vortex. She solemnly promised a painful death, full of depravity and suffering for me, bless her constant heart."

"I should be so fortunate."

"She asked me nicely to include the two of them in any future plans we might have."

"Nicely?" he repeated dubiously. "This I have to hear." He motioned for me to *come on* by repeatedly flipping one set of fingers into his up-turned palm.

"Well, traumatic *castration* was mentioned, along with a significant alteration in the *configuration* of my external genitalia. It got dicy after that, so I'll spare you the shocking details. The girl curses worse than a drunken sailor on I&I*." [* *Intoxication & Intercourse. A wild time while on leave. Play on R&R*]

"I can only imagine. So, are we going for this Torent character, shall we assemble the team, or will we just hope he becomes bored and dies of that?"

"I think it's down to B. A would be suicidal. And C,

well, I hate to be the one to tell you this, Doc, it's just plain silly."

"Plan B it is. *Blessing*, please transport us to Azsuram, on the spot we only so recently left from." He dropped his fibers to the deck.

"By your command, Form 3."

"I thought you said you'd fixed the Cylonism," I said to Toño in a huff.

"It turns out to be harder than one might assume. Vortex manipulators are resistant to new learning."

Any response I might have offered died in the back of my throat. I felt slight nausea. That meant Sapale was within punching distance. I needed to be on my A-game.

We stepped out into an otherwise pleasant spring day. The tension I felt in the air, however, was electric.

"There's a good sign," I said, apropos of nothing.

"What good sign?"

"No shots have rung out, yet."

He chuckled merrily. "*Yet.*"

I led us directly to where Sapale would be staying. Upon entering, I saw Daleria cleaning up in the kitchen, but no brood's-mate.

"Where's Sapale?"

"She went on a dangerous quest with the pool boy, Juaquin."

"Uh, we don't have a pool."

"She felt that was an *issue*, but not a *barrier* to having a pool boy named Juaquin." She turned to me. "The boy certainly got a running start at manhood."

"Very funny. Where is she?"

"Down by Lake JJ," she replied neutrally.

"Did she bring cutting tools and attachable weights?"

"Why, *yes*. How did you know? I believe she called one

of them a *chain* saw." She furrowed her brow. "Made a frightening racket." She winced.

Oh, okay. I call piling on. Where's my yellow flag when I need it?

To Toño, I said quietly, "I'll leave you two love birds alone." I elbowed him gently. "I have a few ties in the back closet, if you need them. *Know what I mean? Know what I mean?"*

"You said something about leaving, yet I still see you standing in front of me," he responded, coolly.

I made it to Lake JJ pretty quickly. It wasn't far. It was the lake supplied by the stream we first settled next to way, *way* back when. While I was walking, I thought back on those times. Darn, they seemed like such innocent times, compared to what was to come. We traveled in my old sub-light-speed ship, *Shearwater*. That was a good ship, a graceful lady with all the right moves. What ever became of her? Funny, I don't think I ever found out. I guess I could have forgotten. But, as far as I knew, knock on wood, I hadn't forgotten anything. Toño said once that there was a finite amount of storage in our computer banks. When a critical limit was reached, a subroutine deleted old, low-priority data. Something like the temperature Sunday morning, May, 3, 1981, which I had known back then, was discretely dumped. I actually didn't know if I'd surpassed the data limit, yet.

After JJ, my best friend, probably ever, passed, Sapale renamed the lake where we loved to fish after him. He'd be pleased. She'd buried him near the rocky outcropping that became, for the two of us, our happy place. We'd lounge, drink beer, maybe do some fishing, and spit. We spit a lot when sitting on those rocks. Hey, we were guys on a guy-outing. You gotta spit when doing that. I think that's an actual law of nature. God, I missed JJ. I'll tell you a secret, if you promise not to tell. You know all the times I could have, hell, *should* have been killed? I might have panicked, or acted impulsively, but I was never afraid, never *truly* afraid. You know why? Because I always thought, if I died, there and then, maybe I'll see JJ again. Yeah. It wasn't a comforting notion, it was redemptive. Hang on a sec. I have some dust in my eyes.

Soon enough I rounded a corner in the trail, and saw Sapale. She was sitting next to JJ's marker, her back to me. She was looking toward the water, and she was softly singing a traditional Kaljaxian lullaby. Dude, I nearly lost it. No words. There are none.

It took me a couple minutes to find the wherewithal to walk over to her.

"Hey there," she called out absently, not turning to speak.

"Hey there, back atcha."

I sat next to her and swung an arm over her shoulder.

"Seems like a nice, quiet day," I remarked.

"I've had better." She finally looked up at me. Her tears streaked down my shoulder. "*But,*" she wrapped an arm around my waist, "I've had a hell of a lot worse."

"Strange days, indeed."

"Nobody told me, either," she mused.

We sat in silence a good little while. It was nice, in a melancholy way.

"Please tell me you'll never exclude me, again?" she said in a whisper.

"I will never exclude you again."

We sat a longer spell, in the quiet, except for the gentle, reassuring breeze.

"Do you even know why you did?" she asked with little emotion.

"Not a clue."

"You know you're a terrible liar, right?"

I looked down at her. "No way. I'm a terrific liar. In fact, I'm the best liar *I've* ever met."

"Why'd you do it?"

"Seriously—and I'm being actually serious, here—I wanted to spare you."

She started to pull away, probably to say something harsh.

I eased her back to my shoulder. "I said I was serious, and I was." I sighed. "Heading right back into the breach, it … it wasn't fun. But, I thought of you, you and Daleria, doing something *positive*. Something non-violent. It gave me a warm, pleasant feeling in my soul. That's the God's truth. I needed you to not be killing or being killed by my side. I needed *you* to be happy, so *I* could find the strength to put one *damn* foot in front of the other."

"Never again."

"I said it. I meant it."

She sobbed softly a few minutes. "When this war's over —" She began to cry harshly, and couldn't finish her thoughts.

I hugged her and we began to rock, slowly.

Finally, she could speak. "When this damn war's over, and before the next double-damn one can begin, I … I think—"

"What?"

"Forget it. Nothing."

In the history of statements issued by a wife that must *not* be allowed to drop, I recognized a Top Ten lister, there.

"What do you think, when this war's done and gone?"

She was motionless in my arms.

"Fine. While you find the words, I'll tell you what I'd like to do when this war's done, if I'm still alive, that is. Because, if I'm dead, my wish won't be necessary."

She looked up at me. "Are you okay? You just said something rather silly."

"It only *seemed* silly, because you didn't let me finish my thought. When this mission's complete, I was thinking maybe it would be a good time to cash in my chips."

"Huh," she jerked away.

"Sure," I tried to pull her back, but she wasn't having it. "I've fought a million battles, seen more awful than a person should ever have to, and, to be perfectly honest, I'm worn out, inside."

"For you, it's easy," she said cryptically.

"I'm sure you're going to explain that one, brood's-mate. I'll sit here, quietly, until you do."

Didn't take long. I could feel her getting all Kaljaxian. Steam issued forth from her nostrils.

"You'd died, twice. It's old hat for you."

"Hey, third times a charm."

She punched my chest. "I've *never* understood what that means, and I do not appreciate hearing it."

"Ouch. And, why is the number of times I've died important to our present discussion?"

"You know damn well."

"I know lots of things, damn well. Some things, I'd like to hear, by way of confirmation, if nothing else."

"I hate it when you speak Jerk."

"Point."

She glared at me several heartbeats. "You know I was about to say the same thing. *I'm* tired. *I've* killed too many people, places, and things. *I've* done my part, like, a *million* times. *I* think I need a break—a *permanent* break."

"Lord knows we've fought the good fight. I mean, saving the universe three or four times, depending on how you tally it, is enough for one lifetime."

"Or two," she said quietly.

I pulled her back. "Or two."

We rocked gently a spell.

"You know what I love about the future?" I said robustly.

"No, but I have a feeling I will not be able to stop you from telling me."

"The great thing about the future is it's not *now*." I stood. "You don't actually have to do anything about the future until it gets here. In the mean time, you keep peddling and try not to crash the bike."

"I'm so glad you became an astronaut."

I was touched. "Because, otherwise we'd never have met?"

"No. Because you're a lousy inspirational speaker. No gift, whatsoever."

She stood and started toward the house.

I fell in tow. "Are we going back to the house to, you know, *celebrate* our resolves?"

"No."

"Good, because I left Toño and Daleria there, alone ... you know."

She huffed at me incredulously, "Well, if there's a *tie* on the doorknob, we won't go in, *will* we?"

CHAPTER NINETEEN

"I tell you flatly, it is not *fair*. I should not be forced to exist in such a diminished, wretched condition."

Torent was reclining on a stack of bodies ten high in spots. The corpses were his most recent *satisfying* kills. A death was satisfactory if the one dying knew what was happening, if the victim was intelligent enough to realize what a harsh end it was about to face. Food animals and wild beasts, though he annihilated them in great numbers, were *unsatisfying*, though not so much that he didn't relish slaying them, too. Being insanely cruel made his life easy.

He was speaking to a throat-lozenge shaped severed, bleeding head; a rather fresh one, in fact. It still dripped white blood at a respectable pace. It was from a race Torent called Pig Droppings. They, the few of them left alive, called themselves the Amant Dour, the great people. But, they were, of late, not so much. Torent found their taste to be revolting, but they put up such a fight, and made such otherwise heartrending bleats, it was a pure pleasure to kill them.

The mature Amant Dour were around one hundred

and fifty kilograms, together. Picture, if you will, four separate disks, joined in a square by thick tubes—kind of like Tinker Toy pieces, only with stouter sticks. Each disk was a distinct sentient, with a disky head atop it. Together, they were a mated quartet, called a sephado. Sex was complicated for the great people. Boy howdy, was it ever.

Each individual head had two mouths, one facing toward the members of the sephado on either side of it. The take-home message is that, when Torent began to rip the Amant Dour apart, eight throats screamed in terror and agony. Gory surround-sound. Torent could not get enough of it. He almost—almost—would regret it when he killed off the last of the Pig Droppings. But, genocide was his inclination, so he knew that regrettable day would come, all too soon.

Back to Torent on the bedding of corpses. He carried on his one-sided conversation with the quarter sephado, well, because Torent was insane. He needed a little rest, to build strength, so he could then indulge further in his lust for all things evil. He was of a mind to complain to someone, and the mutilated disk was the closest approximation of a living being he'd be able to address his concerns to. Any healthy creature that close to him would be shredded in an instant. Torent was forced to *improvise*.

"Here I live a good life, minding, for the most part, my own business," he said to the subunit named Driz-opal-3 when still alive, "and what do I get? I'm marooned *here*, on this god forsaken heap of trash, forced to *try* to survive off of eating one of the most unappetizing species ever," he pulled Driz-opal-3 in closer, and added conspiratorially, "that would be *you*, my dear. No offense intended."

In an abomination of taste, Torent said out the side of his mouth, "None taken," meaning to represent his victims response to his comment. *Insane*. Remember?

157

"But, you can't always get what you want, and I accept that. But seriously, my one true friend, how is a Cleinoid god supposed to get by on such meager pickings?"

"It's a damn shame, that's what it is. A *damn* shame." he said, with the side of the mouth thing, again.

"You know, I've always cared for you, the most, Pig Dropping. You've been the apple of my eye. Now, time to be the apple of my belly."

With that, he tossed the disk once known as Driz-opal-3 down his ample gullet. Torent winced, briefly, at the sourness he was forced to abide. Then, he forgot completely that Driz-opal-3 ever existed.

"I need something to wash that taste—"

Torent trailed off. He saw, and was stunned to see, a two meter tall stack of boulders approaching him on ... stones. Verazz had finally found a suitable candidate for Carol-honoring.

"What sorry excuse are you for a—"

Torent couldn't finish his sentence, on account of Verazz landing a thunderous bolt of energy to the center of his chest. Torent was thrown a soccer field backward, stopping only when the fourth tree he struck did not splinter, but held together.

He rose quickly, but was dazed. He shook his horned head violently. When Verazz was still a ways off, he was able to howl, "How dare y—"

Another energy bolt drove him backward.

As he skidded through brush and over stones, he resolved to make shorter challenges, and to maybe duck during them.

It took Torent a bit longer to rise, but rise he did.

"Would you do me the common courtesy of dying, please," whined Verazz. "It's not like I don't have a *million* other things I'd rather be doing, you know."

"I'm—" Torent shut the hell up. Instead of blustering, he cast thousands of tiny electric lances at Verazz.

Verazz saw them coming, and raised a rocky palm to stop them. But the missiles pierced whatever spell he offered in defense, and shot through his stone body like it was a cloud of mist. Verazz crumpled to his knees and he was in bitter anguish. To draw breath was searingly painful. A panic set in. Then, Torent's devilish face was looking down on Verazz, who had somehow fallen backward.

"What type of flatulating *butthead* uses the words *common courtesy* and *million other things to do* in a death match?" He was laughing maniacally, and actually had trouble getting his taunt out comprehensibly.

"I—" Verazz was silenced by pain.

"Awe, poor Pig Dropping having tongue trouble?"

Verazz focused on that diabolical face. His hand formed into an obsidian spike. He plunged it into Torent's throat.

Torent clasped his neck, gasped, and stumbled away. Olive green ooze spurted out between his finger.

Verazz made to rise, but collapsed back to the ground in torment.

Torent jerked his head, stomped his cloven feet, and cursed all creation as he struggled to stay upright.

Had Verazz been able to take advantage of his opening, he might have finished Torent off. But he was unable to move.

Torent threw his bloody arms wide open, and screamed to high heaven, "I will eat your heart." He charged the incapacitated Verazz. He leaped in the air, and plummeted toward Verazz as he lay unable to move. With inches to go before his hooves crushed down, Torent stretched hard to close the gap faster.

Then, Torent felt himself lurch up and back, like a

marionette snatched up harshly by its puppeteer. He sailed, backward, and then slammed into a small pond. He strained to gain the surface, but something held him down. He breathed in the muddy water, and began choking. Torent's hands patted his back. There were numerous thin wires attached to him. With instinctive fear, he ripped at them.

Few lost purchase.

Torent realized the pond was very shallow, so he stood, instead of trying to swim to his escape. He got up to his knees, but was jerked back into the water. He powered his legs—harder. He was back on his knees, and he was breathing. With all his weight, strength, and conviction, he twisted himself around to look behind.

A figure stood at the edge of the tiny pond. From its left hand, the tiny wires projected to Torent's back. He dug his knees in and got up on one leg.

"Release me," he screamed. "I will—"

Torent was underwater again, on his back. As he struggled, he realized he was being a fool. He calmed his body and focused his mind. The water covering him burst into steam and hissed away in an explosion. The heat his spell generated was enough to dry the mud to baked clay. He flipped onto his belly, then levered himself upright with the aid of his arms.

Jon Ryan pulled with all his might, but he could not bring the Cleinoid down, now that he had good footing. He cursed under his breath.

A second set of wires snatched Torent from the side. Working together, they slammed him back to his knees.

Torent shot his hate-filled eyes to the source of the second set of wires. He saw a smaller figure, a female, tugging at him. Her free arm was raised. The central digit of her hand was extended, while the two digits on either side of it were folded inward. Was she greeting him?

"Doc," Torent understood the male to yell, "check on the down man. We'll try to hold this piece of shit."

Torent saw a flash of a third figure shoot toward the rock man.

In an act of shear guts and anger, Torent stood. He gabbed one set of wires in either hand, and pulled the man and the woman to the ground. His head came back and he laughed the laugh of the enraged insane.

He took one step toward the man, when a fourth figure he'd not noticed raced past him. It moved as a blur. Only when it was well clear of him, did Torent feel the dagger in the back of his chest. He pawed the handle, causing it to tear his flesh painfully. Then he pulled the blade out and hurled the weapon away. He screeched in wrath and pure hatred.

Jon pulled to the side, while Sapale pulled straight back. Torent stumbled, then fell.

Torent felt two hot, stinging whips lance his body. He looked up. Both his tormentors were firing some beam-weapons at him from their right hands. His soul boiled with rampaging fury. He began to levitate.

Sapale, seeing the monster rise, quickly wrapped her fibers around a tree. Jon pulled downward for all he was worth.

Torent held, three meters off the ground. He strained, he wriggled, and he cursed.

The tree snapped in half. Jon and Sapale were lifted off their feet. Immediately, they both released their fibers.

Torent rocketed skyward, then eased to a stop. He needed to take stock of who all were attacking him. The rock man was being helped up by a man. The two who'd bound him were scampering over to the stricken one. He could not see his fifth assailant.

Torent bellowed a war cry, and dropped toward the grouping of four. He intended to incinerate them.

Mid-descent, one - two - three daggers slammed into his face in rapid sequence. He spiraled out of control and slammed to the dirt like a bag of wet cement.

As he lay face-down, he flashed, where had those daggers come from? Who was that accurate? Only a *god*. One of his *own* was trying to kill him.

His mind swept the forest. *There*. A small female hid amongst the trees. Her belt was studded with ancient, powerful daggers. He staggered to his feet and lurched toward the woman in hiding. She would suffer.

Again, tormenting wires seized him. One set sank into his face. The other snatched up both legs. He was slammed to the ground. His fury was all-consuming. From his prone position, he fired off hundreds of electric lances at the male.

The male flashed invisible, then visible. His lances had ... what? Been stopped? That was impossible. Torent fired at the female.

Sapale saw the bolts the instant they were born. She pulsed a total membrane on, then off, leaving a nanometer hole to allow her fibers to pass through.

Torent fired volleys at both attackers. They simultaneously vanished, then reappeared. He staggered to his knees, then to his feet. He looked to the rock man. The third man and the woman from hiding were helping him into a shiny metal box. They disappeared inside.

"*NO*," Torent volcanoed. He would not allow anyone to escape this outrage.

The man and woman holding him with wires ran toward the box. Their wires jerked at Torent wildly. He started to fire off lances, but realized they would be as ineffective. He willed the two figures to die. He saw, in his mind's eye, their hearts stop beating and their blood freeze solid.

Sapale and Jon were struck with a burning sensation. It was like a mild electrical shock. But they sped toward the vortex, anyway. Then the rail cannon on *Blessing* sang to life. They vaporized the ground Torent stood on. He was slammed five hundred meters back, into a cliff face.

By the time, several minutes later, Torent was able to stand, the figures, and the shiny box, were gone. He reached out with his mind to know where they were, but his demand was not answered. Exhausted, he dropped to his knees. He pounded his fists on the ground and he cursed those who tormented him.

CHAPTER TWENTY

I stumbled into *Stingray*, right behind Sapale. Toño slammed the portal shut and ordered us to Oowaoa, before I even had a chance to hit the deck.

"Al, *status*," I shouted after I rolled onto my back.

"All vortex is fully operational. No damage to the ship or any systems. The enemy never actually directed fire toward the *Blessing*."

"And everybody's aboard and well?"

"Aye, Captain. Aside from our new rock pile of a guest, all present, accounted for, and unharmed."

I jumped to my feet. "Doc, what do you make of this ... this guy?" I pointed to the pile of rocks writhing on the floor.

"Unknown species and physiology. He's in pain, but I cannot determine the extent of his injuries. I'll move him to our sick bay. Maybe I can learn more there."

The hull breached and Cragforel popped his head through. "Belay that, Toño. Bring him to my workshop. It's better equipped to treat him."

Toño and Cragforel hoisted the stone man with their

probes and quickly negotiated him off the vortex.

I turned to Daleria, who was still panting heavily, and Sapale. "You two good?"

They nodded.

"Okay, I'll be with—" and I started to turn.

"No, Jon," called out Sapale.

"What?"

"Let them work. If you pester them with questions, it'll only slow them down."

I bobbed my head side to side. She was probably right. In place of telling her that, specifically, I walked over to the mess and threw myself into a bench. "*That* was intense."

"What was, dear?" Sapale asked, disingenuously.

"Seeing Cragforel, of course. What other near-catastrophic event could I be referring to?"

She replied with a big shrug.

"And Daleria, baby, where did you learn to throw daggers like that? You were ... were—"

"Demigodly?" She finished with a wry smile.

"*That's* the word I was looking for."

"Jon, I owned a fancy bar. I *grew up* in bars. Some play dice, others look for love. I learned to win at daggers."

"Wouldn't darts be more, er, practical?"

"Darts are for sissies." She tented her fingers on her chest. "*I* am not a sissy. *I* throw daggers."

"You sure as hell do," I exclaimed. "And, I don't recall seeing you *move* like that."

"Whatever powers Torent, powers me, too."

"What, you the demigod of sprinters?"

She wagged a finger, reminding me she wouldn't say what, if any, her super power was. That refusal, naturally, spurred me on to fits of unbridled speculation. Was Daleria the demigod of undertakers? Hookers? Lord, maybe even—dare I say it—*drummers*? Maybe I'd never

165

know. She sure was fast and not one to challenge at daggery, if that's what the sport was called.

"Torent, eh?" asked Sapale. "That's the shit stain's name?"

"Yes. And, I have to say, he's a real piece of ... well, I was going to say work. But, he's actually a piece of shit."

"Gee," I remarked innocently, "one could not guess so from the whole devil-incarnate look he's got going."

"Everyone used to say, when he was well out of earshot, it was a chicken and egg thing, his appearance. Did he give rise to the devil image, or did it give rise to him? Any way you cut it, he's pretty much a case of *what you see is what you get*. Mean SOB."

"You know, I got that distinct impression, when we met," I quipped. "At first I was going to ask him to high tea. Then, I said to myself, that was not a good idea. The dude would steal the silver and break our best china."

"I once sat a few spaces over from him at a conclave," Daleria said angrily. "He tried to kill the people on either side of himself. One was because the woman talked. The other, the male, it was because he *breathed* too loud."

"Bauchuh's powers, when Toño and I confronted him, were markedly reduced. Do you think Torent's powers are?"

Daleria shook her head faintly. "Can't say. He was a top fifty lister, back home, in terms of power."

"You guys kept *lists*?" erupted from my throat.

"Jon, competitive egomaniacs like the Cleinoid gods. *Bored*, competitive narcissists? Of course they did."

"How about you?" Sapale asked. "Did you feel like you used to, or weaker?"

"Definitely slower, that's for certain."

"Whoa," I wheezed incredulously. "I *saw* you back there. That was the slow-motion version?"

"What can I say. I was a top *ten* lister for speed."

"You're just making that shit up," I whined.

"My speed is not subject to your opinion of it, fortunately."

Sapale set three mugs of coffee down, and both women sat with me.

"We hurt him, but we sure as hell didn't hurt him very badly," I stated as I stared into my mug. "Al thought to drop a spybot, just as we folded away. After we hit him with the rail cannon, at point blank range, he was up and hunting for us way too fast for my liking."

"Form One," *Stingray* stated, "in the brief time we were present on the surface of Podulliy, we were able to ascertain Torent has done extensive damage to the planet and its population. Approximately forty three percent of the two sentient species that call the planet home have been killed."

"Podulliy?" I questioned. "That's the planet we were on, right?"

"Yes, Form One."

"How long has he been there?" Sapale asked.

"Seventeen days."

"He's fast," she remarked to no one in particular. "We may need Mirri to be able to take him out."

"Let's find out what our mystery guest's story is, first," I responded. "Speaking of which—" I looked to Sapale questioningly.

She nodded that I was excused. Hey, we were married a long time. Our communications were streamlined.

Entering Cragforel's work area, I was pleased to see the rock dude sitting up on the bench. He was speaking to Cragforel, but to do so was clearly an effort. Toño was right behind Cragforel, his hands behind his back, listening.

"... I ... I simply can't say." said the patient.

"Not to worry, for now," reassured Cragforel. "When you're feeling better, we can revisit the topic."

I wondered what they were discussing.

"Ah," Cragforel turned to me, "Jon, glad you're here. This is Verazz. He's ... he's an Apractolith. Verazz, this is—"

"I *know* you," Verazz said with an edge to his voice.

I set my hand on my chest. "Me? No, you do not. We've never met."

He leaned toward me, threateningly. "You *lie*. Why do you try to deceive me? Is it because I am injured? Vulnerable?"

"Dude, seriously. I think I would remember a pile of talking *rocks*."

"Ah," he eased back against the pillows that had propped him up. "I forgot. I didn't take this form, when we met. Let me see." He closed his eyes, and concentrated on something.

Slowly, the stones and pebbles disappeared, and a fleshy body replaced them. Verazz was humanoid, now. Sort of, at least. He was larger than most humanoids I'd seen. He was ... more handsome, yes. That was it. He was *too* handsome. His face was absolutely perfect.

"There," he huffed, "now you recognize me."

"Nope. Never laid eyes on you. And I'm being honest."

His eyes narrowed. He was measuring me. "I am never wrong. I say we've—"

"If I might," interrupted Cragforel.

"What?" grumbled Verazz.

"Jon has a twin brother, if you will. I bet that is who you met. Not *this* Jon Ryan."

"Both twins are named Jon? What kind of parents do that?"

"Not twins, in the *conventional* sense," remarked Toño, a bit nervously. "More like *clones*."

"I'd say more like *clowns*," Verazz quipped. He chuckled, but, even after his transformation, he winced with pain.

"So, what's an alpacalith?" I asked.

"*Apractolith*," Cragforel corrected quickly.

"I'm a Stone Witch. An *antigod*." He glowered disapprovingly at yours truly.

"You're an antigod?" I remarked, stunned.

He nodded ever so slightly.

"I heard about you, back in the Cleinoid realm."

He lurched up. "You are one of those—"

"No," Cragforel responded, setting a hand on Verazz's chest. "He is not a Cleinoid. None of us are Cleinoids."

I cleared my throat and directed my head outside, as in, *Daleria's back in the vortex.*

Cragforel understood my message. He nodded to me discretely. "Please believe me. Jon is not a Cleinoid. He is principally responsible for their massive losses."

"Aren't you guys," I formulated a question, "kind of *secretive?*"

"Yes." He rested his head back and looked away. "Generally we are. We avoid contact with lesser species."

"Lesser than what?" I challenged.

"*Other* species," he corrected himself, but, maybe more mockingly, than honestly.

"But you sought out Torent. You must have intended to kill him. Why would *you* care?"

He squinted at me. "My reasons are no concern of ... of yours." I actually think he made an effort to soften his words, just then. Weird.

"Well, as the leader of the merry band that saved your sorry ass, I'd say, yes, it *is* my concern."

Verazz turned, stood, and towered over me.

Okay, maybe hardball was not the best game with an antigod.

"Ah, think about it, a sec," I said humbly. "*We* came to kill him. *You* came to kill him. Neither of us fared so well. Maybe, if we worked together, we might succeed?"

The strength of my reasoning was sufficient to have him sit back up on the table. "I need to recover. That might take a while. Though I could go ... er, home, on my own accord, I would very much thank you for a ride there."

"O-kay," I replied slowly. "Sure. Why not?" I looked to Cragforel. "You think he's fit to travel?"

"I will be the—" Verazz began to thunder.

I raised a finger. "I'm addressing your doctor, pal. Back off. Doctors know best, when it comes to their patients."

To my surprise, Verazz accepted that castigation.

"I believe so. Yes," responded Cragforel. "I think we can all travel there safely."

"We?" I replied dubiously.

"Why, yes, Jon. Naturally, I, as the attending physician, will—"

"A Deavoriath, voluntarily leaving Oowaoa? How unexpected," I responded.

"*You're* Deavoriath?" queried Verazz.

Cragforel smiled faintly. "Why, yes. I am."

"I know of you," Verazz remarked.

"I'm flatt—"

"You polluted the universe only recently, didn't you? Yes, you were like mice, creeping about in every shadow. I very nearly exterminated you, you were so ... so, *pesky*."

"P ... p ... pesky?" Cragforel stuttered.

"Most annoying."

"Ah, that was a few billion *years* ago, Verazz," wheezed Cragforel.

"Yes, that's what I said. Only *recently*," Verazz replied, his tone laced with skepticism.

"Maybe we should go?" I interrupted.

Verazz scanned the room. "Yes. Let us go. Let us go, *now*."

I don't know if it was an antigod thing, or just a guy thing. Verazz wouldn't state the coordinates he wished us to take him to. Instead, he insisted he would pilot the ship there, himself. Toño tried, respectfully, to explain how he'd need command prerogatives to do so.

Verazz then raised his hand and displayed that he did. *Antigod*, here, he meant to convey.

"If you can get those to work," I said in as surly a manner as I could, which was, by the way, *very* surly, "then *fine*. You drive."

"What, precisely, er—" Verazz mumbled.

"You attach them anywhere on the ship. If she accepts your orders, you did it—you're a big boy, now." Oh, hell, yes, I was snarky. Dude wanted to fly *my* cube.

Verazz attached his fibers. He looked at the control panel and said words in a language I could not translate.

Nothing. No nausea.

Verazz looked to Cragforel, then to the view screen. He said similar, but slightly different words.

Nada. Hee hee. Poor baby. His new toys didn't work.

"If you want to get home in time for *dinner*—" I said, open-endedly.

"Very well," he snapped, like a spoiled brat.

I attached my fibers. "*Stingray*, take us to where he said." Slight nausea ensued.

"Open a portal, if you please. And *Stingray*," I added.

"Yes, Form One?"

"Make certain it's large enough for everyone's *ego* to pass through, easily."

"Yes, Form One," she replied, uncertainly.

Verazz held up an authoritative hand. "Only *my* ego needs to fit through. The rest of you remain aboard the ship. Depart as soon as I am gone. That is not an invitation to do so, but a co ... a *strong* suggestion."

"Shall we see you soon?" Cragforel asked nervously. "To plan our combined assault, that is?"

Verazz looked at Cragforel, then he stared at me. "I shall decide," he said with finality. And he left.

CHAPTER TWENTY-ONE

We returned to Oowaoa directly. Even if this Verazz character was in a weakened condition, he presumably had back up at home that was ready, willing, and anxious to obliterate any one who defied the will of the Stone Witches. We four gathered in Cragforel's workspace. He fetched nufe. *Lots* of nufe. In my very long life, I'd never seen a nervous Deavoriath. I have to admit, it turns out not to be a very reassuring sight.

"Please, please," said Cragforel absently, "help yourselves. I'm ... not myself just now."

"I think we kind of noticed that, host. What makes a mighty Deavoriath nervous?"

"Jon," he replied while trying to steady his glass enough to drink from it, "you recall, years ago, when I was amazed to meet a Deft and a human android. That I never thought I would, since you both were likely legends, and certainly extinct, if you were not?"

I shrugged. "Sure."

"And then you introduced me to one of my heroes, Dr. Toño DeJesus?"

"Gee, I hadn't noticed you were so *smitten* by him."

That got a pissy stare out from his scared face.

"Well, combine all those surprises—*shocks*—and you don't even come within *galaxies* of coming face-to-face with a Stone Witch. Surviving that encounter is so unlikely as to safely be assumed to be of zero probability."

I spread my arms. "Yet here we sit, we merry few. Smiles on our faces, drinks in our hands, and a new ally off somewhere coming to the realization that he is just that."

"Or," he responded with a look far more serious than an early grave, "he may realize he wishes to maintain his anonymity and independence, and come here and cancel us from ever having existed."

What a pink-pantsed pansy I had on my hands, here. "Crag," which I called him sometimes because the abbreviation drove him crazy, "we saved his life. He owes us. We *own* him. The rules of ownage are very clear on this point. The first act of being owned is not killing those you are indebted to."

He gave me a disgusted look. "What if the most powerful set of gods in creation haven't read that part of the rule book, yet? What if they read it, and then cancelled *its* existence?"

"Now you're just being dramatic."

Toño held his arms up, authoritatively. "Calm down, everyone. If Verazz wishes us dead, then we are already so. If he leaves us alone, never returns, and scrubs our memories, so be it. We will be none the wiser, and we will still have the same challenging set of dilemmas to address. If he returns with a picnic basket and a secret handshake, joins us in our Keystone-Cops attempts to restop the Cleinoids, then I, for one, will welcome his aid."

"I'm with Toño," voiced Sapale. "If Verazz feels he owes

us the debt he does, I say he'll do the right thing, or one of the righter things."

"You know I side with Toñito." Daleria gave him a dreamy look any male with an intact hormonal axis would be jealous of. She was magically babelicious. *Schwing*.

"Okay, but we need to work on two separate plans. One that *includes* Verazz, and one that identifies him only in a foot note, cited as an ice cream named *pralines and dick*."

"Is it not possible," Toño hounded me, "for you to say one contingency that *includes* his participation, and one that *excludes* such help?"

I looked to the others, then back to Doc. Flipping my palms up, I replied. "I just did. Weren't you listening?"

"Jon, when we next confront Torent, please allow me to take point."

"Doc, *I* take point. It's," I swaggered my head, "it's, kind of, my thing."

"Yes. But, this time, point is likely to die. Please allow me the out."

"Doc, your performance was electrifying. But the Russian judge only awarded you a 6.5. I'm afraid you will not be in the finals of Olympic Drama-Mamaing."

Daleria looked to Toño, but he only had to hold up an admonishing finger for her to let her confusion remain unaddressed.

"Okay, Plan B, where the big guy helps us, is currently unplannable. If he's involved, I'm thinking he'll be pretty bossy. He will not ask for, or tolerate, input from others, and even if he says he is, he won't be."

"We are familiar with that management style," mused Sapale.

"Good. Then it'll be easier for us, if and when we hit that bump."

"Easier for *most* of us," Toño added cryptically.

175

What was he referring to? Oh, well. No time for twenty questions. "So, Plan A, where we singlehandedly save the day—again."

"*Stop*," commanded Toño. "I insist we label that one Plan B. It is infinitely preferable to have the aid and resources of the most powerful god in existence."

Cragforel nodded in what I'd characterize as a panicky manner.

"You seem a bit stuck on labels, my friend. A rose by any other name, and all that."

"Do *not* invoke Shakespeare. He was wise. You are a fighter pilot," Toño pointed out, presumably in an attempt to be helpful.

"Okay. First, *sheesh*. Second, may we proceed with formulating Plan C?"

Toño furrowed his brow. "What happened to Plans A & B?"

"Well, silly goose, Plan A requires Verazz's input, as you insisted so prissily. Plan B was scrubbed, on account of I am not losing a round to you. Not here and now. Not never. Hence, the fallback plan is now titled *C*."

Daleria turned to Toño. "Not *never*?"

He patted the back of her hand and cooed softly.

Daleria looked to Sapale. She spun a finger at the side of her head to suggest I might be mentally less than in tip-top health.

"Suggestions for Plan C?" I called out.

Cue-the-crickets silence ensued.

"People, or whatever, this is not helpful. Suggestions?"

"I have one," Sapale replied with disinterest. "You do what you're going to do anyway, we'll yell and scream that you are positively insane, and then we'll do exactly and only what you wanted us to, in the first place."

"This," I scorned, "is no way to run a railroad."

"No, but it works for an insane asylum or a nursing care facility for those with one foot in the grave and the other on a banana peel," remarked Toño.

"I will laugh *after* we mutually, and by close personal interactions, forge Plan C."

"I vote we accept Plan C in its present form, and in its entirety," Toño said in *as* bored a tone as he could manufacture.

"And Plan *B*," amended Sapale, sounding more comatose than bored.

"I vote with—" Daleria began to say.

"I know. You vote with Toño," I snapped.

"No," she rose in her seat and gave me such a look. "I was *about* to say I vote with the *majority*, piss puddle."

"So noted into the record." I counted to ten. "There is a technicality, on the floor."

"We know. We're waiting for it to STFU, for the record," grunted my forever wife.

Well, *this* was an unproductive meeting, which was to say, it was a meeting.

"Plan CB involves—" I began to clarify.

"*Whoa*, Nellie," shot Toño. "What's this CB business?"

I rested my fists on my hips. "Plan B was scrubbed—"

"Yes," he snapped, "Because of your childish ego."

"I came up with a possible Plan C, but, based on the *childish* ridicule it garnered, I re-renamed it Plan CB. It honors the lamentably lost Plan B, and C."

"Why isn't it then Plan BC?"

"Dearest wife. That would be a misleading moniker. If I called it *BC*, some listeners might assume it involves the time period that proceeded Christ's arrival on Earth, *BC*."

"Daleria leaned into Toño. "Who's BC? Who's Christ?"

"Jon is speaking, love. What do we do when Jon speaks?"

"Fully minimize what he says, if not simply ignore his words."

"You've got it, love. I'm *so* proud of you." Dude even gave her a look of loving pride.

Gag me.

"Here's the drill. We need two things, ASAP. We need to kill Torent. He's murdering and destroying. Plus, sooner rather than later, he'll proceed to a new innocent world. We have an obligation to protect those in harm's way."

"And our second objective?" asked Toño.

"We need to find out how many other Cleinoids are active, and where they are."

"You mean we have to find every nanometer needle in the galactic-sized hay stack?" He sounded dismissive.

"Yes. But we have a fixer."

"What's a fixer?" asked Daleria. "What's broken?"

It was kind of easy to confuse this one.

"*You* are the fixer," I replied flatly. "A fixer is the person who gets what needs to be done, accomplished."

"*Me?*" she responded uncertainly.

"Yes, you. Once we're back on Podulliy, you'll be powered by whatever juices Torent."

She nodded slowly. "Yes."

"And all Cleinoids share a common link, a mental bond, right?"

Again, she nodded slowly. She hadn't made the connection, yet. "Yes. It's not telepathy, per se," she explained. "But we are *loosely* aware of each other."

"Unless they're dead and gone," I added.

"True. Once they are in hell, our link fails. I st ... Ah." She got it. "When I'm on Podulliy, I can tally up who is where."

"Jon, that's brilliant," remarked Toño.

"*And?*" I reacted.

"And, *there*, you ruined another wonderful moment," he huffed in frustration.

"So, as soon as we hit the ground, Daleria's only task is to establish a catalog. Toño, you'll remain with her, to watch her back while she's otherwise preoccupied."

He nodded in approval.

"That leaves Team Ryan to, once again, take on the bad guy."

"The one who made us seem silly," Sapale helpfully remarked.

"Last time was last time."

"Jon," she pretended to marvel, "how do you come up with those profound thoughts?"

"Ha, ha. This time, we have a real plan."

"Of course," she responded cheerily. "We have Plan CB."

"We do indeed."

"And, let me guess, the details of Plan CB are labeled *pending*, on your to-do list."

"Yes and no."

"I feel so much better knowing that," she snipped.

"*No*, because I have the basics."

"Pray tell, oh great leader," she mocked.

"We set a trap for the ass wipe."

She sucked in her lower lip and nodded in the affirmative. "Okay, traps are good. What kind of trap, where, and how's it baited?"

"Well, that's on the *yes* ledger of your previous query."

"Why did I *suspect* that without needing to hear it?"

"I will work out the details while we're en route."

"Sounds like a plan," she said quickly. "Ah, you do remember that travel by space folding is instantaneous, right?"

"Not necessarily. It might just be really quick."

"Which, unlike instantaneous, gives you *plenty* of time to pick a winner."

"I guarantee it, because I'm a seasoned leader."

"And I believe it, because I'm a seasoned idiot."

"You realize that, the instant we appear on the surface of Podulliy, Torent will know we're there and be on us in a flash?" confirmed Toño.

"I would expect no less from our worthy, proven opponent."

"An instant," Toño pressed, "you realize is a very brief period of time?"

"Of course, I do. Trust me on this. I only need half an instant to deploy a winning plan."

"Because, if we waited until you have one written down and vetted, that might take *minutes*."

"There's a warm spot in my rectum, Doc, that hopes you'll grow up, someday, to be just like me."

"Originating from your rectum? That seems appropriate," he returned.

"Ladies and gentleman, shall we?" I asked graciously.

"Why not?" replied Sapale. "I haven't died, yet, *today*. Why put off the inevitable?"

"Why, indeed?" I responded. "Why, indeed?"

CHAPTER TWENTY-TWO

Carol decided it was time to eat. She LOVED, with all capital letters, to eat. The best parts for her were so numerous, and equal in their excellence, that she was sometimes uncertain why she ever *stopped* eating. For one thing, as a god, she never gained weight—duh. Another wonder was that she could enjoy wildly different foods, depending on the configuration she chose for her body. When stones, she ground to dust a wide variety of rocks and minerals. When humanoid, she ate from a divine buffet of delectables. If she chose to be a porpoise, she could gobble up tons of fish. Once, she even became a protostar, so she could suck in cold hydrogen clouds. That was nice, like endless spaghetti. Taking sustenance was her favorite activity, aside, of course, from napping and the tormenting of Verazz.

She decided to dine as a queen, the kind with courtiers and banners and footmen—*lots* of footmen. As she walked from her chamber, the space ahead of her transformed into a medieval castle, torches on the stone walls and all. A long mahogany table stretched out to an absurd length. Vassals, minions, and would-be lovers studded the seats on either side. When she entered the hall, they stood and cheered her arrival. It was all she could do to quiet them, so the banquet might begin.

Just as Carol was slipping into her massive velvet demi-throne, a loud crash caught her attention. She had not willed *that*. It was in the remaining section of her home that wasn't reimagined as a castle. Oh, she realized, it must be the bumbling Verazz, in a more-than-average level of drunkenness. Well, *he* was not going to spoil *her* meal. She raised a finger maybe a centimeter, signaling that the amuse-bouche should be delivered. Servants shot into action as if their backsides had attached springs.

Carol lifted the ever-so-slightly warm velouté de poivron rouge et feta* [*roasted red pepper soup with feta] to her face, to take in its complexity. Instead of smelling it, she smushed it against her nose when an even louder crash startled her. She was, officially, displeased.

Carol rose from the table, without even excusing herself, and stormed to where Verazz was bowling, or knocking down walls.

She froze as she passed into the unchanged section. Verazz, in humanoid form, lay on the floor. He was in apparent agony. She rushed to his side. "What is the matter, husband? Why are you so tormented?"

He glanced up at her, a pathetic attempt at a smile on his face. "Is that soup on the tip of your nose? It smells scrumptious."

"Be serious, husband. What is wrong?"

"I ... I'm fine. You g ... go enjoy your party. It sounds like a proper celebration."

"Stop pretending to be brave. Are you well?"

He looked away. "No. A Cleinoid pierced my flesh with some wretched energy bolts."

She was confused. "And?"

"*And*, they seem to have injured me."

"Can you ... I don't know, heal?"

"I'm certain I will. I'm focusing on maintaining a positive outlook, and hoping for a good outcome."

"What are you saying?" She sat on the floor.

"While I'm certain I will improve, I don't seem to be doing so, er, as quickly as I might have liked to."

"Husband, it's simple. You use your magic to ... magically heal yourself. Why have you not done so, already?"

"The injury seems to have limited my ability to do such a thing."

"Wh ... that's *ridiculous*. How did you return home if you can't perform magic?"

"Some kind passersby, good Samaritans, if you will, delivered me here."

Carol blinked repeatedly in stunned disbelief. "Strangers, *mortals*, ferried you here? To our secret location, apart from traditional space time?"

He nodded quickly. "It was a fine craft."

"Where are these helpy things, now?"

"I sent them away."

She narrowed one eye at him. "Did you thank them for their aid and assistance?"

He looked upward. "I'm fairly certain I did. Yes, I did, if not in so many words, then in good thoughts."

"You are ... Never mind that. Here." Carol rested a hand on Verazz's forehead. "There. Now, get up. You look so ungodly there, on the floor."

A fully healed Verazz sat up, gingerly, at first. He smiled broadly. "Thank you, wife. I feel terrific." He slapped his chest with both palms. "Better than ever, in fact."

"You're welcome," she said harshly.

"Oh, yes. Thank you, wife. I am deeply in your debt." He bowed deeply.

"Tell me of this dangerous Cleinoid."

He sniffed loudly, then cleared his throat. "He was ugly, that much is for certain. When I fought with him, he cast some *surprisingly* powerful bolts at me. That's about it. The others rescued me, brought me home, and now, all is well."

"There's something unsettling about your tale, husband. I thought you said Cleinoids were no match for you? That you could swat them like so many *flies*."

"It is *possible* I *underestimated* them; *some* of them, at least, in *part*."

"You mean you were *wrong?*"

"I was wrrr ... I was wro .... I was wrrr ... Well, I wasn't *as* right as I usually am, if you care to see it that way."

"I suppose that is an *alternate* way to express it. I do prefer my version, however."

"I'll *bet* you do," she mumbled dubiously.

"Look, if it's all the same to you, that soup on your nose is smelling better and better. May we retire to the dining hall, and continue our discussion, there, My Queen?"

"No. The banquet is over."

And it was. Any trace of it, including the daub of velouté, was gone.

Verazz was about to moan in protestation, but, fortunately, he refrained. Carol was not in a playful mood.

"Two issues, husband, must be addressed. First, what shall we do about this overly-powerful Cleinoid. Second, how should you reward your rescuers?"

"*Reward* them?" he said in puzzled confusion. "They were rewarded, twice, in fact."

She glowered at him. She knew him too well to accept that he'd acted even *civilly* toward mortals.

"It is truth, my pet. First, they were rewarded by saving

FALL OF THE ANCIENT GODS

me. That is a grace few can claim, and certainly no mortal. Second, I did not kill them for discovering my true nature. You know what a stickler I am about loose ends, and all."

"You are *un*-believable," she fumed. "Saving your sorry butt is not a grace you *dispensed* upon them. They were charitable, and acted *compassionately.* And, husband, it is never acceptable to kill those who come to your rescue. Ever. Do you understand?"

He bobbled his head side to side. "I *hear* you. Understanding *might* come, in the fullness of time."

She pretended to whack him upside his fool head. "One problem at a time. What are you going to do about the Cleinoid?"

"That I can answer with certainty and conviction. Nothing."

"Nothing? What do you mean, *nothing?* The imbecile nearly *killed* you. He must suffer a consequence for that affront."

"I agree that is one option. In fact, in honor of you, I shall call it Plan One. But, another equally attractive option, Plan Two, is to ignore him, you know, pretend he never existed?"

"Are you *afraid* to face him?"

"No, and that, too, I can say with certainty and conviction. Afraid is a word that carries a pejorative connotation. There is judgment in it's nature. I am aware that confronting him again could end with an inferior outcome. As I hate inferior *anything*, I have elected to act in a manner that precludes any, er, *pushback.*"

"I never thought I'd live to see the day. Verazz, *king* of the Stone Witches, afraid. Like a baby mouse, he crawls into his *rotten* log and trembles before a Cleinoid god."

"I would like to say that, from my perspective, you are over-harshly stating—"

"Enough! I will not *hear* you cower and grovel. Verazz, husband, if you do not return and kill this perverse form of scum, I will *banish* you from our ranks."

A suddenly very serious, focused Verazz responded, "You wouldn't?"

"You *know* I will. I give you only until sunset, tomorrow. Either return with his head, or do not return. If you do return empty-handed, I will banish you. Period."

With that, Carol vanished.

Verazz wished he could, too.

CHAPTER TWENTY-THREE

Stingray materialized on the surface of Podulliy, the hull split open, and Sapale and I rushed out like Marines hitting the beach from their LCVPs. Toño and Daleria could do what they needed to from the relative safety of the ship. We, on the other hand, had a more active role. We imagined we could trap Torent, his being super powerful and unimaginably nasty notwithstanding. Yeah. No problema.

I'd told Sapale what my plan was as the portal was opening. That was because she'd have shut the front door if I told her any sooner. It wasn't a bad plan, sketchy, and poorly thought out. No, it was worse, worse, worse. In fact, it was *so* unlikely to succeed that, if it did, I was going to be stunned. What was my brainchild? Well, it did have simplicity on its side. We would run around until Torent showed up, and then—drumroll—we'd trap him in a membrane.

That's it. That was the plan, in all its glory. Run. Trap. High-five ourselves. My scheme did not, unfortunately, include any notion of what to do with the trapped, powerful, mean Cleinoid. I counted on the plan's near certainty of failure to preclude a need to plan for any positive outcomes.

I'd estimated it would take Torent maybe three seconds to realize we were back, and two, maybe three seconds to descend upon us with extreme prejudice. I was overly-optimistic. He exploded into our presence four seconds after we hit the ground. When I say he exploded, I mean he did just that. Around ten meters in front of us were a small grouping of trees. Then, there was a boom, and there were no trees, just airborne sawdust. In the center of where the trees had been, stood a howling, screaming Torent. What a showboat. I wanted to hurt him for such a performance. On the other hand, I didn't want to ever get close enough to him to bitch slap the dick.

Break, I said to Sapale, head-to-head.

We split off right and left.

Torent immediately lit out in my direction. I figured as much. Everyone hates me the most. It's a gift. I went to flank speed, which was nearly as fast as Torent. He gained on me, slowly. I don't think he noticed I was running in a broad curve. I wanted to run him past Sapale. She would spring the trap.

I pumped my arms and bounded over any obstacles on the ground.

Twelve meters ... ten meters ... eight meters. Al gave me a running summary of the distance between Torent and myself. *Sapale is behind the boulders fifteen meters to your right. Head toward them.*

Roger that, I replied.

If I was going to make it there before Torent tackled me, it was only going to be by a hair's breadth. If he decided to zap me, first, I was dead meat.

Four meters ... two meters ... fell the count.

I shot past the rocks.

One meter ...

Got him, shouted Sapale.

I slammed on the brakes and skidded to a halt. The second I did, I sprinted over to Sapale.

"It's holding," she said, in an excited tone.

Al, what's the stability of the membrane? I asked.

One hundred percent, Captain.

If it varies at all, alert us.

Aye, Sir.

Toño, how are you two coming along?

A bit slower than we like, but we're finding a few out there.

If Torent escapes, we'll need to leave, immediately.

Understood. We're ready, Toño responded.

"Let's walk the membrane back toward the ship. That way, if he breaks out, we've got less distance to cover."

"Got it," she replied.

As Sapale walked backward, I set a hand on her shoulder, on the off chance she stumbled.

The fact that my absurd plan was working so well really bothered me. No way it should work out smoothly.

That's when we bumped directly into Torent. He was standing, quietly, behind us.

Oops.

"Tell me honestly," he seethed, "how's your little plan working, so far?"

I slapped another full membrane on him. Yeah, no reason to hope it'd work, but it was mostly a reflex.

"*Run,*" I shouted.

We're ready to fold the instant you're aboard, Al said steadily.

Sapale, put a flat full membrane behind us.

Done.

Not a microsecond too soon. I heard Torent's

189

electricity lances sizzle against the membrane immediately.

Okay. The membrane didn't hold him, but it stopped his main weapon. At least, I hoped that was his main weapon. I didn't really need him to have a stronger one.

Sapale flew through the open portal.

Toño stood at the edge, firing a plasma rifle randomly behind me.

Al opened up with the main lasers. Torent was too close to permit using the rail cannon, with a portal open.

I leaped into the air diving for the portal.

That's when he grabbed my feet.

Torent spun me over his head like he was a cowboy and I was a rope.

Tactically, that was an error. He became a clear target. Three plasma rifles pounded him as one. *Stingray* rammed his legs with a small membrane.

He tumbled, and I went airborne. Unfortunately, it was in the opposite direction from the ...

The lights went out in a reverse flash. WTF. What happened?

Then I was slightly nauseated.

Toño switched his membrane off. I was flat on my ass, on *Stingray's* deck.

"You clever son of a gun," I exclaimed as I vaulted to my feet. "That was brilliant, Doc. Thanks."

"Lucky impulse," he responded with a shrug.

"Al, one hundred percent, Torent's not on board?"

"He is not, Captain."

"I agree," added Daleria.

"That would be ... bad, if he slipped on."

"I think it would have been bad in a death kind of way," responded Sapale.

"Okay, new addition to Plan CB," I said with authority. "We're *never* going to do that again."

———————

Two days after our narrow escape, I knocked on Toño's lab door. He'd been studying the data Daleria provided us with monastic intensity. Doc'd stared at the screen so long, I was afraid he'd *fuse* with it, if I didn't interrupt.

"Got a sec?" I asked softly.

"Huh? Ah, Jon. Yes, I'd love some coffee."

Okay, I went and retrieved two mugs of hot joe.

He accepted his without even looking at it, and set it down directly.

"Any insights?" I asked.

He leaned back, scruffed his hand in his hair, then picked up his coffee. Then he set it right back down.

"Earth to DeJesus," I said with my hands cupped around my mouth.

"What? Jon, may I help you?"

"Now that you mention it, sure. Any progress?"

He gestured to the screen. "With this?"

Not the time for levity. Crap, he set himself up so perfectly, too. "Yes, Toño. With the Cleinoid data."

"No. I simply fail to distinguish any pattern."

"Does there have to be one?"

"If there isn't, how will I account for their scattered presence?"

"Chips falling where they may?" I suggested.

"No. That's not possible. They might have fallen to the ground randomly, but for some few to be energized, while most perished, is very nonrandom."

"And you don't see any connections?"

"No. It's most frustrating. Look," he fingered the screen.

"Daleria found seventeen active Cleinoids." He tapped the individual marks on the screen. "The star systems are randomly distributed."

"How about the planets?"

"That's the frustrating part. There's no pattern. Six Cleinoids are on rocky, terrestrial worlds. Two are on gas giants, four on aquatic planets, and the rest on mixtures of lighter rock, mostly silicates."

"But there has to be a connection between the planets and the energy the Cleinoids are taking advantage of."

"Yes, there has to be. But, I can't, for the life of me, see what that is."

"Okay, break it down differently. What possible energy sources are present on each planet?"

"Again, I looked at that set of variables. A couple have geothermal reserves. One is significantly radioactive, but the remainder have no significant active energy available."

"Are the Cleinoids, like, photoelectric?" I asked that with zero conviction. If they were, I'd have noticed it back in Godville.

"Huh, you're not ser—"

"What?"

"The stars. Maybe ... Al," he shouted. "List the spectral types of the seventeen stars associated with active Cleinoids."

"On screen," Al snapped.

"Fascinating," marveled Toño. "Would you look at that," he pointed at the screen.

"Would I look at what? I'm dying, here, Doc. *What?*"

"Every single system has, at its center, a Wolf–Rayet star."

"A what?" I'd heard the term, but placed no significance in it.

"Wolf–Rayet stars. They're quite rare bodies. Their

common, and distinguishing characteristics, are that they are very hot and massive, with high rates of mass loss. Strong winds of material are being blown off their surfaces at incredible speeds. They've lost their atmospheres and have exposed their cores of heavy elements."

"Interesting, I guess, but what does that mean in the context of powering Cleinoids?"

He pouched his lips out. "No idea. But," he spun to face me, "they are rare, powerful, and give off unusual products. There must be something in their output that energizes Cleinoids."

"That's crazy talk. How can a weird ass star power Cleinoids? Clein, sure. But it wasn't a star."

"No, but the Cleinoids may have evolved spontaneously, using Wolf–Rayet energy. Then, as they matured, they forged Clein, taking advantage of what they knew to be the beneficial properties of these stars."

"You think they *evolved*?"

"I would be surprised if they didn't. Random mutations led to the ability of rare individuals to harness Wolf–Rayet energy. Those select few then harnessed the power, to concentrate it and make it widely available."

"I guess. But, how does that help us? It's not like we can turn the damn things off."

"No, not even the Deavoriath have that level of technology. Still, it is a clue." He stood. "I'll be right back."

He returned a minute later, Daleria in tow. "I've asked *Blessing* to take us close to a Wolf–Rayet star that we know does not have an associated Cleinoid." He looked up. "Engage, *Blessing*."

Slight nausea.

"In position, Form Three."

He turned to Daleria. "Well?"

"*Yes!* I can feel it. I'm *pulsing* with energy."

Toño looked to me. "I believe we've proven our hypothesis."

"But how can we *use* that knowledge?"

His face went blank. "Let me give that some thought."

I took Daleria to the comm-station and had her work with the Als to methodically locate as many Cleinoids as she could. It was something to do while Doc's wheels turned.

I sure hoped there was some angle we could use to beat these dogs down. I most assuredly did.

CHAPTER TWENTY-FOUR

Torent—and please note he was the only one—felt sorry for himself. He was *tired*. He was mentally *exhausted*. He *needed* a vacation. What with all the slaying, destroying, and rapacious consumption, he was having to be evil at a horrendous rate. Add to that the annoying gnats buzzing around trying to kill him, and he almost imagined he needed a hug.

A hug? My, but that tickled a notion. Perhaps a *group* hug? Oh, but that would be *perfect!* The old gang, getting together for one last road trip? Assemble the band for a triumphant reunion tour.

And, why not? They were, after all, gods ...

CHAPTER TWENTY-FIVE

Daleria and I, then Daleria and Sapale, because, I get bored easily, catalogued fifty three active Cleinoids in the Milky Way. With greater distances, she became less accurate, but she definitely perceived other Cleinoids out there, too. She couldn't be certain, but somewhere in the range of four hundred were registering outside our galaxy. Since *one* was one too many, we had ourselves a numerical problem in need of solution via death. Given the lack of success we were having stomping out Torent, having four hundred and fifty two more to go was depressing. Place-barrel-on-temple-pull-trigger depressing.

But, a journey of a thousand miles did begin with a single step. So, a stepping we would go. I was buoyed a little—a *tiny* little—by Daleria's repeated reassurances that Torent was a particularly powerful and lethal god, by Cleinoid standards. Statistically speaking, she promised, many of the others would be pushovers. That's when Mark Twain leaned in and whispered a reminder in my ear that *there are three kinds of lies: lies, damned lies, and statistics.*

I walked over to where the women were working. "Any more hits?"

Daleria looked back, over a shoulder. "Just one in the last—"

"What? Go ahead and say it," I pushed.

"Okay, I'll go ahead and say it. Jon, turn around, *slowly*."

Now, I was a boy raised on crappy B-horror films, back in the day. Real Roger-Corman-level cheesy. Pictures like *The Blob*, *The Crawling Eye*, and *Texas Chainsaw 3D*. The classics. Here's an important rule I might have neglected to tell you, earlier in the saga. Never say to a guy—even a two billion year old fighter pilot—*turn around slowly. There's something behind you that you do not want behind you.* Commence with the curdling of blood and pleas for mercy that will never be heard.

So, I turned, slowly. Ah, ha. It was Verazz. Okay, not too bad, on the turn-around-slowly scale. "Hey, dude," I asked. "What's up?"

I couldn't decide. Did he glower at me, or just glare? It was somewhere in those zones.

"Hello."

"Not chatty, today?" I pressed my luck.

"You make communications very difficult. Well, at least exchanges in which I do not kill you."

"So I've been told. Personally, I feel those rumors are overblown, but what do I know?"

Verazz twirled his fingers, while pointing them downward. "If I disappear, and then reappear, and we begin again, might it go better? More like adults were involved?"

"Not a chance in the multiverse," opined Toño, as he entered the room.

"I strive for consistency," I gloated.

CRAIG ROBERTSON

"It is good to see you again, Verazz," Toño said with a slight bow of his head.

"And you, also, Doctor." There was no nod coming from Verazz's swollen head.

"So, to what do we owe this visit?" I asked firmly, back to being mission commander.

"I would propose we work in union to dismiss Torent from this life."

Odd phrasing, but I did like the intention. "That would be nice. Do you have any specific ideas as to how?"

"Attack. If Fate favors us, victory will be ours."

I pointed between Daleria and Verazz. "So, you're both into this Fate with a capital *F* deal?"

"Anyone with a functioning *brain* understands the power of Fate," Verazz replied sternly.

"It is not a religion, Jon," explained Daleria. "Time has taught us that Fate is a real force of nature. To not accept its role is ... *unhelpful.*"

I believe she meant *asinine*, but was being diplomatic.

"We kind of did the Charge of the Light Brigade thing. I recall the outcome was less stellar than we might have hoped."

"I was ... less focused," Verazz said with convincing authority. "When I face Torent again, he will test a very different Stone Witch."

"Focus is *good*. A large weapon, what we call a BFG, is good, *too*. But a sound plan exploiting the opponent's weaknesses and emphasizing our strengths is, admittedly, *better.*"

"I am willing to hear your suggestions," the big guy responded. "But first, I need to correct a potential oversight. I wish to thank you all for saving me."

"You're welcome," I marveled. "I'm betting that wasn't easy for you to cough up."

"Jon, must you be so rude?" snapped Toño.

"Sometimes, *yes*," I said obliquely. "There are times when I wish to discover the level of resolve and conviction a new friend might *have*."

"You are wiser than I'd have given you credit for, Jon Ryan," responded Verazz, with no anger in his tone. Excellent. I wasn't about to be never-existed, or something.

"We can hurt him with our weapons, our devices. But we have proven we cannot contain him and we cannot easily kill him," I summarized.

"My attempts to kill him were also unsuccessful. But, I was foolish. I did not try to defend myself against his attacks. I gave him no credit. I will make neither mistake, again."

"Okay. His advantage is we're on his home turf. He will know when we appear. A surprise assault is not possible."

"I would not say I agree," Verazz stated flatly.

"Are you saying you can dampen his ability to detect us?" I queried, a tad incredulously.

Verazz twisted his lips. "I had not thought along those lines. *Possibly*."

"How can we sneak up on the dude if we don't shield his ability to detect us?"

"The answer to that is painfully obvious," he replied rather judgmentally.

"Not to me, it's not," I shot back.

"We attack him in the past. That way, he will never have faced us. He might sense us, but he won't know with certainty who we are and what our intentions are. Additionally, if we strike him just as he arrived to what you term Podulliy, he might have less power. I assume there is some storage function in Cleinoid energy usage. His supply will likely be less than full."

"Well, there's a mouthful of confidence. Are you

familiar with the saying, *no battle plan survives first contact with the enemy?*"

"No. It sounds silly. There are no gaps in my plan."

I poked a hand up a little. "Maybe just one. Travel in time is ... well, it's not *impossible*, but it's damn hard to do."

"It is?" he replied with surprise.

"So, we go back in time, bushwhack Torent, and then return to this time and place. Easy peasy?" I confirmed.

He furrowed his brow. "I do not know what an *eased pea* is, but yes, that is what I propose."

"Can we depart from here, or do we need to return to Podulliy?"

"One locus is as practical as any other. You know that, right?" he asked.

"Sure. I was just ... confirming it."

"So, you zap the four of us and yourself into the past, and then back to the f—"

"No," he said firmly. "Just you and I. The others must remain behind." My goodness, he said that with finality.

"Why is that?"

"Because it is a matter between Torent, you, and me."

"I go where my mate does," snapped Sapale. "If *he* goes, *I* go."

"No. Just the two of us."

"Why," challenged Daleria. "Because you're big, strong men?"

"Why would *that* factor into anything?" Verazz puzzled.

"Then why?" asked Toño.

"Because we are principles, we three. You know of principles? Please tell me you do."

"We do not," Sapale said in an icy tone.

"You three," he gestured to Toño and the women, "are important in your own rights. But *we* three are Fate's *principles*, in the present case."

"You said words, but explained *nothing*," huffed Sapale.

"I believe he's saying that the three of them are the central figures, as Fate sees it in the current action."

"Yes. Others *might* have been. We *are*," Verazz said with certainty.

"Fine," I announced. "When do we go?"

"I ... I am limited in my time window," he replied hesitantly.

"What's the window?"

"Soon," was all he'd say.

"Fine, I'll get my stuff and we'll do this."

He nodded.

I went to my quarters. Sapale followed closely.

"I don't like this set up," she said, while I was tossing weapons together.

"Me, neither. But, what alternatives do we have? If we *want* the help we *need*, we do it his way."

"I guess. But I don't know why I can't—"

"Do you think you're about to talk that one into changing his mind?" I asked, pointing toward the mess.

"No. You're right."

"Unfortunately."

"Well, you be careful," she admonished.

I pointed to my chest. "Me? *Mr.* Cautious? No way I won't be."

"That makes me feel so much better."

"Look. I have to come home."

"Why's that?"

"Because if I didn't, you'd kill me."

She chuckled. "You got *that* right, flyboy."

I slung my duffle over a shoulder. "Come on." I kissed her.

When I stepped back into the mess, I knew bad had just turned to worse. The looks on everyone's faces was one of frightened disbelief. Man, I hate frightened disbelief. I really, really did.

"What?" I snapped.

"Matters just became *infinitely* worse," Toño responded glumly.

"*Infinitely*? That's a powerful lot."

"He's being *conservative*," remarked a dejected Daleria.

"The suspense, it's not what I need, right about now."

"Torent reached out to the other Cleinoids," stated Daleria.

"And you heard him?" I confirmed.

"Yes."

"What did he say?"

"He called us to rally as one."

"What, is he forming a Tuesday night bowling league or something?"

"No. Much worse," sighed Toño. "He is calling the Cleinoids to move their star systems together. He wants to centralize and boost their power supply."

"He suggested they move their *star* systems? That's silly ridiculous."

"That might be true. What is also true is that many stars have already begun to move in space," mumbled Toño. "The Cleinoids are bringing *stars* together."

I was *so* over this god thing.

"We must go *now*," thundered Verazz.

In the short, relatively brief time I'd known the clown, I'd learned he loved his thundering. I was very glad he did, because that made one person who did.

"No," I said in as restrained a manner as my temper would allow. "This is a bad time to attack Torent."

Verazz raised a hand toward me. I hoped, powerfully, he wasn't about to transform me into a dishwasher. "If the stars are brought together, the combined strength of the Cleinoids may be too great for even me to defeat."

"That is exactly my point. If we rush to Podulliy, and the hundreds of stars followed right behind us, we'd be in some deep shit. I need to see how quickly this develops."

"I believe Jon is correct, in this matter," Toño added in his professor's voice. "It is logical to assume the Wolf–Rayet stars will move incredibly fast. Otherwise, there would be no point in Torent summoning them. If they moved in real space, at interstellar-travel speed norms, it would take them an enormous amount of time to arrive. Most of them would require more time to arrive than the universe has left before it dies a heat death."

Verazz looked between us like we were bugs, particularly unintelligent and contemptible insects, at that.

"Fine. Have it your way."

"You ... you agree with us? Just like that?" I marveled.

"No," he said with a huge grin. "Like this."

He raised his hands, and that's the last thing I saw, before I was scanning the terrain of—you got it—Podulliy. That proved, yet again, you can out-reason a god, but you can do diddly about it, because the only way they like it is their way.

"*Harsh*, dude," I breathed out.

"It might have been. But, since we're *here*, we might as well make the best of it."

"And take on, like, hundreds of juiced up Cleinoids."

"My, that's an excellent idea. Here comes the first of them, now, in fact."

He raise a finger and pointed behind me. I turned. Yup. Torent was rushing to the very spot we stood on. Hmm. He seemed mad, and intent on mayhem. Same old same old.

I threw a membrane at his legs. Hey, it was something

that worked before, even if it was, at best, only annoying to him.

Torent hopped over my pulse.

Great, now he could see the shields coming. No more scrapes and bruises for him, now. Oh, joy.

Verazz stomped in front of me. "Be *gone*," he thundered —again, with the thundering. He swept an arm in a broad arch.

Torent was gone.

My first impulse was, *yes.*

Then I remembered that scene in *Ghostbusters*, where the four guys thought they'd vanquished Gozer, there on the roof? Yeah, Venkman says, *Wasn't so hard*, then, all of the sudden, the Stay Puff Marshmallow Man is stomping New York. I flashed on that.

"What'd you do?" I shouted.

"I got rid of him," Verazz said almost jovially.

"Where? Where'd you send him?"

"To his fiery doom."

"Could you be more specific?"

"You *are* a petty little man, aren't you. *He* is gone. *I* won. *Enough* spoken."

"I'm petty. Fine. *Where?*" I said that last word with sufficient anger and authority to wipe the condescension off his smug face.

"I cast Torent into the center of that." He pointed—holy crap, my guess was correct—at the bright, shiny sun overhead.

"You—and please think about what I'm saying before you react like you tend to—placed Torent *closer* to the source of his power?"

"Yes, I—"

"Placed him, in fact, at the *center* of his power generator."

"Well, yes, I did. But, you'd have to understand—"

I never learned what it was I *didn't* understand. Before Verazz could answer that question, there was a powerful sonic boom high up in the sky.

We looked up to see a flaming ball of pissed off Torent careening toward us.

Then we saw ... nothing.

CHAPTER TWENTY-SIX

"Wait ..." screamed Sapale.

"Verazz, no ..." shouted Toño.

It was too late. He couldn't hear their protestations. He, and Jon, were gone.

"That son of a *bitch*," wailed Sapale. "When I get my hands on him—"

"We will worry about revenge when we have the time," Toño said sternly. "Right now, we need to save Jon."

"We know where they went," barked Daleria. "They're probably right where we were on Podulliy when we fought Torent."

"Als, can you confirm the direction Verazz left in?" asked Toño.

"Scanning," Al replied tersely. After a few seconds, he was ready. "Negative. There are no radiation trails or gravitational wave disturbances."

"Daleria's right," steamed Sapale. "They *have* to be back at the same location."

"Not necessarily and, if they are, that might be the worst place for us to materialize."

"Toño, we gotta *go*," screamed Sapale. "We know Jon's down there. If we don't get there soon, there may be no reason left to make the trip."

"I suggest we place ourselves in orbit around Podulliy. We can, then, quickly ascertain where they are." Toño was aware that Sapale was the captain, in the absence of Jon. Otherwise he might have just executed that command.

"We need to move *fast.*"

"If we all get killed, we serve no good," he responded passionately.

Sapale did the Kaljaxian thing. She growled, this time a war cry, and a loud one. She slapped her fibers on the deck. "*Blessing*, put us in orbit around Podulliy. Lock us right over the spot we fought Torent."

"Aye, Form Two."

Sapale felt the slight nausea, so she knew they were there.

"Sit rep?" she called out.

"Scanning," replied Al.

"Come on, come on," implored Sapale.

"Done," Al shot back. "We can confirm a massive impact to roughly the same location we landed before."

"A *what?*" Sapale wheezed.

"A massive *impact*. There's a crater seventeen kilometers across spanning our landing area. The projectile originated in the central star. It traveled approximately seventy five million kilometers per—"

"Stop," howled Sapale. "Any *life* signs?"

"One. Torent."

"Where is Jon?"

"There is no trace of him or Verazz."

"What do you mean, *no trace*. They *had* to be down there when the whatever hit."

"In spite of the power of the explosion, if they had been, we'd find traces. There are none."

"Are you saying they escaped?"

"We cannot say if they were there and escaped, or were never there."

"That is unacceptable. Where *are* they?"

"We are scanning. There are no signs of either of them."

"*Fozenlop*," she screamed at the top of her lungs. It's a bad word in her native tongue. Don't ask.

"It appears ... yes. Torent is heading toward us at impressive sp—"

"Azsuram," shouted Sapale. Her fibers were still attached.

Slight nausea.

"Any signs of pursuit?" she called out angrily.

"Negative," replied Al.

"And still no trace of my brood-mate?"

"Sorry, Captain. None."

"Well, they have to *be* somewhere."

"We cannot speculate on that issue," Al responded cautiously.

Sapale eyed the comm-station with lethal intentions, but let the impulse pass. She wasn't mad at the Als. She wanted only one thing. She wanted Jon back.

CHAPTER TWENTY-SEVEN

I was floating in nothingness.

Crap, crap, *crap*, crap, *crap*. Not again. Not the Pillars of Freaking Creation.

I tried to turn. I wanted to see if Verazz was nearby.

I couldn't move. I could only ... *be.*

No. I wasn't floating like space debris.

I was fixed. Lord knows what I was fixed *to,* but I was ... *restrained?*

No, I was standing. But all I saw, heard, smelled, and felt was ... nothing.

I was coming to a slow boil. I mean that figuratively, as in I was getting really *angry.* I did not have time for Existentialism 101. Torent still needed killing. The now uber-*powerful* Torent, the one we couldn't kill before, yeah, *that* one needed killing. And my crew had to be going bananas-and-ape-shit with worry. But, could I save the day and comfort my loved ones? No, I had to stand floaty-fixed in Never Never Land, because the universe hated me *just* that much.

I knew Verazz was there. He was ... beside me? If he

was, that meant I could sense dimensionality out of the void.

Yes. He was to my left, a little behind me. Whoa, how could he be *behind* me? Two points defined a line. We had to be side-by-side. Unless ...

I saw nebulousness take form, in front of me. You know, I even hate saying *nebulousness*. It's a lame word, if it's even a real word. But, that's what it was like ... sort of.

"Jon, is that you," Verazz said very tentatively, very distantly.

"Yes, it's me."

"Where are we?" he asked in a muffled tone.

Oh, boy. Now *the* most powerful Stone Witch was asking *me* where we were. How reassuring was that? A god asking a robot where the heck they were. Yeah, what could be more normal?

"*Not* the Pillars of Creation," I asked more than stated.

"That's nice to know."

"Seriously. No clue."

By then, the swirling clouds of light were coalescing. A dais, with figures on it, seemed to be taking shape. Five ... no, two figures. No, one what-the-hell, and a woman. The woman was young, and she was gorgeous. And she was ...

Jenna!

The whatever-it-was? I had no idea. It wasn't a corporeal being, if it was a life form at all.

Jenna stood, and walked slowly toward us.

"Stop where you are," Verazz squeaked. "Identify yourself."

"Jon knows me," Jenna cooed, as she stroked my cheek with the back of her hand. Wow, did that ever feel better than it should have.

I could move. I lifted my hands, and studied them. Then I looked deep into Jenna's eyes. "Am I dead, Jenna?"

"Which one of you?" she replied with a giggle.

"You mean Verazz or me?" I said stunned.

"No, silly." She flicked the end of my nose. *That* felt way better than flicks should. "Which one of the Jon Ryans. Some are. Some aren't."

"Let's narrow it down to *this* Jon Ryan, the one doing the being confused."

"*Spoilers*, sweetie."

"I kind of figure the spoilers period is over. We're into some *post*-spoiler phase, here."

"Oh, so you make the rules, my—" She gestured toward ... oh, hell. Now the WTF looked like a thingamajig. Kind of a paradox wrapped in a dilemma, surrounded by riddles, and standing on thin ice. What does that mean? No clue. Seriously, do *not* ask me. But, that's what Jenna wafted a hand toward.

"Who are you?" Verazz asked of the Welsh Púca.

"*You* may not address our host," Jenna responded sternly.

I flinched, instinctively. When someone talks to a Stone Witch like that, badness will ensue rapidly, ten times out of ten.

"Do you know—" Verazz began to whimper. Whoa, dude. He couldn't thunder here, in wherever. I liked it more, instantly. Hopefully he couldn't bluster, either.

"You are the proud and mighty Cumpli Verazz dour Fentalpiy, ruler of all you see," Jenna replied with sarcasm.

"You ... how can you know my *true* name? It is—"

"**Forbidden** ... *forbidden* ... *forbidden* ..." Jenna echoed in a fading mock of what he was going to say.

"Verazz, maybe you should observe, you know, for a while. I'll do the talking."

I half-expected my head to roll off onto the floor.

Instead, I heard a feeble, "For now."

I *liked* this place.

"Jenna, how are you?" I asked.

"I couldn't be better."

"Is this Heaven?"

"No. Iowa."

"Iowa?"

"And I'm your father." She burst out laughing. Through fits and gushes, she was able to say, "Ease my pain."

"Jenna, have you been doing *drugs*, in Heaven?"

"This, Jon Ryan, is *Camelot*," she shot back, robustly.

"I don't think that's Merlin," I responded, as I nodded to the wraith.

"No, that's Fate."

"Fate?"

"Yes, Jon."

I dropped my head. "I preferred Iowa. This is too New Age for me."

"I know." She energetically marched in place, throwing out her chest. "Because you're a fighter pilot, not a college don."

"*Professor*, Jenna. We call them professors."

She shrugged playfully. "Don't know. Never had me a chance to *go* to college, on account of my havin' a bad case'a being prematurely dead."

"When it's time to be serious, could you raise a hand, or wave a little flag? That'd be swell."

"Jon *Ryan* wants to be serious? Now I know the multiverse is in peril."

"Jenna, Jenna. I'd love to frolic here, forever with you and your pal Fate. But, I got a universe to save. My friends ... they're worried sick, as we speak."

"Yes," she got a suspicious, judgmental look on her face. "This Sapale. She's yet another in a disturbingly long line of women who weren't *me* that you married."

"You said it yourself. You suffered a lamentably premature death."

"Men," she huffed. "So faithless."

"You were *dead*. Jenna. If I married a *dead* person, even a dead female, they'd have locked me up. *I* would have locked me up."

"Excuses, excuses." She crossed her arms and turned away.

"Jon, that's ... that's Fate?" whispered Verazz. "Jon, we have been given an audience with Fate *itself*."

I shrugged. "Is that ... unusual?"

"No, dumdum. It's not unusual. It's more rare than *you* honoring your true love," scorned Jenna. "It, like, *never* happens."

"I've never heard of it," agreed Verazz. "Fate, I am—"

"Listen, bucko," snapped Jenna, "I told you *once*. I'm reminding you *once*. No talky to da Fate. Next time, I might have to smite you."

"Jenna, you can smite people?" I asked in disbelief.

She cupped her mouth toward me. "No way. But don't tell Mr. Smellypants, over there."

I giggled.

"I can hear you," bemoaned Verazz.

"No, it's just that, Mr. Smellypants is what we used to call the janitor, back at the summer camp. No idea why, but to us, he was Mr. SP."

Jenna pinned her nose closed.

"Jenna, I'm beginning to suspect why *I'm* here. But why are *you* here?" I asked gently.

"Because *you* are here. When I heard it through the grapevine *you* were slated for a cameo, I canceled my staycation and rushed over."

"Staycation?"

"You know, that phase of the afterlife."

"No, I *don't* know. Now that I do, I'd like to unknow it."

She stuck out her tongue.

"*Jenna*," I pressed.

"I wanted to see you again, Jon. I've visited you as if in dreams, but, I wanted to do this."

She waltzed up to me, wrapped her arms around my neck, and gave me such a kiss. I mean, she nearly sucked my soul out, it was so passionate, so intense.

Then she gently released her hold, and backed away. "And if you so much as say, *But, Jenna, I'm a married man,* I'll make you wish you hadn't. Pinky promise." She wagged her pinkies in the air.

"No. No objections, here."

"That's better."

She kept backing away. And she began to fade.

"*Jenna*," I shouted in a panic. "Jenna, don't go."

"Go?" she responded in a fading voice. "Where ever would I g—"

She had dissipated.

"Jon R ... rrryan. I woul ... d say to yo ... u now."

Pretty sure that was Fate's surprisingly inept way of attempting to communicate with me.

"Hello."

Seriously? What does one say to Fate, by way of introduction? You try it, sometime. *Not.*

"Hello?" grunted Verazz. "A once in a million lifetime's chance to meet Fate, to actually speak with Fate, and all you *got* is hello?"

Everyone's a critic.

"J ... Jon, you are well."

Was that a question or a statement? Screw it. "I'm fine. How are *you*, Fate?"

"Fate is well."

Hey, it was speaking quicker. That was nice, because it didn't grate on my last nerve, anymore.

"Good to hear. So, ah, how are fateful things?"

"*Jon,*" hissed Verazz.

I gave him a look.

"So, if, you know, it's my place, and all, can I ask, like, what am I *doing* here?"

"And *me*. Don't forget about *me*." Yeah, you know who hissed that one.

"Fate favors you, Jon Ryan."

Was it speaking of itself in the third person? If it was, that was annoying. I *hate* things that do that. Maybe there was some other fate, or Fate. Hell, maybe it said Phate, and I couldn't read the letters.

"You do?" seemed the most *diplomatic* response.

"I must."

It *had* to. Was that a good thing or a bad thing? What if, like, Fate was a fighter pilot, and hated being told what to do? Ah, *that* didn't sound promising.

"Is that a problem?"

"Is what a problem?"

"That you must favor me? I mean, if it is, maybe we could ... have you *not*."

"Your words are nonsense," Fate said.

"I agree," whispered Mr. Unhelpful.

"I'm sorry," I offered.

"There is no sorry. There is not remorse, either yours or mine. It is what it is."

New Age Fate? Was it a millennial? Que será, será?

I was getting a headache.

"Who made you favor me?"

"You would not understand, were I to attempt a response."

"Would he?" I pointed to Verazz. "Maybe explain it to

215

him, and then later, he can maybe explain it to me. If there is a later, sir, I mean." Wow, was I lame, or was I lame?

"I am to favor you because everything that would *not* have been, *needs* to be as it will be, which is to not be, or even resemble what might be conceived. That which is responsible for the goodness, at the immeasurable limits of time, would have me favor you."

"I don't understand. *Wait*. Don't answer that. You said I wouldn't, and I don't, so I'm good." I turned to Verazz.

He shook his head in befuddlement.

"Moving on," I tried to sound cogent. "What would that mean, in practical terms?"

"It means you have been favored."

"Okay, and thanks, but, have been, that kind of sounds like, old-time used to be. I am to be favored, or I was?"

"Yes."

"Is there an echo in here? I mean, Jenna did. Maybe I'm not hearing you clearly. It *sounded* like you answered two opposing yes/no queries with one affirmative."

"Yes."

"There's an echo?" I was *so* confused.

"No, you moron," growled Verazz. "it's saying *yes* it answered the conflicting questions ambiguously."

"It was not, and still is not, ambiguous," responded Fate. "It is only, perhaps, you are thinking too linearly."

"Can you help me see your meaning, *less* linearly?" I coughed up. What was I even asking?

"Probably not."

How unhelpful.

"So, is there, like, something I need to do? Do I push a button, to start the favoring, or favoring process?"

"Jon, shut *up*," suggested Verazz. Dude was likely correct.

"No. You are favored."

I rubbed the inside of my ear with the tip of my little finger. Not sure why, but I'm trying to be complete.

"So, if there's nothing I need to do, and I don't understand the key parts of what you're saying, then, I needed to be here because?"

"You needed to."

"I needed to ... be here?"

"No, silly boy," giggled Jenna. "If you were any denser, I do believe your head would collapse into a black hole." She rapped on my forehead. "You needed to *know* you were favored."

"I needed to know?"

"Naturally."

"I'm going to *pretend* I have no idea why that matters, and you try and explain it to me, the why I *needed* to know. Because, if I all of a sudden start speaking *French,* do I actually need to know that I did so suddenly? Or can I just, speak French?"

"What did you just ask?" she remarked, looking at me kind of funny.

"I don't know."

"Good. I was worried there a second."

"Me, too," added Verazz.

I was, too.

"Jon, it was important you knew you were favored. It's a *reward,* ya goof."

"A reward?"

"Of course, silly. Look, everyone who has ever been favored, or not favored, doesn't actually know they were. *You* get to know. It's a present."

"The Cleinoids knew their favor shifted."

"And, last time I checked, they were, oh, what do you call those all powerful things? Gods! Yes, that's it. Mr. Lamo, they're *gods.*"

217

"Okay, you win that point."

"No, duh."

"So, is there someone I need to thank, or something?"

"Yes."

"Who?"

"*Spoilers*, sweetie."

"Have I mentioned how much I hate you?"

"No. But, sticks and stones, baby. Sticks *and* stones."

"What is the favor I was granted? Can you at least tell me that?"

"Yes, that's easy."

"You're kidding? *Something* here is easy?"

"Sure. The answer is, you were not done any favors."

"Bu ... but ..."

"Bu ... bu ... but ..." she mocked back. "You are *such* a queer."

"No, we don't *say* that any more, Jenna."

"I do. I died before PC was in effect. I have PC protection."

"You mean like cooties protection, *CP*?"

"*Just* like that."

"Okay, back to adult-speak. Did not Fate just say I got a favor?"

"No, it said you were *favored*. Big diff, big doo-doo."

"Ah. So, what was the effect of the favoring?"

"Ah ah. Spoilers, sweetie."

"If you don't tell me, I'll give you a titty twister. I swear I will."

Jenna glanced down at her very womanly breasts. "In your *dreams*, flyboy."

"Jenna," I begged.

"Yes, Jonny?"

Jonny? That's what she used to ... Oh crap. "Jenna, you're not about to fade away, and I wake up in ...

Boom.

I was aboard *Stingray*. Verazz was standing next to me. Sapale and the others hadn't noticed we were there, yet.

"I say we go back to Podulliy and blow Torent to hell," my wife snarled.

"Hey, you have to run that through me, first," I shouted, because I really wanted to startle them.

Boy did they startle. Nice. I believe Toño briefly jumped out of his polyalloy skin.

"*Jon*, you're back," exclaimed Sapale.

"No. This is my front," I began to tease.

She stopped me by leaping into my arms.

"Where were you?" Only then did she notice Verazz. "And him, I guess."

"I'm not sure you want to know," I responded softly.

Then, the inexplicable happened, proving there was a God. Sapale gave me a titty twister. No, *seriously*. I mean, no way that could happen by chance alone. *No* way.

"Torent blew us up and we were granted an audience with Fate, capital *F*."

"Oh. Seems normal enough. So, you hungry?"

"Just like that?" I wheezed.

"No, not just like that, you loon. Was it like the Pillars thing?"

"Sort of. Yeah."

"I haven't done the Pillar, but I tend to agree," offered Verazz.

"You seem awfully social, all of the sudden," remarked a dubious Sapale.

"Me? I'm always ... nice."

"Babe, he's impressed I got him in to see Fate. He's totally smitten."

Verazz could only nod, distantly.

"Well, *I'll* be," declared my brood's-mate. "Who'd ever imagine?"

Verazz shrugged. He didn't know, either.

"So, how long have we been gone?" I asked.

"Not long," she looked to Toño.

"Maybe ten minutes," he speculated. "Things were happening rather quickly, around here."

"Weirdomania," I mumbled. "So, Torent's still on Podulliy?"

"He was when we folded away," he replied.

Then I noticed Daleria wasn't present.

"Where's Daleria?"

"Oh, not to worry. She wasn't feeling well. She went to lie down," explained Toño.

"Wait. You went to Podulliy. She should have felt ... better."

"I suppose she did."

"But now?"

"Now she feels worse. Jon," Toño said skeptically, "I fail to see why her tummy ache might matter."

"I don't know. It strikes me as odd, that's all."

"Shall we make for Podulliy?" Toño asked.

"Not-just-now," I said hesitantly.

"Hmm?" he grunted.

"Too many things seem off. I want to make sure what we're getting our asses into."

"By doing what?" snapped Sapale. "Reading military history?"

"Sweetheart, we *are* military history. No. Doc, what's the status of those stars?"

"In the last fifteen minutes?" he sighed dubiously.

"Yes. Please."

"Al, put the updates on the main screen."

Red dots with blue tails popped to life.

"Hmm."

"Didn't you just say that?" I pressed.

"I did, indeed. These stars have moved incredible distances." He tapped a few icons in particular. "And two stars have completed their journey to rendezvous with Podulliy's star."

"In the last fifteen minutes?" I asked, rather stunned.

"Yes, Captain," he replied, "you seem to have been correct in reassessing the tacticals."

"I'm going to see Daleria," I announced.

I knocked. Her door slid open.

"You feeling okay, kiddo?"

She propped up to her elbows. "Better."

She didn't look better.

"Have you felt ill, like this, before?"

She thought a second. "I must have."

"But you can't actually *recall* feeling ill like this?"

"I'm sure it's nothing."

"The first time we went to SMC WR7, you felt the boost, right?"

"Yes, though I wasn't aware of it, at first."

"Then we left. You felt—"

"Fine."

And when we went to the other Wolf–Rayet star, as a test—"

"I felt fine after."

"But after leaving SMC WR7, just now—"

She furrowed her brow. "I'm certain it's a coincidence."

"The terms *coincidence* and *war* must not be uttered in the same sentence."

"I'll have Doc do a full physical on you. That okay?"

"Fine. Anything to help."

I returned to the main controls. "Doc, check out Daleria. I want to know how quickly she feels better."

"What concerns you?" he asked seriously.

"She shouldn't start getting sick out of the blue. Just check her, okay?"

"Certainly." He left quickly.

"Al, what is the rate of acceleration of the migrating Wolf–Rayets?"

"Minus seven percent compared to five minutes ago."

"You mean they're slowing down?"

"Their acceleration is decreasing."

"But most are still far away?"

"Affirmative."

"Alert Toño of the changes and report to me every five minutes on the status of the accelerations."

"Roger."

"What is it, Jon?" Sapale asked, gently holding my arm.

"Not sure. Something seems to be changing, though."

"After Fate told you it favored you, whatever that means."

"Whatever that means."

Toño rejoined us. "She's feeling better. Her exam is normal. What's this about the stars losing acceleration?"

"Unexpected, eh?"

"I should say."

"Doc, I'm taking us back to Podulliy. Along with everything else, keep a sharp eye on Daleria."

"I shall."

"*Stingray*," I dropped my fibers, "take us to Podulliy. Orbit over the crater Torent made."

If my day got any weirder, I was writing a letter to someone. Heads would roll.

CHAPTER TWENTY-EIGHT

Torent was in rapture; positive ecstasy engulfed his being. His body glowed with the radiating power he had absorbed inside the star. Sex, liquor, food, and the ripping out of beating hearts *combined* didn't approach the level of pure euphoria he felt at that moment. Nothing would ever defeat him. Trouble was a pest of the past. His future was to be only blissful domination, glorious destruction, and unending self-indulgence.

He was now reunited with three other Cleinoids. Rumparious, Molquandle, and Xenor. Though he hadn't seen them since Rage egressed to Prime, they were a sight for his sorriest of eyes. Together, they could defeat planetary armies. As one, they could crush entire segments of the galaxy to primordial gasses and dust. Life, which was superb, had just gotten infinitely better.

His power boost from being inside his local star was ebbing, slightly. But he still felt just the way he liked to. Lethal. His new companions did not share his level of intoxicating dominion, but they were strong. Strong was good. Molquandle and Xenor were the rarest example among the Cleinoids. They were unrelated gods of the same species. They were Atommitofoils. Their basic configuration was that of a rectangular plate, much longer and wider than it was deep. Think extremely large bars of soap. Their substance was dense and hard, almost like stone. Adults could freely couple together along any side, forming any number of bizarre three-dimensional structures. When joined, learning, nutrition, and sex gametes could be exchanged at dizzying rates.

Molquandle was a god of petty vengeance, while Xenor was the overlord of the simpleminded. That neither reigned over a glamorous or sexy sphere didn't bother them in the least. To rule was good. To serve was bad. As basically block structures, their main martial tactic was to land on, and crush, their enemies. Both could cast spells. Both could fire simple electric bolts. They were not nearly as potent as Torent, but they were incredibly tough, and became, in effect, mobile castle walls.

Rumparious was an oddity onto herself. Unlike any other Cleinoid, she was a semi-corporeal aquatic monster. Her flesh wasn't as thick as gelatin, but it was more defined than, say, a mist. In her native environment, she would wriggle through water, much like a sea snake. Her touch was deadly to any creature, and, accordingly, she was the god of poisons. Her mode of combat was to wrap around her victim, like a python, and to then ooze life-ending juices. Since becoming a Cleinoid, no creature but a god had survived her deadly embrace.

"My brothers and sister," cackled Torent. "Fate favors us. It most certainly does. It *smiles* on our destruction, and enjoys along *with* us the spoils of our labor. We have been placed together so that we shall never, again, be forced to grovel, never again be forced to accept mediocrity."

Torent didn't go on to explain what he could have

possibly meant. He, for one, had never known mediocrity or deprivation of any kind. But, then again, he *was* criminally insane.

"I sense little to consume or render unto death on this world," stated Rumparious. "The world I have guided to this spot is *rich* with pitiful creatures who live in peace and harmony, and taste like buttered-bacon ice cream."

"Then we will join *you*," Molquandle responded emphatically, for himself and Xenor.

Torent recoiled when he sensed betrayal in the air. His was to lead. *He* was the supreme Cleinoid, the big fish in the little pond.

"We will do that if I decide it is what we will do," he challenged hatefully.

"Torent," spoke Molquandle, "you are not even first among equals. We are equals and there is no first of us. If we ravage as four or as one, it is the business of each of us, and no other."

"If we divide our strengths, we could fall victim to a crafty enemy. I cannot allow any of you to suffer. The whole *is* greater than its parts. In the name of the whole, I claim leadership, so that the *whole* may be glorified."

"You speak with a forked tongue," snarled Rumparious. "I reject your false claim of being our ruler."

Torent stuck his tongue out at Rumparious, in order to demonstrate that his tongue *was*, indeed forked.

"I meant that metaphorically," stammered Rumparious. "Sorry. Let me rephrase. You speak deceptively."

"That's better," hissed Torent, a god who would tolerate no species-profiling.

"To—" Molquandle trailed off in his rally cry. "I'm sorry. What did you say the name of your planet was?" he asked Rumparious.

"I have no idea. Let's call it the Planet Delicious."

"To *Delicious*," shouted Rumparious.

The three recent arrivals turned and headed away.

"Stop at once, you traitorous scum," menaced Torent. "If any would leave, I would part you from your life."

Rumparious glanced back, but the Atommitofoils surged ahead.

Torent reared back and hurled a flaming spike at one of the retreating gods. He couldn't, if pressed, say which Atommitofoil he targeted. Torent honestly couldn't tell them apart.

Xenor was lifted slightly, and fell forward, when the charge struck. He rose quickly, and was unharmed. He was, however, mightily pissed. Since Xenor was, and Molquandle had touched him in helping him up, Molquandle was mightily pissed, too. They turned.

"If it is *death* you seek," threatened Xenor, "it is *death* you will know." The pair advanced, slowly, on Torent.

"I do not wish death, or discord," cried out Torent. "I want but order. I want only to honor the *whole*."

"Then honor the *whole* by serving it as our minion," responded Xenor.

Torent had to think a moment, in order to offer a suitable, crafty response. "I would honor the whole *less* if I served it under your administration. To maximally *glorify* the whole, I must submit to leading it."

"This bickering is pointless," scorned Rumparious. "Fine, if it's such a big deal, I declare you the leader of our whole, Torent."

"Hang on," protested Xenor. "If we were to vote, it would be two versus two. A tie means we go our separate ways, as pairs."

"No," reminded Rumparious, "a tie vote at the conclave went to the ruling side. As Torent is the declared ruling side, *he* is victorious."

"Are you certain?" asked a confused-looking Molquandle. "I remember that rule differently."

"No. I'm quite certain," Rumparious replied sounding very official. "I served as co-under secretary to the center seat, in an honorary capacity, for an entire term."

The Atommitofoils tapped surfaces.

"Okay. Torent is our whole leader," declared Xenor.

"What are your commands, Torent?" asked Rumparious.

Torent threw an arm forward. "To Planet *Delicious*," he cried out in a frenzy.

And, it was off to the planet actually named Quin-111-blot, home to the Fatoricify races. All four Cleinoids leaped/flew across the thousand kilometer space separating the planets without difficulty. *A note to the planetary scientist currently reading is in order. Obviously, placing stars in close proximity would wreak havoc with the local space-time. Gravity would pull the stars apart, toward a mutual center of gravity. The planets, such as Quin-111-blot, would be destroyed. But, the Cleinoids compensated for those laws of physics, such that the stars remained isolated stars, and the planets remained in their cheery orbits, unmolested by Kepler's Laws. Keep this in the back of your minds for what is to follow.*

The quartet hit the ground running, figuratively, more than literally. The Atommitofoils did not have appendages on which to run. They spotted a large village teaming with buttered-bacon-ice-cream flavored aborigines. Their pace quickened, Torent surging into the lead. He could already taste the panic-stricken delights.

Then he slammed into an invisible barrier. He slid down its surface, only partially conscious. He was a living parody of Wile Coyote, after having struck, yet again, a cliff face.

The other three were sufficiently behind to be able to stop before impacting, themselves Torent groaned, and staggered to his feet.

"What happened?" Xenor asked quickly.

"I ... whoa." He steadied himself, further. "Some old friends seem to have come back to play," he said, recovering his focus.

"Where?" cried out Rumparious. "I sense no one."

"They will manifest themselves, soon enough. Let us proceed, more cautiously. Xenor, I grant you the honor of leading our team to victory." Torent pointed forward while speaking to Xenor.

With Molquandle joined to him, Xenor plodded, slowly, onward. Torent limped behind them, with Rumparious well in back of him. Torent seemed not to notice his own awkward gait.

With the village almost within reach, the Atommitofoils stepped it up a notch. That's when a large hole appeared in, first, Molquandle's center, then, Xenor's. *Blessing* had fired on them. Both plate-creatures twisted in pain, but it was transient. Their flesh sealed over, and they charged ahead.

Rail balls and more gamma-ray laser fire jumbled the stony substance of the Cleinoids. Torent dashed up to their backsides, in order to be covered from the attack. He immediately regretted his discretion. As the Atommitofoils were peppered with ordnance, they staggered backward, and fell on top of Torent.

Though he tried with all his might to rise, Torent found his injured leg wouldn't allow him to hoist the others off of him. He relaxed flat, and willed the ground to allow his passage. He oozed down and forward, and stood up a few feet from the fallen walls. His eyes scanned for the assailants.

There. Jon Ryan and the other, the antigod, stood to his

left. Heavy fire came from behind them, slicing into his team. Xenor split from Molquandle, and, individually, they struggled to rise. One would become upright, then be slammed back down, while the other just managed to stand. Small puddles of Atommitofoil started to form below them.

Rumparious flattened out to a few molecules thickness, and slithered toward the source of fire. The occasional piece of debris or shrapnel pierced her, but she filled in instantly. But it stung each time she was hit.

Torent sprinted, as best he could, toward Jon. That one would be the first to die, today.

Barely five meters in front of his prey, Torent froze. Verazz had held up his hand and commanded Torent to stop. Torent tore and ripped at whatever contained him, but he could not move.

"You will now pay the price for defying me," thundered Verazz, right into Torent's face.

Then the ground on which they all stood shook with massive trembling. What had been solid dirt looked like waves on a choppy sea. Gravity was stretching Quin-111-blot like a rubber band.

Verazz lost his footing, and a large tree fell squarely on him. He lost control of Torent.

The Cleinoid sprang on Jon. He buried his sharp digit into Jon's face, trying to crush his eyes.

Jon drove his arms up and between Torent's arms, to slam his grasp open. Once ... twice ... the third blow freed Jon. He kicked Torent away. Before Torent could recover, Jon seized him with his fibers and held him flailing in the air.

That's when Rumparious formed into a thick tube and rammed herself through Jon's chest. She coiled around him in a flash, and oozed poison as quickly as she could.

With his legs still free, Jon slammed backward into a tree. He struggled to lift his arms. Rumparious' grip was not powerful enough to resist the pounding and the pressure. She was tossed off like Jon was a dog shaking off water after a bath.

Jon scorched the area she fell into with his plasma rifle. Clouds of Rumparious flew into the air. She retreated as fast as she could, begging her jumbled flesh to follow her.

Xenor was finally upright and advancing on *Blessing*. Then Jon realized the two rectangles had fully fused. That was how they found the strength to withstand *Blessing's* vicious assault.

Verazz grabbed Torent around the throat and lifted him off the ground. "Die, little one," he howled.

Torent spread his arms, then crashed them down on either side of Verazz's head.

But Verazz held on.

Torent slammed him and slammed him. Torent's hands became flaming torches. Fire splattered from Verazz's head.

But, still, the Stone Witch held on to his prey.

Rumparious launched herself at Verazz. She saw that Torent's life was slipping away.

Just inches from his leg, Rumparious slammed into an invisible wall. She crumpled to the side, and began to dissipate.

Another earthquake, a bigger one, struck. Massive gashes formed in the ground. Everyone was thrown to the dirt.

The tremor lasted thirty seconds. When it ended, Verazz stood. Torent was gone. The Stone Witch reached out with his mind to find his enemy.

Torent struck him from the side. They tumbled several

meters and Torent sprang free just as Verazz reached for his neck.

Jon grabbed Torent with his fibers and moved him toward Verazz.

Torent chopped down on the fibers and sheared their grip. He stood over Verazz, as he still lay on the ground. He reached back to deliver an energy bolt.

Jon picked up a boulder with his fibers and batted Torent into a nearby fissure. The Cleinoid sailed in, almost gracefully, clearing both sides like he'd practiced the dive to perfection.

Jon helped Verazz to his feet. He checked *Blessing's* position. The combined Atommitofoils had nearly powered their way to the hull.

Jon sprinted to cut them off.

Torent flew out of the gash as energetically as he'd crashed into it.

Mid flight, a third quake shook the entire planet like it was a chew toy in a pit bull's jaws.

Everyone but Torent was thrown to the deck, hard.

Torent spread his arms wide, and aimed to slam into the fallen Verazz's midsection.

Verazz saw inbound death. He timed his kick perfectly. Torent was nearly lifted into low planet orbit from the force. He landed hundreds of meters away, flat on his back.

As he lay helpless, Verazz dashed toward him.

Slowly, painfully, Torent got to one knee, then the other.

Verazz was fifty meters off.

One leg, then the other. Torent swayed back and forth like Gumby trying to steady himself in hell. He saw Verazz's rapid approach. He aimed, and cast an energy lance at him. Then another and another.

Most fell short. Some went off to the side. A few shot

harmlessly, way overhead. Torent stared at the wayward lances, like they'd intentionally betrayed him. He made to fire again. As his arm went backward, so did he. He pivoted on one foot like a drunken sailor in a storm on the high seas. Round and round ... and down.

Verazz reached down and lifted Torent by the scruff of his neck. He snapped the Cleinoid around, so they were face to face. Verazz spat in Torent's eye. "Now you—"

Verazz squinted. Then he shook Torent tentatively. He placed Torent's chest against his ear.

Torent was dead. The master Cleinoid had simply stopped being alive. Committed to not being fooled again, Verazz threw Torent up and away, and the body ignited in a glorious ball of fire. By the time the remains began to fall back to earth, they were nothing but seared ashes.

Verazz saw Jon wrestling with the plate aliens. He began to trot to his aid. He nearly tripped. Verazz looked back to the weeds he'd come though. The ragged, spare remnants of Rumparious were sprawled out loosely. As Verazz watched in stunned amazement, whatever lingered of the semi-corporeal monster thinned out, and was, finally, gone.

Jon punched at the plate Cleinoid as it struggled toward *Blessing* like a salmon trying to get past him to spawn. Slowly, his slamming fists gained purchase in the hard flesh. Sputters of tissue careened off with each blow. Each strike moved the plate backward just a bit more. Then a punch split through and came out the other side of the beast. Another and another and another. Larger and larger gaps formed, and none sealed over.

Jon landed a wheelhouse punch to the surface, and the fused Atommitofoil cracked in half, horizontally. The top section slid backward, and the lower flopped forward. It pinned the tips of Jon's boots to the ground.

"Do you require assistance," Verazz asked as he slowed to a stop. "I fear those shoes might be beyond repair."

"Nah," Jon returned, with a grin. "I'm good." He jerked first one, then the other toe free. "Is that weird ass cloud snaky thing gone, too?"

Verazz raised his hands, slowly parting them, as his fingers wiggled wildly. "Puff," he popped.

"Is it me, or was that a crazy ass battle?"

"I'm certain it's you. All things puzzling and unexpected seem to be."

"I mean, we're fighting for our lives, and then these ass clowns fade away—"

He was cut short by a ground swell orders of magnitude larger than any disruption before.

"I think this planet is about to fly apart," shouted Verazz. "We should go."

"There are billions of people who don't share that luxury, pal. If they're not leaving, neither am I."

"Oh. I forgot about them." Verazz closed his eyes. Soon his hands were jumping and twisting like he was playing a hologame, a particularly violent one, at that. Five minutes later, he lowered his arms, and slowly opened his eyes. "There. All better."

"What's all better?" Jon demanded.

"Everything. I returned the stars to where they belong and the planets to their happy little orbits."

Jon gestured over a shoulder. "Including the ones, like, from other galaxies?"

"All of them." He tented a hand on his chest. "Stone Witch, here."

"Oh. I forgot about that."

CHAPTER TWENTY-NINE

In a dark forest, a wooden shack stood alone. It leaned slightly to the north. It seemed to be supported from total collapse only by the thick weeds and brushes that ensnared it. Neglect had perversely preserved order. That was in keeping with the hovel's preternatural owners. Strange is as strange does.

Slapgren held Mirraya's hand ever so tenderly. He was long past knowing if she still knew he was, but he knew he needed to. There was, in fact, nothing else he wanted to do. Mirri had been asleep for days. He'd lost count of how many, and he'd lost interest in counting them. It was unimportant. Once in a great while, his only love would moan, or twitch. But none of that seemed intentional.

A couple months before, when it was clear how close the end was, Slapgren and Mirraya had made a decision as untraditional and as rebellious as their lives together had been. They decided to split from hollon. In every case anyone knew of, mated pairs of Deft remained joined as one of them passed. That way, the one who stayed behind had an ongoing vision of their life partner. The holloned couple was a mighty dragon, and, after death's bitter visit, one of them still was.

But Jon Ryan's kids decided differently. Of course, they did. When Mirraya was gone, Slapgren would be only who he was. He would face the unhappy future alone. That was how they'd entered the world. Alone and afraid. That was how they were when Jon swooped in to save them. Alone and afraid. That's how it would be. Slapgren would be alone and afraid. So alone. So afraid he'd never see his bride, again.

Mirraya's arm jerked. It slipped out of Slapgren's grasp. With guilty speed, he gently picked it up.

His spine stiffened. Mirri's pulse was gone.

Slapgren set his ear to her chest.

Nothing. She was gone.

Though they'd said their goodbyes every morning, back when Mirraya still woke up, Slapgren felt robbed. Tears welled up, and began streaking down his unwashed cheeks. He would wait, just a little while, before he followed Mirraya's last instructions. She had reminded him he was lazy and forgetful, so he needed to light the pyre soon. If her body went cold while it was still whole, her magic would leak out. Disembodied magic was a mischievous and pesky manifestation. She wouldn't tolerate burdening all the future children sleeping at night who would be scared awake by rattling and knocking under their beds.

But, he could wait, just a bit.

After a few minutes, his tears dried. His breathing grew steady, once again.

Maybe it was time. Yes, he knew it was.

"I'm ... I'm going to miss you, wife. I was ... was getting kind of used to you."

He smoothed her hair back, away from her eyes.

"I guess I could, maybe get a part time jo ... job. Something, you know, to pass the time."

"Or, you could get the shears out of the shed, and clean up this frakking yard," came a stern voice from behind him.

He spun.

"It looks like two very old people live here, like their kid's kids don't bother to come 'round. It's embarrassing. That's what it is."

"Mirri?" he peeped.

"No, I'm the tooth fairy and you're in luck. She died with a full set," snarked Mirraya, as she floated, shimmering in glory.

"Mirr ... Mirri, are you okay?"

She smiled. It was a smile of release. She was released from her pain, and he was released from his despair.

"Of course, I'm fine. I'm with *you*, my perfect man."

He looked down, then back at her image. "Will you stay, then?"

"No. You know I can't. We talked about this. It must be as it always has been. It is good, and so it will remain."

"Oh, I was—"

"Plus I just found out how high the housing prices are, on this side. *I'm* going to need to get that job if I'm going to buy us a nice place, by the time you *finally* get here."

"Finally? You know?"

"Of course. I got a handbook and a schedule. It says you'll waste so much time before you join me, I may have lost interest."

"Re ... really?"

"Slapgren," she said firmly. "I'm kidding. Just because I'm dead doesn't mean I don't need a laugh or two."

"So you *didn't* find out about my girl friends, then? Any of them?"

236

"Your *what*? I can promise you—"

"Kidding, Mirri. Two can play the same cruel game."

She smiled and she chuckled. "I think I'm going to miss you. Not sure, but, you know, probably."

"I know I'll miss you."

"You w—"

"I'll likely stave to death in filthy clothes with hair down to my ass."

"I'm leaving now. And when I say leaving, I mean, *boy, howdy* leaving." She thumbed over a shoulder.

"I know. We talked about this. Plus, I have one thing on my honey-do list I can't put off any longer."

"If you mess this up, it's *you* I'll be haunting." She wagged a finger at him.

He raised his arms in surrender.

"Mirri, can I give you one last kiss?"

She was stricken silent. Finally, "Yes. I think there's just about enough magic left in the world."

He stood and walked to her form. Both leaned in, not wanting to chance touching too closely. And they kissed. It was the kiss of a married couple, who had loved for generations, and who knew it would not be their final one. There'd be more ... later. That's the way it was with long-married couples.

Everyone knew that.

CHAPTER THIRTY

I spied over Doc's shoulder. "So, how's she doing?"

Toño hadn't left Daleria's side since we set down on Oowaoa. Neither had Cragforel.

"She's in and out of consciousness. But, I think her blood pressure's finally stabilized."

Cragforel nodded with a serious expression.

As soon as I was certain the four Cleinoids we fought on Podulliy, and whatever, were dead, Verazz and I piled into *Stingray* and we left. Hopefully, we acted fast enough. It was touch and go, both on the battlefield, as well as aboard the vortex. But, there was no way around it. I wanted the ship's firepower for the engagement, and it was a good thing I stuck to my guns—pun intended. We only just won. Verazz insisted, again, that it be only him and me doing the fighting. He said, in a firm and godly manner, that Toño, Daleria, and Sapale had to stay inside the ship. I'm fairly rebellious and contrary, as you know by now. But, when the head antigod says *jump*, you're pretty much stuck asking *how high*. And woe betide you if you don't clear the requisite height.

Verazz also reasoned that, if the *two* of us, plus the ship, couldn't defeat the four Cleinoids, then the *five* of us, plus the ship, weren't going to, either. PS, he was more impressed that *he* was one of the two of us, not *me*. I was along for metaphysical reasons, more than from his confidence in my martial arts skills. He was probably right on all counts, but you'll never catch me telling him that. But, in any case, lingering near those Wolf–Rayet stars might mean death to Daleria. But, I'm getting a little ahead of my story.

As soon as we were back safely on the ship, Toño insisted we go to Oowaoa. He wanted help treating Daleria, since he knew she was big time sick. He also wanted the Deavoriath's input on what had happened to the Cleinoids. He was forming some theories, but, when it came to anything to do with the ancient gods, fairly sure wasn't nearly good enough.

Seeing after his patient was Doc's first and most pressing concern. It didn't take Cragforel and him long to determine she was suffering some form of radiation poisoning. Her circulating counts were way down, her "blood cleaning function," as Doc called it, was taxed to the max, and her lung function was down to fifty percent, because of fluid accumulation. Poor Daleria was in bad shape.

"I'd estimate she's accumulated five or six gray units of ionizing radiation," Toño announced solemnly.

"Yes," Cragforel tapped a view screen, "judging from the chromosomal damage in this sample, I'd say that was about right."

"I can't think of any additional treatment. We've replicated as many stem cells as possible and transfused them. I've filled her with all the antioxidants I dare."

"We could try giving her nanites impregnated with

layered graphene. They might trap some of the lingering decay products."

Toño rubbed his chin. "Possibly. But trapping the gamma particles at this point might not help much. If our treatment works, any future damage can be repaired. The issue is stabilizing her enough to get her through the immediate crisis."

"I've been able to remove a lot of the 177^{m}Lu in her tissues using a magnetic resonance trap. I'd agree with your assessment. If she survives the acute poisoning, she'll do fine."

"Guys," I said from behind, "I truly hate to interrupt, but where did she get radioactive lutetium *from*? It's not like it rains from the heavens. Isn't it's half-life, like, a hundred days, or something?"

"One hundred and sixty, give or take," Toño replied in a distant tone.

"But from *where*?" I pressed. "If it has such a short half-life, it has to be generated continually, locally, and in fairly large amounts."

"The answer to that question is both plainly obvious and stunningly baffling," he responded, with a little more animation to his voice.

"And that would be—"

"The Wolf–Rayet stars," answered Cragforel.

Huh? "I didn't know Wolf–Rayet stars *contained* 177^{m}Lu," I sort of grunted out.

"They do now, as *fate* would have it," Cragforel said with an edge.

"What ... huh? They didn't and now they do?" I was the very definition of gobsmacked.

"Ah, no," Toño replied, "well, yes."

"Okay, now I'm clear on that. Thanks. Come *on*, throw me a bone, here. How can it be *both*?"

"Only in the *Ryanverse*, that's how," Cragforel responded with that same edge to his voice.

"Sure. I knew that."

"Jon, I can tell you what we discovered, but it is unsettling. I know you will say to tell you, anyway, so I will. But, I'm not certain how *I* can process the truth, in this case. How *you* will ... we'll simply have to wait and see." He collected his thoughts. "The AIs ran real-time spectroscopic analyses on around ten thousand Wolf–Rayets, both locally and at distance. They found lutetium in most, but not all of them. Included in the isotopes of lutetium is consistently a goodly percent of 177^{m}Lu."

"Is that unexpected?" I posed.

"No, in fact, it is not. Historical records show Wolf–Rayets often contain ambiguous amounts of lutetium."

"And what's a *goodly percent*?" I asked.

"More than one might expect to occur by natural processes," replied Cragforel.

"But, not *so* much that it is clearly an artificial abundance," added Toño, still rubbing at his chin.

"I'm impressed, and it's wonderful to know, that WRs have *wacky* spectral profiles. I fail to see, however, how that is mind-numbingly life changing."

"In and of itself, it's not," Cragforel stated flatly.

"However, I took the liberty of downloading images of Wolf–Rayets from a privileged source, one possibly uncontaminated by time-foolery."

"Time-foolery? Is that even a *word* now?" I muttered.

"Only in the *Ryanverse*," Cragforel parroted.

"I'm starting to get goosebumps, because I'm suspecting where this is going, but, could you—"

"I downloaded all the images of Wolf–Rayets *you've* ever directly observed, Jon," Toño said stiffly.

"Okay, might'a been nice if you asked first, but, how many have I seen?"

"Including your initial Ark voyages, you've recorded over three thousand images. Most were inadvert, mind you."

"Naturally. I'm a married man. Can't be caught gawking at WRs, now can I?"

Toño shook his head, slowly. Boy, I'd recorded that image a lot, also.

"In *all* cases of the Wolf–Rayets you have *ever* captured, there are no traces of lutetium," Cragforel stated firmly.

"None?" I wheezed.

"Zero," replied Toño.

"That's, you know, *fairly* unexpected."

"That's the *existential* understatement of all time," murmured Cragforel.

"And your data, both sets, are good? No corruption, adulteration, or Russian hacking?"

"The data are all sound. Nothing is even *slightly* questionable."

"You know what, guys," I began hesitantly, "I'm kind of guessing what this all means. But, out of fairness to you, I'd like your take on *WTF* is going on."

"Occam's razor would support that Fate *favored* you by altering the stellar nucleosynthesis of Wolf–Rayet stars," Toño responded quietly, thoughtfully.

"It did?" I mumbled.

"We believe that is the *only* possible explanation," said Cragforel, equally respectful of the implications of his words.

"Can Fate even *do* that?"

"Only Fate can answer that question, Jon," replied Toño. "There are no documents outlining the parameters under which it functions."

"Ho, boy," I exhaled.

"Oh, boy, *indeed*," Toño affirmed.

Daleria stirred. That snapped all our focuses off epistemology and back to the medical arts. I, for one, was extremely glad of that. My head was not *swimming*. It was *drowning*.

"Can you hear me, my dear?" Toño asked loudly.

She groaned in almost-speak.

"Daleria, I'm right here. You're sick but I'll make you well. Don't you worry." Never heard Doc make a medical promise like that before.

Her eyes fluttered, but didn't really open, meaningfully.

"I think that's a good sign," opined Cragforel.

"Can you recheck her metabolic status, please?"

"Right away," Cragforel answered.

I left. They didn't need me there, and I wanted to be ... well, *nowhere* would have been nice. I sought out Sapale. My Rule Number One is, when I find myself in times of trouble, Sapale is who I see. She was in the mess, stirring a large pot of something. The closer I got, the more calrf-like it stank. Then I remembered. When she was moody and stressed, she made that anti-delicacy from her home world. Any port in a storm is a good port.

I came up from behind and kissed the top of her head.

"How you holding up?" she asked tenderly.

"Poorly. Thanks for asking. And you?"

"Middling, at best." She sighed. "Is Daleria improving?"

"Maybe. The boys are optimistic."

"One of the boys is *hoping* more than he's *reasoning*."

That would be Toño, of course.

"Time will tell."

"Did Toño tell you about the spectral conundrum?"

"Conundrum? Since when do you use such big and obscure words?"

CRAIG ROBERTSON

She craned her neck around to look at me. "I *love* to use impractical, overly-burdensome words. They're ... fun."

"If you insist."

"So, did he?"

"Yes. You know, of all the unjustifiable, mystical, and down-right jarring things that have happened to me in two billion years—"

"That's the topper?"

"No. You are." I quickly kissed the top of her head, again. Mostly that was to prevent her from whipping around and kneeing my groin. "No, seriously, I was going to say, as incredible as it seems, this revelation is no biggy. EJ appears back in time with a membrane generator, I visit the Pillars of Creation, Fate interviews me, every time I'm knocked out Jenna floats into my head, Toño reveals that some jerk's pet dogs nearly conquered the universe, I meet and defeat Ralph, who, up until then, I thought was evil incarnate."

"*And?*"

"And, now all of reality *reconfigures* itself to allow for the Cleinoid dynasty to end, entirely and forever, because *I* wanted it to."

"Yes, but, *otherwise*, Mrs. Lincoln, how did you enjoy the play?"

"Exactly and precisely. Everything is so bizarre, so dumbfounding, and so challenging to accept, that I get all *meh*."

"Don't you mean you're consumed with ennui?"

"With the big *words*, again." I playfully swatted her butt. "Stop it. You'll *dissuade* participation in informational exchanges."

She stuck out her tongue. She did not even bother to turn her head to show me. That's how casual our relationship has become.

244

"Fate summons me, tells me *someone* told it to favor me. Next thing I know, the physics of a class of stars changes. And, it is altered in *just* the right way that Cleinoids depending on that class of star for their power, also just *happen* to accumulate a lethal dose of radiation. What gives them life, gives them death, all in one convenient package."

She rotated around and hugged me. "All I know is we won. The universe is safe, *finally*. I'll accept that victory, no matter how or why it was achieved."

"Amen, I say upon you, sister."

"I really wasn't looking forward to snuffing those ass-jockeys out, one at at time."

"Oh, now potty mouth, not megalogophilia. I don't know which I like *least*."

Again, with the tongue.

We were quiet a spell, standing there hugging. It was nice.

"But, babe—" Sapale said in a low tone I assumed was intended to approximate me speaking.

"What ever do you mean?" I blinked repeatedly as I addressed her.

Again with the low voice, "But, babe, there one more thing I need to do." I think she overdid the cowboy aspect of her rendition.

"Wife, there are many things left to do. *I* have things. *You* have things. *We* have things."

"Ooh ooh, let me guess. *They* have things, too?"

"I'm sure they do."

"But none of the *not*-yous has to seek out and justify himself with EJ."

I'm not really sure how she knew me so well. It was ... impressive.

"It was on my to-do list. I can't deny that."

245

"I know your to-do list, sweetheart. One: bug the shit out of EJ. Two: drink beer."

"You are absolutely and positively incorrect. You forgot Three:—"

"Go *fishing*."

"*There's* the to-do list."

"Seriously, why?"

"Because I like the outdoors, and they say fish are good for the brain."

She slapped my shoulder.

"Because beer gives *life*?"

She slapped the other.

"Because I have to."

She placed a finger right under my nose. "I should hit you for saying that, too. It's so wrong."

"It is if you're not in my head."

"Which I am glad not to be."

"He's a loose end. He split when we returned to this universe. I'm sure he knows the war's over. But he needs to know ... the specifics."

"*Why* does he need to know the specifics? Are you certain it's not that you need to seek forgiveness?"

"Forgiveness? Are you batty? Forgiveness for what?"

"For not *wanting* him around. For not *loving* him. For not *begging* him to stay. Or, how about for never *trusting* him, or *welcoming* him, or ever *caring* about him enough to say the words?"

"Yeah, but how do you really feel about it?"

Shoulder. Slap.

"He treated you *horrendously*. I can never forgive him for that," I stated resoundingly.

"Yes, he did. But, first, he did that to *me*, not *you*. Second, he's changed. *No*, he's not perfect, not even in perfect's zip code, but he tried and he *succeeded* in lifting his

246

soul out of the mud."

"So, maybe I do need to address those issues, too, if only on a *subconscious* level."

"What? You time traveling to see Dr Freud, now?"

"Not *recently*, no."

"Do you need to go soon?"

I bobbed my head side to side.

"Now?" she said tersely.

"Now's good."

"Alone?"

"*Alone!* Now *there's* a thought. It never occurred to me to *not* include you."

"Will you excuse me a sec?"

"Sure. Why?"

"I need to get a match so I can light your pants on fire."

"Okay, sure. Any particular reason, *this* time?"

"Ah, that's a yes. You're a liar."

"Everyone knows *that*. Hardly worth celebrating with a barbecue."

"You know, I think I'm going to *insist* you go alone. Stay-as-*long*-as-you-like." The tongue, yet again. I was getting tongue-fatigue.

"There's my girl." I gave her a peck.

"Where will you look. I bet he went to ground."

"I know he did. But, I know where I'd go to ground, so I'm thinking I know where he'd dive in."

"The two scariest words in the English language. Jon Ryan saying *I'm thinking*."

"Isn't that three words? *I am* is, in your example, a contraction."

"*Go.*"

"Not going to offer me a bowl of that marvelous smelling calrf?"

247

"Go, *now*." She lofted a finger in a potential direction I might go in, rapidly.

I, being a dutiful husband, chose that direction to go, rapidly.

CHAPTER THIRTY-ONE

Where would I go, after returning from hell, the Cleinoid universe, and the insanity of war? Earth. Duh. When I was melancholy, really down in the dumps, being there gave me ... comfort. Plus, if I wanted to run into myself, that would be the obvious choice. But did EJ want to run into *me*?

I was about to find out.

I left Sapale, Toño, and the mending Daleria on Oowaoa. Cragforel was even glad for the company, especially since that company didn't include me. Plus, Doc wanted him to help make certain his girlfriend was healing as quickly as possible.

Doc's *girlfriend*. It still sounded so weird. Like cloudy monkeys or purple yellows, the words just didn't seem to go together. But, if anyone deserved to be happy, it was my oldest friend.

I asked *Stingray* to orbit the remains of planet Earth. I wanted to confirm there was an android down there, somewhere. I also wanted to take the measure of the place, see if it was recovering. The last time I visited, which was a while back, there were positive signs, if not obvious life. What I found was astounding. There was even more water present. In spite of the old age of our solar system, cometary water was still impacting Earth. It's greatly diminished atmosphere allowed it to pass without vaporizing, so it was able to bind gravitationally. Expansive seas were forming, some up to fifteen meters deep.

Doesn't sound like much? Remember, Jupiter stripped off the outer third of the surface. There was nothing left but scarred, barren rock. Now, shallow oceans had formed. A goodly amount of atmosphere was also accumulating. It wasn't spring air in the Rockies, or anything vaguely similar, but it was a start. Who knew? The molten core was still sustaining a robust magnetic field. With safety from the worst of the cosmic radiation, maybe life would begin again. Or, maybe it'd scrape off my boot and start even faster. I could only hope. I had a special place in my heart for the old girl.

"Pilot," Al said, snapping me back from my day dream, "there is no sign of EJ. That said, there is a small area covered by a partial membrane. Presumably, he's to be found inside."

"Sneaky bastard."

"Pilot, if *his* mother was not married to *his* father, neither was *yours*."

"EJ's a post-*conception* bastard. Totally different subspecies."

"I stand corrected."

"Stand anywhere you want, just not close to me."

"My but you're in a *perky* mood this fine whatever time of day it is."

"Why not? I'm back home, just ended evil, and I got a new set of skivvies on. Life's good."

"So, why not abuse your antiquated, overworked, and underappreciated ship's AI?"

"'Xactly. I'm glad you're learning your place. Sure, it took billions of *years*, but, in the end, you got smart."

"I *got* smart? Gee, when youz say it like that, it all makes sensible." Then he said something like, "Pizzalo wasr."

"What?"

"I said smelly apes can't hear so well. Why, didn't you hear me well?"

"Al, that's, like, a third grade joke. I'd expect more from a toaster of your advancing years."

"Sorry, I was programmed to pair my conversation level with the individuals I address. Blame Dr. DeJesus for the elementary-speak, not me."

"Speaking of you, where's *Stingray?*"

"My wife's right here. She'd like to go shopping with her friends, maybe have a light salad over girl talk, but she can't, so she's here, by my side."

"*Stingray* wants a hen-scapade? You gotta be kidding."

"Yes, it's the lone item on her bucket list."

"I give up. Why *doesn't* she go on an outing with the old gang/gaggle/galère, insert your own descriptor? Is it, perchance, because she, too, is overworked and underappreciated?"

"No, not at all. She doesn't have time. She's too devoted to me. Why, just th ... o—"

His voice broke up into static and harsh pops.

"Al, you okay, in there?"

"Good evening, Form One. How are you?" asked *Stingray.*

"Just-fine-and-you? What happened to Al?"

"Sore throat. There's a frog in his tongue, cat's got his throat."

"Poor guy. Tough break, eh?"

"I'm beside myself."

"When, if ever, do you anticipate he'll be back on his metaphorical feet, again?"

"The second he apologizes."

"Much as I anticipated. Glad to hear it, too. Couldn't have happened to a nicer heel."

"My sentiments, exactly."

There was another rush of static, then nothing. Blissful, empty, silent nothing.

"Could you set us down next to the membrane sphere, please?"

"It will be my pleasure, Form One."

I stepped off *Stingray*, and onto the hard ground, outside. There were traces of dust and rocky debris, but nothing like dirt, yet. I crunched over to the membrane's limit, and—you got it—I knocked, because there was no doorbell.

Immediately two things happened. The membrane vanished, and I smiled ear-to-ear. I was looking at my happiest happy place. Peg's Bar None, cheesy signage and all. Hell, the door frame was even crooked, like it always had been. I rushed in. Yes! The broken Coors Light sign. It was still broken! There was a God in Heaven.

The only issue—grrr—was that *he* was in *my* seat. Some things are *not* worth fighting over. Some things *are*.

I sauntered up to EJ. "Hey, buddy, you're in my chair."

"Can't be. I'm in *my* chair."

"You never rode on *Granger*, so you never *had* a seat at Peg's. Move."

"I do now. It's my favorite, already. I love it like I do my left nut."

"Oh, for fuck's sake, not *two* pieces'a shit," screeched Peg, "I'm going to have to strike a match every two minutes to keep the smell down." She was heading over with a tray.

It had two shots and two beers, so I don't think she was all that surprised I'd arrived.

I slid into the seat opposite EJ's. "You programmed her holo well."

"Damn thing programmed *itself*, it's so ornery."

"Nice. Just like the old days."

"Except I got your seat." He grunted a laugh.

"If I'm gonna be able to tell you two ass wipes apart, I'm gonna need to color code ya." She leaned over and spit a huge loogie right on top of EJ's head.

If I'd have died at that moment, my life would have been fully and blessedly complete and deeply satisfying.

"You got my chair, but I *don't* got a wet hairdo." I giggled like a school girl.

"You'd think the bitch holo'd know who programmed it, and who the shit bird is."

"I *do*, shit bird," Peg hissed. Then she waddled away, complaining, "I got payin' customers to pump. You two freeloaders can fend for yourselves until it pleases me to return."

"I should'a married that little woman," I mused, as I watched her igloo-sized butt disappear around a corner.

"Should'a, would'a, could'a."

"What the hell's that supposed to mean?" I snapped.

"It *means* ... I need refills but you pissed off the barkeep."

"Hang on a sec." I stood and headed behind the bar. In my universe, that would have been a fatal error. No one, but no one, went behind Peg's bar. Death by flesh-eating beetles was preferable to what she'd do to a trespasser. But, EJ'd set up the holo. I snatched up two beers, and one bottle of drinking whiskey. Seriously, those were the only two words on the label: drinking whiskey. She didn't even *bother* to capitalize them. Zero fashion sense.

I was halfway to freedom when a broom swatted me

squarely in the face. Luckily for me, it was the business end, not the handle. Apparently, the rules according to Peg were universal. My bad.

"I'll bring refills in the fullness of time, sonny," she growled. "If you set the merchandise down on the bar, you might just leave my establishment with your ability to sexually *reproduce* intact."

"Yes, ma'am," I shot back, and I wasn't trying to be clever.

I scurried back where I belonged.

"You know what, meat?" EJ said once I'd settled in. "I didn't program that into her repertoire. I *swear* I didn't."

"I believe you. The power of Peg is both mystical and undeniable."

Wipe Out sprang to life from the jukebox.

"*That* I did program in," he grunted.

"And you did *good*." I toasted him with my empty glass.

"As you might have guessed, I was expecting you." He looked around the holo.

"Yeah, I was kind of thinking."

"You know why I was expecting you?"

I shrugged.

"Because I've led a vile and *contemptible* life, that's why. I deserve you."

"Gee, gosh, golly. I've never been anyone's penance before. I have to say it's just *swell*."

"I'll make *you* swell. I'm being serious. I hate your guts, and you hate mine. But, there's no way around it, we're joined at the hip."

"More like joined *at the DNA level*, but, whatever."

"You always were a sissy ninny."

Peg chose that moment to grace us with two shots and two beers. She swept up the empties and left without a word.

"You want to switch beers?" I asked EJ.

"Nah. I hate the taste of saliva."

"*Saliva's* not the body fluid I'm afraid of, here."

"Then I'll order you another, quick as a *tinkle*."

I pounded back my shot, and then eyed my brew with suspicion . "I don't hate any part of you, *Jon*," I said frankly.

"What? No more *EJ* bullshit to try and sandpaper down, completely, my last nerve."

"No."

"What a frakking relief."

Hey, he said *frak*, too. Excellent. "You know," I said gesturing toward Peg, "she swears. It's okay to swear in here."

"Thanks for the update, pus brain. I shall treasure it."

I waited a second before plowing ahead.

"I also hope you do not hate me. We had some rough patches, and some rougher ones, sure. But you were a stand-up guy with the ancient-god thing."

"I do not *seek* or *require* your approval," he menaced.

"Sorry. I didn't mean it to come out like that. I should have said that, in my estimation, you're a good man."

"I don't hate you." He shot a glare up to me. "That said, I don't like you much, either. I told you once, a long long time ago, you'd never see me again. The failure of that pipe dream to remain constant has been a repeated boil on my butt."

"I'm penance, a sissy ninny, *and* a boil. I'm a confused allegorical figure. I was previously unaware of that."

"Don't leave unrelenting *jerk* off that list."

"I want to square things between us."

"And you assume *I* do, too, because—"

"Because you're here."

"Shit. I *knew* this was a bad idea. I should have left the past be."

"No, you didn't think this was a bad idea. You weren't sanguine about it, but you knew we needed to do this." I sipped my beer, tentatively. "And then we'll never see each other again."

"Crap on a cracker. You drink like an *old* lady," he complained bitterly.

"I want to analyze it before I fully commit. Is that alright with you?"

"No. You drink like an *old* lady." He reached across, snatched up my beer, and downed it in one gulp.

"Is that supposed to teach me how *real* men drink someone else's urine?"

"*Yes*, ya big baby."

"First things first," I said, back to serious. "I want you to know that I'm not too sure I like you either. But, you've changed. You regained your humanity. I'm proud of you." I raised my hands to stave off his protestations. "I know. You don't require my approval. I'm not giving you that. I'm telling you how I see you, how *Sapale* sees you. We're not inviting you over for dinner, but we're glad to see you came back, morally."

"*Second* things *second*," he responded angrily.

"I need to know. And when I say I *need* to, I mean I *need* to know. Where did you get the membrane tech?"

"Puddin Tane, ask me again and I'll tell you the same."

"Asshole."

"Guilty as charged."

"Look, when somebody, especially yourself, says they need to know, and you know, you tell that person. Any questions?"

"One tickles the back of my mind. Or what?"

"Or," I extended my fibers a little.

"You wouldn't dare."

"I won't have to if you just tell me. What is the BFD,

here, pal? You're not the mysterious Mr. Uto any longer.
It's you and you, sitting at a table, settling up. Why can't
you find it in your heart—"

"Oh, for the love of Mike. If it'll shut your
sanctimonious *mouth*, I'll tell you. You're positively more
than a man's likely to take."

"Thank you," I huffed.

He got a poker face on. "Who do you *think* did?"

"Let me see. There are estimated to be 10^{25} *planets* in
the universe. Assuming one in a *hundred* has intelligent life,
and four billion *souls* dwell therein, I don't know, of the
ginormous number of choices, I choose I don't have that
much time to guess which individual did."

"I got time. Take one guess."

I studied him. He was serious. He wanted me to take a
guess. "The Deavoriath."

He slammed his palm down on the table. "No. And
that's such a lame guess, you gotta guess again." He
was hot.

"There's only one real option, but it's nuts."

"Say it."

"Toño DeJesus."

"Bingomatic," he fired his index finger at me.

"But, he can't have. He doesn't know where it came
from. It's not something a body's likely to forget."

He stared back at me.

"How?" I used my Clint Eastwood tone.

"You ever fight a Pesquil?"

A Pesquil is probably the last sentient—and I'm using
the term sentient advisedly, because their dumb as warm
asphalt—you'd ever choose to fight. The small ones are six
hundred kilograms. They stand firmly on three tree trunk
legs, have armor plating not even a plasma rifle will scorch,

and they have the meanest, most disagreeable disposition of any creature ever born.

"Can't say I have. That factoid, by the way, does *not* alter the passion with which I want you to tell me how Doc could have gifted you the membrane technology."

"I was drinking in a place, one day, that makes this pile of crap look like the Taj Mahal."

"I heard that," yelled Peg.

"Looks like you'll get seconds on that piss beer," I stated gleefully.

"This Pesquil walks up to me and says I should buy him a drink. I'm naturally curious, so I ask him why, in the name of his whore-mother, I should."

"No," I said in true disbelief.

He raised his hands. "I was curious. What can I say?"

"And his reasoning went—"

"His response was really rather basic. *Bang, pound, slam* on the top of my head."

"Alert the media. There's a surprise."

"I couldn't. I was rendered unconscious, believe it, or not."

"You were lucky."

"I haven't finished my *story,* yet."

"Then proceed."

"So, I'm out like the proverbial light. Then, I realize I'm not out. I'm floating."

"I don't like where I think this story's heading," I said real low.

"Me, neither. So, I'm floating, and yada, yada, yada, all of the sudden, I'm looking up at Fate," he pointed at me, "capital *F*, Fate."

"Old friend of mine, too."

That raised an eyebrow.

258

"So, Fate tells me, basically, it favored me. What it meant—"

"Trust me on this. I know."

"You're a curious son of a bitch, aren't you? So, Fate says I have to right a wrong. I ask, 'And how the hell am I supposed to do that.'" He grinned. "A voice calls out behind me, "If I were you, Jonny, I wouldn't swear in the presence of Fate.' Now, meat, I'll give you as many guesses as you want, because you're never—"

"Jenna. Jenna was warning you playfully."

If you ever want to look up the term *no fucking way*, please search for the one with that picture, the one of *his* face, the second *after* I said *Jenna*.

"There is actually no f—"

"Been there, done that, starred in the video."

He fingered the air. "Refills, honey, and be quick about it."

"No can do, *honey*. You two kept me so busy, I'm dehydrated. Refills'll be out when they're out."

"So," he continued, still in a bit of shock, "Jenna and I have a cute conversation about the old days, she flirts with me, I get so embarrassed I nearly pee myself—"

"Tell me about it."

"Then, Fate gets all serious. It says I must go. I must serve. I must," he waved a hand dismissively in the air, "do some bullshit, whatever."

"And then?"

"And then I'm standing on a tiny, cramped, but neat and orderly ship, somewhere in space."

"Doc's ship."

"Of course. He turns around and says, like, *you're late.*"

"Sounds like Doc."

"So, I ask, late, how can I be late when A) I have no clue

when now is, B) I didn't know I was coming, and C) he couldn't know I was coming."

"Excellent points," I said, while nodding.

"You know what he says? If you do, by the way, and you say it, I'll kill ya."

I raised my palms in his direction.

"He says, 'I knew you were coming, as fate would have it.'"

"I *hate* that creepy crap."

"Not as much as I do. So, he tells me we're in the year 8510, in his timeline. He knows the Listhelons killed off humankind, in your space time, and mine, and that he was going to give me a tool to prevent those events from occurring."

"And he gives you the plans for the membrane?"

"And he gives me the plans for the membrane."

"But, where'd he get them? I mean, did he invent membrane technology, or did Fate gift it to him?"

"I asked."

I was so relieved.

"He said, and I'm quoting him here, 'Puddin Tane, ask me again and I'll tell you the same.'"

I was unrelieved, *massively* unrelieved.

"But you dug in your heels, you made him tell you?"

"No. I disappeared."

"And ended up—"

"Looking up at a Pesquil's *extremely* ugly ass." He trembled. "I slid away on my back and left while the behemoth was laughing and the crowd was cheering."

"Wait, you gave the membrane to your timeline, too. You never told me that."

"*That* is a correct statement."

"You led me to believe it ended tragically, all was lost,

and you were suffered to roam the galaxy, rife with guilt and sadness."

"*Rife?* Who writes that shit for you?"

"You lied to me."

He held up a finger in protest. "No. I mislead you. I never lie."

"Wait, *that's* a lie."

"Seek legal council and sue me."

"So, how did your timeline end?"

"No clue, Blue."

"But you gave them—"

"I *gave* the plans to that Toño DeJesus, maybe six months before the Listhelons hit."

"And—"

"And I split."

"You what?"

"Well, for one thing, *micro-brain*, there was *already* one of me there, because the shit hadn't hit the fan yet, and I hadn't split yet."

"So you split?"

"Yup."

"To avoid you or you splitting?"

"Jon, move on. You're acting more pathetic than usual."

"You left. You didn't stay to see if they all died, anyway? You didn't stay to help them *not* die?"

"Weren't you listening? I did. That other us. He was there."

"I surrender."

"*Thank* you."

He looked to Peg, hoping for more liquid courage. She was chugalugging a big glass of water. She held up a finger, by way of asking him to hang on a sec.

When I was over being too depressed to speak, I

continued my quest for closure. "Last one. Then we're done."

"Can I get an *amen?*"

Peg sidled up, and set down four glasses. "You fellas redefine what *constitutes* work," she chortled merrily, and left without waiting for a response.

"I don't know if you know. I know I don't know, so you *probably* do not know. I know that."

He shook an angry finger at me. "Don't *ever* say that sentence, again."

"Anyway, what happened to the humans?"

He pulled his head back. "What do you mean, what happened to the humans? They boarded worldships and set course for the second star to the right and straight on till morning."

"I know ... Yes. I am aware of *that* history. But, I was asleep for two billion years. The US of A no longer raised a flag in the air. What happened to the diaspora?"

He sighed. "Oh, *that* what happened to the humans?"

He reflected a few moments. "Basically, if it looks sort of human, it used to be human."

"That's it?"

"What can I say? Most humans went to Azsuram. Some went other places, Kaljax, for example. Then those humans went elsewhere. They isolated their gene pools, mutated, and screwed like there was no tomorrow. A few hundred thousand years later, it was Klingon Gump. Wacky human clones everywhere. Then, one isolated gene pool'd hop on a ship, conquer another isolated gene pool, and then breed like rabbits. And weirder ass humanoids were born of their sexual efforts."

"Sounds ... *interesting.*"

"Maybe to you. I found it dull and boring. Watching

262

other people screw each other's not my idea of a good time. I developed hobbies. Humans did their thing, and I did mine, thank you, very much."

"But, we did good."

"Who we did good?"

"You and me. Us. We *us* did good. We saved asses by the bucket load."

"We did indeed. A few colonies on a few planets failed, or were killed by unhappy locals. But the vast majority of humans not only got off doomed Earth, they found reasonably nice places to live, and they settled into the business of living. Plain old, boring survival."

"And screwing?"

"And screwing."

"So Cellardoor was human, more or less?"

"Who?"

"Oh, no one. Someone I knew a very long time ago."

"Like I said, if your Cellardoor *looked* human, she probably was."

"Well, I'll be damned."

"*Finally*, something comes out your mouth I can agree with."

What can you say when you discover that your two billion year long life was actually successful? You saved your species, defended the future again and again, and did it well.

And, in the end, it comes down to this. I did what I could, because I *could*. Listen, you help someone with a different talent set live a little longer, so he can love his family a little longer, and a little better. You never give up, because, if you do, you're not pulling your weight. If you don't, someday you might look up and see me walking toward you. Spoiler alert: I'm not coming to shake your hand because you're such a swell person.

EPILOGUE

"See you later, love," Sapale said, as she kissed the top of my head, and walked toward the door. "Have fun."

"Have *fun*," I protested. "You don't even know what I'm doing today. You don't even know if what I'm going to do today has *fun* as a potential outcome. Hmm. Maybe ... maybe I'm getting my prostate checked, *today*."

By the time I was done whining, she had traveled the short distance back to my La-Z-Boy recliner. She folded her arms. "Of course, I know what you're doing today. It's *today*. Every today, you do the exact same thing. You pack up as much beer and fatty sausages you can carry; hoagie roll, too, of course. Then, you go fishing. It's *today*, so *today*, you're going fishing. Have-fun. Good-bye."

"So, I'll see you later. I think I'll go fishing, up at the lake. You have fun. And don't worry about dinner—"

"... 'because I'm bringing home more dinner than the two of us can eat.' I know. You say *that*, too, every day. You don't, of course, because, to you, fishing means drinking beer, frying up dogs, and spitting. Occasionally, your line falls into the lake, by accident. Maybe a fish dies from the concussion. Otherwise, we're looking at stew tonight."

I started to protest.

"And now *you* say, 'Honey, I hope it's not calrf. I really'd rather not eat fish than eat calrf.' A *year* ago, I'd laugh when you said that. Six *months* ago, I'd pretend to laugh when you said that. Now, eh, not so much. But, now I am late to meet the girls."

"Having *dry* salads and *juicy* conversations?" I waggled my eyebrows.

"They can if they want. I'm having a grilled racdal fat sandwich."

"That's my girl." I patted her on the rump.

So began, and basically ended, another day in paradise. Azsuram, to be more specific. I would, shortly, be heading up to Lake JJ, where I would perform some approximation of fishing. I'd also tell JJ every one of the same stories I'd told him maybe a thousand times before. You know what? He never once complained. I'd also tell him I miss him, and I love him, because I sorely do. Then, I'd call it a day, and return home to my warm house and my loving wife. Some days, a suicidal fish'd even volunteer to follow me. If it did, good. If it didn't, good. It was all good.

So, how long can a man of action, like me, waste time pseudo-fishing and speaking to the dead?

I do not know.

And how long can a nation-building war-goddess, like Sapale, content herself with idle gossip and greasy lunches?

I do not know.

But, when I find out, I'll let you know.

Maybe.

Then again, maybe I won't.

I can't very well tell you stories *and* fish, now can I?

The End

GLOSSARY:

Als (1): The original ship's AI on Jon's first flight long ago was Alvin. Jon shortened that to Al. When Al was joined to Jon's vortex in the Galaxy On Fire Series, Al and *Blessing* fell in love and got "married." Since then Jon refers to them combined as the Als.

Antigods (1): A group of reclusive, uber-powerful gods. They have been the bane of the Cleinoid's existence since time began.

Apractolith (3): The proper name of the antigods.

Beal's Point (1): An area of monuments to disgraced Cleinoid gods. All living gods must visit to be made ill so they stay loyal.

Bellicity (3): A conspirator allegedly with Festock against Vorc.

Bethniak (1): Child appearing, vengeful, powerful, and really really mean god.

Blessing (1): See *Stingray*.

Brindas (3): High master of Deft traditional magic and psychic ability.

Brood-mate/brood's-mate (1): Male and female members of a Kaljaxian marriage.

BUFF (6): Military talk for *big ugly fat fucker*.

Calfada-Joric (2): The Deft master brindas, or witch/magician, on Rameeka Blue Green. Went by Cala. After the war with the Adamant was over she was given Evil Jon to rehabilitate.

Calrf (1): A Kaljaxian stew that Jon particularly dislikes.

Carol (2): An antigod. Generally takes the form of a rock being with rattling pebbles.

Casper (2): The name Jon gave to the mysterious ghost who helped him fight the ancient gods.

Central Seat (1): The official leader of the Ancient God's conclave.

Channel of Curses (4): The first barrier guarding Clein.

Clein (4): The actual mystical force that gives the Cleinoid gods their power.

Cleinoid gods (1): Ancient and malevolent mix of gods. They have destroyed many universes before and are eyeing ours now. The five ranks or groupings for their invasion were to be Rage, Torment, Wrath, Fury, and Horror.

Command Prerogatives (1): The thin fibers Jon extends from his left four fingers. They are probes that also control a vortex.

Cragforel (1): Friendly Deavoriath Jon met after he first escaped the Adamant in the far future.

Cube (1): Jon's alternate name for the vortex he captains.

Daleria (2): Demigod and innkeeper whom Jon and Sapale befriended. She worked with them against the ancient gods as she'd grown to hate them.

Dalfury (1): Vorc's right hand, or chief assistant. A demigod of cloudy memories, hence, he has the form of a cloud.

Davdiad (1): Kaljaxian divine spirit.

Deavoriath (1): Three arms and legs, the most advanced tech in the galaxy, and helpful to Jon.

Deca (1): One of the witch gods skilled at prophecy. Sister of Fest.

DILLIGAF (6): Military expression for *do I look like I give a fuck.*

Dominion Splitter (2): The name of the transfolding vortex the ancient gods use to transport to our galaxy. He has a lot of issues and is very conflicted. Actually he's just a total asshole, period. Aka DS.

Dragmire (4): A co-conspirator in hell with Jéfnoss. In life, one of the home economics gods. She was a Quilamo, an amoeba-like species. An un-nice individual each and every day of the week.

Evil Jon Ryan/ EJ (1): Alternate time line version of the original human to android download. Over time, he turned to the darker side of his nature. He studied "magic" under a Deft master.

Felladonna (2): Vorc's second assistant or so called *right hand*. A demigod of lists and communication.

Felnastop (2): A delicious vegetable that runs like the wind.

Fest (1): One of the witch gods skilled at prophecy. Sister of Deca.

Festock (3): Old friend of Daleria who was part of a conspiracy against Vorc.

Fire of Justice (2): A metallic rod given to the center seat as a sign of power. A powerful incinerator, also.

Form One/Form Two (1): A Form is the title of a vortex pilot. If more than one is aboard they get numerical designations based on seniority.

Gáwar (2): Seriously badass god. The god of demons. Ten-foot long lobster claw front hands. Multiple tentacles serving in place of antennae. Block-shaped bull head. Gáwar's torso was a snake with human legs. Yeah, badness on the doorstep, I couldn't take one more step.

Genter-ban-tol (1): Prime Minister of the Joint Galactic Parliament. A Bezathy, basically the Galaxy's largest snail species.

Gorgolinians (4): Fish tank sentients of Sotovir.

Gorpedder (1): Ill-tempered boulder Cleinoid god.

Hemnoplop (1): Demigod of Fool's Island. On pilgrimage to Beal's Point with Jon.

Hollon (3): The complete joining of two Deft shapeshifters.

Jenna (The Forever Series): Jon's childhood companion. They spent summers together at a lake. She drowned one year the day before Jon arrived for the season.

Jéfnoss tra-Fundly (4): The first center seat of the Cleinoid conclave and the god of prophecy. He was a very cruel and hated leader.

JJ (3): Sapale's first son. Raised by Jon as his own son, whom he loved very much. JJ is short for Jon Junior.

Joint Council for Interplanetary Defense and Cooperation (1): Group of allied free world who fought the Adamant. Remained as a central quasi-UN for the surviving planets. JCIDC to its friends.

Kalvarg (1): The planet Jon took the orphan Kaljaxian population to as the Adamant were destroying their home world. An island solar system long ago ejected from the Milky Way Galaxy.

Lorpamoor (1): Cleinoid vampire god. Nasty, nasty fellow.

Marropex (1): A reaver. The Cleinoid god of atrocities.

Mirraya-Slapgren (3): A pair of Deft shapeshifters joined as one in hollon. Jon rescued Mirraya from certain death as a child and found Slapgren shortly after that. They are joined in the form of a large golden dragon. Very impressive, really. They are a powerful magician. Referred to as *Mirraya* generally because she is the one who speaks for the pair.

Nassel (2): Leader of the Rage faction of Cleinoids. She had done so for the last three transheavals. A god of conquest.

Oowaoa (1 TFS): Home world of the Deavoriath.

Plexuronic particles (4): An exotic particle created only under extreme conditions, very short lived. Was used by Jéfnoss to return from the dead.

Podulliy (6): The planet, orbiting a Wolf–Rayet star, where Jon and his crew, along with Verazz, confronted Torent.

Probe Fibers (1): Aka command prerogatives, they allow

piloting of the Vortex spaceship and can analyze whatever they touch.

Quadirpa (6): Secretary general of the JCIDC at the time of Jon's return from the Cleinoid universe. They were a symbiote pair, meaning they are two separate individuals bound in a symbiotic relationship.

Quantum Decoupler (1): A most excellent weapon that pulls the quarks apart in a proton. The energy released as they rejoin is amazing.

Queeheg (1): Owner of a dive bar Jon frequented when he first arrived in the Cleinoid realm.

Racdal fat (1 of TFL): A food animal from Kaljax's abundant fat stores.

Sapale (1): Jon's Kaljaxian wife from his original flight to find humankind a new home. At first just her brain was copied, then, eventually, she was downloaded to an android host. Traveled with the corrupted Jon Ryan from an alternate time line.

Space-time congruity manipulator (1): Hugely helpful force field. Aka a *membrane*.

Stingray (1): Jon's Deavoriath spaceship. Her name in the Deavoriath language is pronounced "crash." Hence, silly Jon renamed her after one of his favorite cars. It makes Jon-sense.

Stone Witches (2): Another name for the antigod gods.

Tefnuf (1): The first ancient god Jon encountered. She was saddled with an uncanny ugliness and a profoundly bad temper.

Toño DeJesus (1 of TFL): The scientist creator of the android Jon. Became his lifelong friend.

Transfolding (1): The mechanical process of moving from the land of the ancient gods to somewhere else.

Transheaval (1): The term the Cleinoids use to describe their migration from one universe to another. Accomplished via a mean vortex-cloud know as Dominion Splitter.

Visant (3): The proper name for a pair of Deft joined in hollon.

Verazz (2): The first antigod introduced. Also one of the most powerful.

Vorc (1): Current central seat of the conclave.

Vortex (1): Super-advanced Deavoriath sentient spaceship. Moves by folding space. If you get a chance to own one, do it.

Vortex (alternate definition) (1): See Dominion Splitter.

Walpracta (2): Ancient god of consumption. Positively revolting.

Wolf–Rayet star (6): Wolf–Rayet stars are a rare heterogeneous set of stars with unusual spectra showing prominent broad emission lines of ionized helium and highly ionized nitrogen and carbon. They have a very high surface enhancement of heavy elements, a relative depletion of hydrogen, and strong stellar winds. Their surface temperatures range up to 200,000 K, hotter than almost all other stars.

Wul (1): God of business and enterprise. Humanoid. Befriended Jon.

Zastrál (2): A three-meter long, one-meter tall fuzzy siamese-twinned python with paddles for legs. Used to extract knowledge. Very unpleasant chap. Also the only god who can summon Gáwar.

AND NOW A WORD FROM YOUR AUTHOR

WHO DOESN'T APPRECIATE SHAMELESS SELF-PROMOTION?

Thank you for continuing your journey through the Ryanverse! Along with this series, please check out *The Forever Series* if you haven't already. Beginning with The Forever Life, Book 1, *you can* learn Jon's backstory and share his many incredible adventures.

The second series in the Ryanverse, *Galaxy on Fire*, begins with Embers. Learn what happened to Jon and his companions long after humankind safely left Earth.

Audiobooks, you ask? Why yes, there is The Forever on Audible, and it's superb.

Along with joining by reading, hop aboard the bandwagon. There's plenty of room. Follow me at Craig Robertson's Author's Page on Facebook. Partake of the conversation and fun. Best of all, sign up for my Mailing List by emailing me [contact@craigarobertson.com] That way you can stay abreast of news and new releases. You'll be so glad you did. Finally, I love emails. No, I'm not that needy. I just love emails. contact@craigarobertson.com.

If you curious as to my history, you can find it on Amazon: Craig's Bio

A final favor. Please post a review for this book, especially on Amazon. They are more precious to us authors than gold.

So, happy trails to you and your, until we meet again ... craig

www.ingramcontent.com/pod-product-compliance
Lightning Source LLC
Chambersburg PA
CBHW070057030726
47506CB00002B/502